IN THE WOODS

IN THE WOODS

CARRIE JONES
AND **STEVEN E. WEDEL**

TOR
TEEN

A TOM DOHERTY ASSOCIATES BOOK

NEW YORK

IN THE WOODS

A Tor Teen Book
Published by Tom Doherty Associates
120 Broadway
New York, NY 10271

www.tor-forge.com

Tor® is a registered trademark of Macmillan Publishing Group, LLC.

The Library of Congress Cataloging-in-Publication Data
is available upon request.

ISBN 978-0-7653-3655-2 (hardcover)
ISBN 978-1-4668-2847-6 (ebook)

Our books may be purchased in bulk for promotional, educational, or business use. Please contact your local bookseller or the Macmillan Corporate and Premium Sales Department at 1-800-221-7945, extension 5442, or by email at MacmillanSpecialMarkets@macmillan.com.

First Edition: July 2019

Printed in the United States of America

0 9 8 7 6 5 4 3 2 1

*To the awesome people out there who try super hard to not
suck. Thank you for trying.*

—CARRIE

*To all the young people trying to make the world around
them a better place despite the odds against you, keep it up.
It matters.*

—STEVE

IN THE WOODS

1

LOGAN

I look at the lines I've just written, read them again, then again. I don't like them. Walt Whitman and Robert Frost probably never wrote such horrible poems. Maybe if I add one more couplet to the one I have, it won't be so bad. I tap the eraser of my pencil against my chin, something I always do when I think. Studying the early night, I look for clues, searching for something that will move me. It's a hot, still night in late May, the first weekend of summer vacation. Off to my left, somewhere in the pecan grove, a cricket is singing. It'll have to do.

Sitting on the grass beneath a full moon,
I think about you, hope to see you soon.
A lonely cricket sings a lonely song;
I know he'll be singing it all night long.

The lines stare back at me. I murmur them to myself, not bold enough to shout them to the stars. They're soooo bad. I don't understand it. Every line has the same number of syllables. The rhymes are real and aren't corny, like when I once rhymed "short stack" and "six-pack." That was back in freshman year, though. That's when my Robert Frost kick began, all because of one silly report about how landscape is a metaphor for human things. It felt like some sort of magic language that poets spoke. I thought maybe I could do it—make the metaphors, make the magic. Like crickets can be hearts singing or something. I don't know. By this time, as a high school junior ready for my senior year, I should be able to do something better than the words staring back at me from the lined paper of my composition notebook.

Somewhere behind the barn a cow lows. No way I'm adding that to my future trash can ball. Nobody wants to read about contented cows standing around at night. Maybe that's my problem. All I know are dairy cows, pecan trees, and farm machinery. And fishing. And hunting. But those are things every farm boy in Cherokee County, Oklahoma, knows. No magic. Nothing special.

I close my notebook. The problem is that I can't write about being lonely and longing for somebody because I'm really not. Sure, it'd be nice to have a steady girl, I guess. Maybe. I don't know, though. Me and my best friend, David Thompson, used to hang out all the time, fishing in the morning and hunting at night. David got a girlfriend, Yesenia, and I hardly ever see him. He goes to a lot of movies up in Tahlequah now.

I lie back on the old blanket I spread on the lawn and stare up at the stars. Thunder, my bloodhound, takes that as a sign that I need his attention. He burrows his nose in my armpit, then runs his snout under my arm until my hand comes to rest on the back of his head. I scratch behind his ear, but I'm not really into it.

Maybe there's something wrong with me. I mean, really. Here I am lying on a blanket just out of sight of the house where my parents and sisters are sleeping, staring up at the stars because I can't write poetry. Poetry! It seems almost ridiculous. My best friend has a girlfriend, and all I really feel is jealous that I never get to see him anymore.

"Wow. Thunder, am I weird or what?"

His only answer is a snort, which is pretty appropriate given the question. Then he looks at me with those sad brown eyes. There's not another dog in the world that looks as sad as a bloodhound. I laugh at him a little, then bring my other hand over to grab the skin behind his face in both hands and push it backward, pulling out some of the wrinkles. He patiently stares at me, waiting for this old and silly game to be over.

Last summer at this time, David would have been over here spending the evening with me. We'd play video games and eat popcorn (and anything else that we could sneak) and talk about fishing and hunting and girls. But David doesn't have to talk about girls anymore. He has a girlfriend.

"Remember when David pulled that snapping turtle out of the river?" I ask Thunder, who continues to ignore me. That had been a good day last summer. We drove my pickup truck over to the Illinois River and had our lines in the water way before the sun came up. At about dawn the fish started biting and we pulled out channel catfish and sand bass for a while, then the day got hot and the fish stopped biting. But David swore he could still catch something.

"You won't catch anything until it cools off," I told him.

Still, he kept casting his line. Finally he put a regular old earthworm on the hook, set the weight so the worm would go deep, and threw it in and sat down beside me and our lunch. He was halfway through a ham-and-cheese sandwich when his line jerked.

"Ha! Told ya!" He jumped up and started reeling. Ah, but he was too proud. He kept turning around and taunting me and didn't even look to see what was on his line when it came out of the water. "Who said I couldn't get another fish?"

Then he reached for his line. When his hand touched that turtle's belly, the thing let go of the worm. The hook never set. The turtle fell to the ground. Snapping turtles can be aggressive, and pretty fast for turtles. It went after David's foot.

I laugh out loud remembering David dancing around on that ledge a few feet above the water until he finally got a good angle and kicked the turtle back into the river. "That was a good day," I tell Thunder.

Another cow lows. I check out Thunder, who has perked up. That cow isn't simply making a contented noise in the night. Another cow, a little farther away, moos. Thunder jerks his head out of my hands and jumps to his feet. His nose twitches as he scents the air. Zeus, our cranky old bull, bellows a challenge, then comes the sound of many hoofed feet running.

"Coyote!" I yell, rolling to a sitting position, then jumping up. It's not magic, but it's something. "Let's get him, boy."

Thunder barks once. Behind us, Galahad and Daisy answer him. A second later Galahad streaks past us, running for the northeast corner of the fence. A mostly blue heeler mix, he's younger than Thunder, and not the smartest dog I've ever seen. Daisy is old and no longer interested in nighttime activities that don't involve table scraps. I'm sure she's settled herself back down on the porch, but is listening. Thunder looks back at me, then after Galahad, then back at me again.

"Go on," I tell him. "Get him!"

Thunder takes off and I follow at a trot. My dog slips under the bottom strand of barbed-wire fence. With the help of the thick corner post, I vault over the top, out of the yard, and into the hilly cow pasture. The cattle are still running and Zeus is still bellowing. Galahad's short, sharp barks come back to me from the darkness ahead. He's already vanished into the thick night of the trees beyond the barn.

Then there's another sound. It's not a roar, really. No way it's a cow, or even our angry bull. It's not a coyote, either. I slow down as I pass the backside of our milking barn.

Panther?

No, I don't think so . . . the sound's not high enough in pitch, though I've never actually heard a real panther. The most likely animal is a black bear. In the back of my mind I remember a report saying the black bear population here in the Ozark Mountains has been on the rise.

For a moment I think about going back to the house for a rifle, but the sound of a screaming calf stops me. Blackness nestles under the trees some thirty yards from where I'm standing. Something's got one of our calves. No way I want to face off against a bear without a gun, but it's not like it'll be a grizzly bear. You can scare away black bears pretty easy. And I'll have Thunder and dummy Galahad with me. I take off running into the dark.

The sound of panicked hooves is moving northwest, out of the trees and into the grass pasture. The calf still bleats. A cow, no doubt the calf's mother, moos frantically. Galahad's barks are constant and fierce. Then Thunder opens up with his deep voice, baying to let me know he's trailing something. I follow the sound of his voice into the dense forest of sycamores, oaks, maples, and other trees, watching for roots and rocks, whooping to encourage Thunder.

"Get him, Thunder!" I yell. "I'm coming."

In my pocket, my cell phone bursts out with a snatch of Toby Keith. I pause long enough to dig the phone out, then keep running.

"Logan?" Dad's voice asks. "What's going on? You're not coon hunting around the cattle again, are you?"

"No, Dad," I say, panting. "There's something out here. Do you hear that calf?" I hold the phone in front of me for a second, then press it back to my ear. "Sounds like a bear or something."

"Get back here, Logan," he warns. I can hear Mom beside him, asking what's going on.

"I can't, Dad. It's got one of our calves. Can you bring a gun?" Thunder's baying turns into a serious of deep, frightened barks. That's not good. "Thunder's found it."

The calf's screaming stops suddenly. That's *really* not good. Then the predator makes another sound. It's almost a howl, like a coyote or a wolf, but different. It sounds . . . almost human.

"Holy crap, Dad! Did you hear that?"

"Logan, you get back to the house right now," he orders.

But it's too late.

Oh God, it's too late.

I see Thunder first. He's standing between two trees, the hair all along his back standing straight up, his tail out stiff behind him as he looks ahead of him. Galahad is running in half circles around a tiny clearing in the woods, barking, barking, barking at something in the deep shadows.

The Holstein calf is elevated, its shoulders about four feet off the ground. The white hair on it seems to glow in the darkness, making its black spots even blacker. Its black eyes are so wide, the white rims are visible. The calf's mouth is open and it's bleating in fear, its long pink tongue protruding and curling up at the tip. The clearing smells of fresh cow poop and pee.

I can't quite see what is holding the calf. It's huge, though, and dark. Starlight reflects in moist black eyes. The eyes. I swear they are at least seven feet off the ground. I'm six feet, and they are way higher than my head. The thing's eyes are shifting from Thunder to Galahad and back again when I walk up, but then they fix themselves on me. From the darkness under the eyes comes a low, angry growl. Teeth flash in the moonlight. Could that be a man? That can't be a man. Could it?

"Holy crap," I murmur. "Holy crap. Holy crap."

Involuntarily, I back up a step. It doesn't seem far enough away. Five thousand miles doesn't seem far enough away.

The dogs are still barking. Thunder crouches low. He growls and barks. Galahad keeps running from place to place, lunging forward, retreating, repositioning, barking with every breath.

And the calf is screaming again.

The white pattern on the calf's face disappears as something covers it up. Then, even over the dogs, I can hear the sharp *crack* of the calf's neck breaking. The screams stop. I look again at the Holstein calf's head, and for a moment in the moonlight I see what looks like hands.

Not a bear! My mind screams this brilliant realization over and over.

"Galahad!" I call. "Thunder! Come on!" I back away another step, my eyes fixed on the blacker-than-black shape in the shadows of the trees. The calf is quiet. Dead quiet. The shadow shifts, bending over the calf's neck. There is a ripping, tearing, wet sound. The blood runs off the calf, onto the ground, and then I can smell the copper of it.

"Oh my God. God help me," I whisper to the night.

The thing shifts again. The calf dangles by its head for a moment, then is caught up, and much of it disappears into the shadows. There is more of that tearing sound.

The calf's head flies out of the shadows and rolls to a stop inches from my boots.

I almost pee a little.

Then I can only hear the sounds of heavy feet running away, old leaves crunching, and tree branches whipping back into place as the giant dark shape pushes through them.

Behind me, Dad yells my name.

Galahad starts after the thing. I try to yell at him, but there's no sound. I lick my lips and try again. "Galahad! Come back here!" Thunder takes a step forward, but I stop him. "No, Thunder."

The calf's big, dead, scared eyes look up at me, asking me why. *Why am I dead? What killed me? Will my mother ever stop calling for me? I can't go with her anymore.*

"Logan." A hand falls on my shoulder. I jump forward and scream. My foot hits the severed head and it trips me. I fall onto the hard ground, twisting around to see what's behind me, sure it's the monster, but it's only my dad.

My dad.

He's wearing his work boots, unlaced, and his pale-blue pajamas. He's carrying a pump shotgun in the crook of his right arm.

I don't know if I should cry or laugh or scream or what.

Dad looks from me to the head I tripped over, then to Thunder, then to the clearing, where Galahad is sniffing at the pool of blood in the grass beneath where that thing was eating. "Galahad! Come here," Dad snaps, and the dog obeys. Galahad doesn't really obey anyone else.

"Was it a bear?" Dad asks me.

I suddenly realize I'm lying down, defenseless, and that thing might not be too far away. I jump up and look behind me, toward the place where the thing disappeared. "No. It wasn't a bear."

"Panther? You shouldn't have gone after it alone, especially without a gun. Logan, we've talked about this. There are dangerous animals out here sometimes."

Now I do laugh. I can't help it. It's a scary laugh, though, and I'm really worried I won't be able to stop. Finally Dad's voice cuts it off. "Logan!" he commands. One more laugh escapes, a twisted, frightened thing. His hand squeezes my shoulder. "What is wrong with you?"

"Can we go home?" I ask.

Dad looks back at the head, then at the pool of blood. "I guess so. I'll get the sheriff out here in the morning, let him call the state wildlife people."

"It wasn't a panther, either, Dad," I say as we start walking downhill, toward home.

"Not a bear or a panther? What was it?"

"I don't know," I answer honestly. "A hungry shadow with wet eyes and big teeth."

2

CHRYSTAL

Dead cows.

Instead of hanging out at Moosehead Lake with Zoe and the rest of my friends . . . Instead of getting tan and working to pay for gas money and new strings for my bass . . . Instead of being in New York City with Mom and Husband #3, also known as Bill, jamming up a storm with a bass legend . . . Instead of all these things, I am sitting on an unending stretch of interstate in a car that smells like my dad's cinnamon gum because of dead cows and some crazy boy's imagination.

"So many dead cows," Dad murmurs as he maneuvers the station wagon around a piece of blown-out tire that lies flat and dead-looking in our lane. His voice loses its murmur and gets all excited. "Not just regular animal bites either . . . but mauled. Incredibly vicious. Chrystal! It's amazing. You should see the photos. A calf's head was ripped clean off its body."

His eyes go all big the way they always do when he's excited about something that's absolutely weird-slash-disgusting.

He says, "Really. You should have a look. The folder is in the back."

"No, thanks." I peek over my shoulder at the manila folder he got at Walmart. I already know what will be in it: photos, copies of articles from newspapers or that he compiled off the Internet, addresses and phone numbers of witnesses. And it's all there because of some dead cows.

We're in Oklahoma to do some weird paranormal, crypto-zoological research. He's big into that, which is something I try not to share with people. He's even got a blog called *Strange Maine*. My dad is a cryptozoologist, which means that he studies things people don't believe in: werewolves, bigfeet, bat boys, vampires. It's sort of cute the way his raspy dad voice will get all excited and he'll point as he drives, talking, talking, talking, but I am not supposed to be here. I am supposed to be in New York. I want to be in New York. I want to be practicing bass with real mentors.

My dad is not the world's weirdest person, and he is not the world's skinniest person, but I think the combination of weird and skinny make him seem like he should be the star of a British science-fiction television show instead of a kindergarten teacher/ Bigfoot enthusiast in Maine.

It wasn't until fifth grade that I realized quite how weird he was. That was when I did my mammal report on Bigfoot. I got a zero because the teacher said Bigfoot wasn't real. And I said, "But we have Bigfoot hair and a footprint in our house." Everyone laughed. The teacher called me a liar. Then I did some back tucks at recess and everyone forgot to make fun of me.

Gymnastics is good like that. So is the guitar. Sometimes when you have skills—even minimal skills like doing a back tuck—that other people don't have, they forget that you and your dad are just on the other side of normal. My bass skills were *going* to be insane, because I was heading to New York City, specifically Manhattan, to hang out with Mom this summer and work on my music and check out the indie scene and it was going to be amazing.

But that ended up being a nonstarter.

And here we are.

Like I said, Dad teaches kindergarten. When people ask me what he does in the summer, I tell them he's an amateur animal behaviorist and that usually stops the questions. It's lying, but I think it's the kind that God forgives pretty quickly, not the kind that keeps you in the eternal fires of hell, which is basically where we are right now.

Hell.

Also known as Oklahoma.

Honestly, I'm sure Oklahoma is a fine place when it's not early summer and when you aren't stuck in a Subaru station wagon with the heat rippling into the car in waves you can almost touch with your fingers as your dad babbles on and on and on about werewolves. Yes, werewolves.

"A werewolf is also called a lycanthrope, from the Greek λυκάνθρωπος: λύκος, as in *lukos*, "wolf," and άνθρωπος, *anthrōpos*, 'man,'" he says. "How fascinating is that, Chrystal?"

He guns the Subaru around a truck full of cows. They are adorable, actually. I wave at them. I hope they don't die via Bigfoot or other means. I hope they don't feel as powerless in their summer as I do in mine.

"It's fascinating, Dad." I pull my leg up so that I can inspect my toes. I took my flip-flops off states ago. "Are we almost there?"

"That we are, my little helper! I know you're disappointed that your mom and Bill went to Europe, but I'm excited to have you with me." He reaches over and rubs my hair. "It's an adventure, right?"

"Right."

I must not sound too excited because he goes, "Try not to be too disappointed, dear one. It'll hurt your old man's ego."

"Sorry." Guilt pushes into my chest. It's not his fault Mom and Bill ditched me for Europe, and it's not really even Dad's fault that he's so into weird. So I give him my best happy face and say, "I love you, old man, but you probably shouldn't call me 'dear one.' It makes you sound silly."

We can't pass, so we're stuck behind another cow truck for a while.

"Good, I love you too." He smiles back. "Silly is a good thing. I noticed you have a tattoo on your ankle. Isn't it illegal for minors to get tattoos in Maine without parental written permission?"

I suck in my lips, lift my eyebrows, and try to look innocent. "It's a lollipop, though."

"You are a sucker for lollipops!"

"Ha!" I punch his arm and then we sort of just drive more. I watch the cows' faces. They are all so alike, stuck there staring at a landscape of green trees and rolling hills. "You know, 'Boredom is the root of all evil—the despairing refusal to be oneself.'"

"You are still on the Kierkegaard kick, aren't you?"

"Yep. All Søren Kierkegaard. All dead philosopher. All the time."

"'The task must be made difficult, for only the difficult inspires the noble-hearted,'" Dad quotes at me, as if I don't know it by heart.

I let that one settle for a second. "Is that why you do this? Search for weird things that don't exist. Because it's difficult?"

"Partly." He turns his head to look at me. For a second there is a strange, almost sad look in his eyes, but he blinks it away and then there is only a hint of mischief. "And partly because being bored is the root of all evil. Don't want to become evil."

"You couldn't ever." I turn away and reach out toward the cows. The wind whips my hand backward and pushes my hair toward my dad, who has *finally* had enough, and guns the Subaru in front of the cow truck. It's a bit close, so the cow truck driver blows his horn. I jump. My dad laughs.

"I'm refraining from giving him the finger," he says.

I've turned around. "He didn't hold back at all."

"Two-fisted one-finger salute? Did that fellow give me the two-fisted salute?"

"Totally." I wave at the truck driver in a way that I hope seems apologetic and not obnoxious. Then I sit back in my seat, readjusting my seat belt and starting the examination of my toes again. I'm a bit obsessed with my toes when I'm bored. Weird runs in the family, I guess. I give it up and grab my bass from the backseat. I will practice even without a mentor until I can get one.

Dad said if we have any summer left after this case, he'll bring me to New York himself. He hates New York and its "teeming humanity," so this is a big deal. Unlike Mom, Dad keeps his promises and he doesn't forget me. He's weird, but not that kind of weird.

A couple years ago, Mom forgot to pick me up from school and bring me to a bass lesson. She was still living in the state then. I texted her and texted her and finally got a ride with Zoe's mom.

My mom picked me up from Zoe's, and as soon as I climbed into the car she looked at me all bright eyed.

"I have met the most interesting man," she said.

"That's why you forgot me?" My voice was tiny and angry. I belted myself into the car and hugged my bass in front of me. Usually I put it in the backseat, but not that day.

"Oh, honey. Mommy didn't forget about you, but he was just so interesting." She looked at me then, finally, and I guess she realized how shattered I was because she said, "Don't worry. You come first with Mommy. Always."

She lied.

I strum the memory away, and as we loop and climb and coast down green slopes on the hilly highway, Dad starts again. "I like to think about how many places in this world have Bigfoot myths. There's . . ."

From the way he's going on and on, I think I'm going to be inspecting my toes a lot this summer.

We have to slow down for a truck loaded with logs that's going, like, twenty miles per hour around a sharp curve in the highway.

"I thought Oklahoma was all prairie," I say as I text my friend Zoe another positive affirmation about her character and how no, she should not go out with the guy who does the go-karts at Seacoast Fun Park. When I'm done, I add to my dad's conversation further. "You know, just flat and covered in waving strands of golden wheat. Like in the song."

"That's the western part of the state," Dad says. "The east is pretty much all like this, according to what I read. We're still in the Ozark Mountain range."

"I wonder if they drive faster in the flat part of the state."

He laughs at me. I finally put my bass safely away and reach for the manila folder behind me.

"I knew you'd succumb to curiosity," he says.

"Succumb to boredom is more like it," I retort as I open the folder.

The first page is not mutilated cows, thank God; it's just facts about Cherokee County, Oklahoma. There's a mere forty-two thousand people in the entire county: half are white; a third are Native American. It doesn't say what nation, but I'm assuming Cherokee, hence the name.

"Not a lot of people here, Dad," I say. "I think the werewolves would get bored. All the bigfeet, too."

"Funny." He smiles. "The horse who starred on *Mister Ed* is from here. That's something."

I must give him a blank look because his face turns into disappointed-dad mode.

"You have no idea who Mister Ed is, do you?"

"Nope."

"I've totally failed as a father." He groans and turns down the radio. "How about Robert J. Conley or Jackson Narcomey or Hastings Shade or Sonny Sixkiller?"

"Nope. Nope. Nope and . . . nope." I flip to a new page. It's a contact list.

"Wilson Rawls?"

"He wrote *Where the Red Fern Grows*." I act incredibly triumphant about knowing this because I know Dad will love it.

"Finally," he says, all pretend-exasperated-father.

"That was the saddest book ever. We read it in fourth grade.

Why do they only make you read sad books in school? Someone always has to die."

"Not in kindergarten," he says proudly.

I nod and start perusing the new page, which is a newspaper article. "True. It's *The Cat in the Hat* and *Fancy Nancy* all the time in kindergarten. You know, it's never too early to teach those developing minds that life is full of tragedy and horror. Give them some Stephen King. Some *Hamlet*."

He laughs and scruffs up my hair.

"Dad?"

"Yeah." He switches into the fast lane of the two-lane highway again. This time it's to go around a big green tractor. A guy is driving a tractor on the highway! I resist the urge to text this info to my friends.

Instead, I ask, "All your stuff. This is mostly all about Bigfoot. I thought you said this was a werewolf sighting."

"Well, not technically. I have a theory about Bigfoot and werewolves and it's really pretty interesting, but it's not an accepted theory at all, Chrystal. I'm still developing it, you know? And anyway, once we start investigating I would rather if you didn't say 'werewolf' to anyone. I think it will spook them and maybe undermine our credibility."

"Dad . . ."

"What?"

"'*We* start investigating'?" Seriously?

He gives me his best win-you-over smile, which is half four-year-old boy, half Cookie Monster. "I don't want you to just hang out in the hotel room playing your bass the whole time, Chrystal. That's not social. When you were little, you loved helping me. Remember when we looked for Gourd Head in Brazil?"

Gourd Head is a humanoid cryptic that is supposedly about three feet tall. He has been spotted in Brazil, where they call him *negro d'agua*, which means "black man of the waters." His head is super-big and looks like a gourd and he has webbed hands and feet. Needless to say, we didn't find him.

"You liked Brazil," my dad offers. "We had fun there."

"Dad. I was five and you dangled me over the side of the boat as bait."

"No, I did not."

"You totally did."

"It was because you liked to be dangled over the side of the boat. You thought it was fun."

I don't respond. It's not really the best social policy to spend the summer looking for monsters with your dad. Plus, it usually means intruding on people's lives, or even worse, talking to stuffy professors.

Finally he says, "I'll pay you if you help."

I smile because I need money for gas and strings and a new amp. Seriously, what choice do I have, anyway? "Deal. Plus, with my mad skills, we might get to New York sooner."

"Right." He pulls off the highway and onto an exit ramp, which is a minor miracle because we've been traveling for-freaking-ever, and says, "But only if it doesn't get too dangerous. If it gets too dangerous, all bets are off."

"No dangling me over the side of the boat for bait this time," I tease.

His face loses all its jokey dadness and becomes deadly serious. "No way in hell."

"No way in Oklahoma," I rephrase. He doesn't get the joke.

3

LOGAN

I don't know," I repeat. "I never saw anything like it."

Dad. Mom. The sheriff. The lean, weather-beaten guy from the Oklahoma Department of Wildlife Conservation. A reporter for the Tahlequah, then the Tulsa, newspapers. I told them all the same thing over the course of a week. Now I have to say it again to Mrs. McKee, Mom's friend from church.

"Did you read about it in the Tulsa paper?" I ask.

"No, Logan, I saw it in one of the supermarket papers," she answers, her voice full of awe. "The ones that go all across the country."

This makes no sense. "What?"

"The *National Enquirer*, I think it was. Maybe *Weekly World News*," she confides. "'Boy Sees Bigfoot Eating Cow,' the headline said. The paper said your dogs saved your life. Is that true?"

"Not exactly, Mrs. McKee," I tell her. I can't believe this. They'll be saying I partied with Elvis on a UFO next. Mom finally comes out of the bathroom, her head wrapped in a fluffy pink towel, so I hand the phone off and go to my room.

The notebook with the horrible rhymes about the moon and crickets is in the drawer of my night table. After church, I take it out and flop down on my bed, opening to the page after the poem, the page where I wrote down everything that happened that night. I've read it several times since seeing the thing the papers want to call Bigfoot. I couldn't sleep at the time. I was awake all that night, afraid I'd hear that horrible yelling howl again. So, I wrote. I don't think I could ever forget the details, but I wanted to write them down anyway. It's nothing like a poem. It's details with no meaning. Words that make no sense. I want sense. I want to understand what happened, what that was, why I saw it.

I haven't heard the monster again. It sounds so babyish to say "the monster," like what I saw is a boogeyman hiding in my closet. But, like I keep telling people, I don't know what it is. Could it be Bigfoot, like Mrs. McKee said the tabloid paper called it? The sheriff and the wildlife guy didn't suggest that. None of the reporters had, either. I never called it Bigfoot, and I didn't even talk to a reporter from the *National Enquirer*, or whatever paper it was. I should probably go into town and get a copy of it to see what it says. I kept saying I didn't know what it was, but people in town had jumped on the Bigfoot wagon right off, too. Could it have been? Or was it just some large dude hopped up on roids, pulling off calves' heads for kicks or his YouTube channel or something.

Eight days have gone by since that night. We haven't heard the thing, and no more of our cattle have been killed. Everything has been very peaceful, except for the reporters and people calling because they read about me in the papers. My family is acting like everything is normal, even though reporters randomly call. We do chores. We sleep. We eat together. Life goes on, even though there are monsters.

I read my description of the monster again. It was extra dark that night because of the cloud cover. *In the woods. Maybe it was just a bear. A bear in the dark, seen by a farm kid who has a good imagination and a knack for bad poetry.* Maybe I'm just obsessing about it because it's like a good poem. I know it exists, but I can't make it. I can't understand it. I can't . . . Maybe it's just me imagining away my humdrum life where every Sunday we go to church and have roast beef for dinner. Who knows?

Bears can stand on their hind legs.

They can.

The whole thing is just crazy. I start to close the notebook, but then see the poem again. I try reading it aloud, just in case it doesn't sound so bad. It's horrible. The theme and scheme aren't so different from, say, Robert Louis Stevenson's "Summer Sun," but while his lines shimmer with brilliance, mine seem to give off rays of garbage stink. It's almost enough to make me wish Mrs. Walker had never praised a poem I wrote in her creative writing class a couple years ago. It was supposed to be a blow-off class, an easy A, not a class that would lead to frustration years later.

"The poem you judged to be the best in class is . . ." Mrs. Walker had really drawn it out for effect. Our poems had been typed and posted around her room for a week, and all her students got time to put a mark on the one they liked the best. I remember how nervous I was, waiting, watching her eyes twinkle behind her thick glasses. Then she said it. "'Moonlight Dancer' by Logan Jennings."

The class had clapped half-heartedly as Mrs. Walker handed

me my prize, a denim-covered journal, like a real hardcover book, with blank lined pages. That journal is in my underwear drawer, its pages reserved for final drafts.

My winning entry wasn't very good, but I was one of the few students to take the assignment, and the contest, seriously. I wrote about an imaginary girl and gave it a *Lord of the Rings* kind of feel. I remember the first couple stanzas. Idly, I copy them into this notebook, under the thing about the crickets.

In a meadow in the forest of my mind,
Among winter flowers of unknown kind,
A spritely maiden dances all alone
In fragrant evening, all alone.
Flashing feet—my graceful elf—
She dances there, dances for herself.
Her laughter blinds me to my way.
When she sees me, she will not stay.

Won't you dance for me?
Won't you stay with me,
Tonight?

And do what? There was something in the poem about dancing together under the stars. My friends harassed me for a while over that poem, teasing me for getting in touch with my sensitive side. More than one had asked friends to ask me if I'd written it about them. I was flattered at first. Until I found out they hoped I didn't write it about them.

Why write poetry, anyway? Girls? Money? Nobody makes any money at poetry. Yeah, I've checked that out. Even poets who have won Pulitzer Prizes and been named poet laureate of their states don't usually make a living at it. They're professors or something. But it's not the money. Can anyone really write for money? Doesn't it have to be for love? Or at least the need to say something? I feel like I have something to say, but I just can't get it out.

Or maybe I just don't know what it is I have to say yet. Maybe that's why everything I do write seems so forced. So bad. So very, very bad.

I put the notebook away and go downstairs. In Tahlequah, David and Yesenia are probably snuggled together in a movie theater, watching a romantic comedy. On the Jennings farm, however, Saturday night is game night and it's my turn to choose. My sisters, fifteen-year-old Kelsey and ten-year-old Katie, are already sitting at the dining table, munching popcorn as I go to the coat closet, where the games are stored on a high shelf.

"You just watch," I hear Kelsey tell Katie. "He always gets the same one."

"I want to play Sorry!," Katie calls to me.

"Sorry, Katie," I say as I pull Risk out of the closet. Ha! I made a pun.

"Not Risk again!" she wails. "Why do we always have to play that war game? I hate Risk!"

"Katie," Mom calls from the kitchen where she's frosting cupcakes. "I told you, it's Logan's turn to pick. You picked Sorry! last week."

"I picked Life the time before," she pouts. "I don't always pick the same game every time, like he does."

"If you don't want to play, you can go on to bed," Mom answers.

For a minute I think Katie might go. Ultimately, I think it's the popcorn and the promise of chocolate cupcakes that keep her at the table.

"We can team up against him," Kelsey whispers. Big surprise there. They always do that anyway, and I still win.

I spread out the board and distribute the plastic cases of colored numbers that represent armies. Within fifteen minutes I've captured all of Australia. A couple turns later I've amassed a big enough force to launch my invasion of Asia.

"Here he comes again," Dad says as he passes me the red attack dice. He winks. I wink back.

"Ew! Logan tooted!" Katie crinkles up her nose. "That's nasty."

"I did not, Katie," I protest. I'm not above claiming it when it's my crime, but the noxious odor did not come from me.

"Dad?" Kelsey eyes him.

"Not me!" He holds up his hands in mock surrender while Kelsey makes sort-of-fake and sort-of-real gagging noises.

I shake the three cubes in my hand, ready to announce my attack on India. It's right when I'm rolling the dice that the noise happens. We freeze. The dice land by the board. The sound gets louder. It's a roaring—something primal and horrifying and coming from south of our house, in the direction of the 720 Road. My mom's face loses all its color. Katie immediately starts crying. Dad stands up and grabs the rifle by the front door, but he doesn't go outside. Kelsey whispers, "It's in our driveway."

Dad yanks the door open. I'm right at his heels, but nothing's out there—nothing but darkness and smells.

About four years ago a tornado ripped through our town. Dad and Mom yanked us all out of bed once the warning siren sounded, and hauled us into the basement. It was dark. It sounded like a train was roaring down the road outside our house. Not just any train—but something nuclear. David had been sleeping over, so he was there too, and when it was all over and our house was still standing, I noticed he had wet his pajama bottoms. His face was a horrified mix of embarrassment and fear. I threw a pillow at him. I'd been clutching that pillow because I was so scared. Anyway, I threw that pillow at him and he grabbed it and held it in front of the stain on his pajama pants. My dad left the house to go help with the cleanup and my mom and the girls went to bed. I snuck downstairs and washed David's pj's. We never said a word about it to anyone, and not to each other, either, except when we put the washer on and David whispered, "That was the worst thing that ever happened to me."

I wish I could say the same. I wish that would be the worst thing that happens to any of us, but I somehow doubt it, you know? That howling makes me doubt everything.

"Sure, it's a great idea, Ronnie, but you're not the first one to come up with it," Sam Davis, owner of the feedstore in Forest Road, says to my dad. Forest Road is a few miles south of Tahlequah, the county seat and it's the closest town to our farm, and it's barely a town. Basically, there's a post office, the feedstore, the Baptist church almost everyone around here goes to, Gus's Grocery— which is really a convenience store with one gas pump beside it—and a little beauty salon run by Mr. Davis's daughter. The feedstore is the closest thing we have to a hardware store.

Dad sighs deeply. I can feel his disappointment.

"Nothing?" He leans against the counter, then seems to think better of it. He straightens up and rubs a hand over his eyes.

"I have two lights left. Shop lights you clip to a workbench," Mr. Davis answers, rubbing the gray stubble on his dark face. "They take a regular bulb. Everything I had that was bigger, and it wasn't much, was snapped up within twenty minutes of opening the store this morning. And posts to mount them on? Shoot, I could have retired if I'd had enough of them."

"I guess we could go to Tahlequah," Dad says. I stand away from them a bit, looking out the window of the front door, not really watching anything.

"That's what lots of people are doing," Mr. Davis says. "If it was me, I'd head for Wagoner. Maybe Fort Gibson. One of those mega stores, Lowe's or Home Depot."

"That'll take hours of daylight," Dad argues.

"I'm sorry, Ronnie. Really, I am," Mr. Davis says. He's an older guy, probably in his sixties, bald but with gray stubble on his cheeks no matter the time of day. The patriarch of one of the area's only black families, he always wears pin-striped bib overalls with a chewed pencil in the bib and a tape measure clipped to his right hip pocket. Mr. Davis is the only person I know who calls my dad Ronnie. To most people, Dad is RJ Jennings, but Mr. Davis has been calling him Ronnie since Dad was a little boy.

"Well, give me what you've got," Dad says. "It's a start."

Mr. Davis ambles toward the back of his small store. Outside, a red Ford F-250 crunches over the gravel drive and stops beside Dad's black F-350 diesel. David and his dad get out and come in.

Mr. Thompson, wearing a battered straw cowboy hat, nods at me then goes to shake hands with Dad.

"Hey," David says. "You hear that thing last night?"

"Yeah," I say. Dad and Mr. Thompson are having the same conversation. "I guess everyone around here heard it this time."

"Nobody's gonna think you're a weirdo anymore. That's for sure," David says.

"You thought that?"

"Nah. You don't make stuff up. Not like that, anyway. You just make it up for your poetry." He grins at me. "Hey, you know that one you wrote? The one about how a tree smells wet after it rains?"

"Yeah."

"I thought of that the other night when we had that little bit of rain. Me and Yesenia were in her yard and I was pushing her on the tire swing. I said the lines I could remember and she really liked it."

"She did?" I ask. Somebody liked my poem? "Does she want to read the rest of it?"

"Well, man, I didn't tell her you wrote it. She just thought I made it up, so I let her think that. Is that cool? You okay with that?" His face is earnest, hopeful.

"I'm your Cyrano?" I say, joking, but not really feeling it.

"What's that?" he asks.

"Oh, he was an ugly guy who wrote poems to help his friend get a girl."

"Oh. Yeah, I guess. You're not mad, are you?"

"No," I tell him. I guess I'm really not. At least he remembered a little of what I wrote, and when he recited it, the audience liked it. "So, how much did she like it?"

David glances over at our fathers, then says real low, "Third base."

I laugh, but don't say any more. Mr. Davis returns from the back of his store with the lights in cardboard boxes. He calls out, "Hello there, Billy!" to Mr. Thompson. "I hope you're not here for lights, posts, extension cords, or .30-.30 shells."

"Well, I was," Mr. Thompson drawls. "RJ here done told me you're cleaned out."

"Yep. Whatever you folks up north heard musta scared the bejesus outta everybody," Mr. Davis says, then looks at me and David by the door. "Excuse me," he says. "Anyway, everybody up your way is wanting to put lights around their houses today."

"What was it?" Mr. Thompson asks. "Anybody see anything?"

"Nope," Mr. Davis answers. "That young feller over there's the only one to have seen it." He points at me. "We all read the papers. Whatever it was killed Ray Cheever's bull calf last night. The bull was pretty near nine months old. It wasn't a little thing anymore. Bo Sanders and Jed Fields both have stock missing. Bo's been missing a couple goats for close to two weeks now."

The thing is: animals have been going missing for a long time, way before this. Nobody thought anything of it. Coyotes can run stock way out into the hills, wear out a cow, a goat, sometimes even a horse, and then, when their prey goes down, they'll kill it. Bears get a few, and some get shot for wandering into remote areas where people are growing pot. Nobody'd thought much of a missing calf here and there. But maybe . . .

"What'd it sound like to you, RJ?" Mr. Thompson asks Dad.

"I don't know," Dad answers. "Sounded . . . I don't even know. Almost like a man trying to sound like a bear but not doing a real good job of it."

"Yeah." Mr. Thompson nods. "That's about it."

"What kind of setup are you planning to do around your place?" Dad asks.

"Gonna put up some lights around the house and barn. The chicken house is already pretty well lit because of the coyotes and varmints," Mr. Thompson answers. "I just got the four head of cattle I can run into the little pasture by the road. I figured a half dozen of those halogen lights, just mounted on the sides of the barn, and some of those motion-sensing lights on the house. How about you?"

"I'd like to set posts around my west pasture, light up the whole thing, but it seems like that's not going to happen," Dad says. "I've got a hundred and fifty head of cattle. I guess I'll still run them in there after the evening milking, put up all the lights I can find, and me and Logan'll have to watch over them at night."

Mr. Thompson emits a low whistle. "Stay outside with that thing loose? No, thank you."

"Has it got any of your chickens yet?" Dad asks.

"Thank God, no."

"When it does, you'll probably think different," Dad promises.

David bumps my arm and motions for me to follow him outside. I'd rather stay and see how the men decide to handle the situation, but I follow my friend out to the gravel parking lot. "You and your dad are going to stay out all night waiting on that thing?"

"Sounds like it."

"You scared?"

"Yeah." No use lying about that.

"What did it look like, man?"

"I told you," I say, but I describe it again anyway.

"Do you think it was Bigfoot, like the papers say?"

"I don't know." I've seen shows on TV where people went hunting Bigfoot. I think again about what they said about the creature. "This thing seemed, I don't know, smarter than Bigfoot. But that means it wasn't a bear. I want it to be a bear."

"It's messed up," David says, then reaches into his back pocket and brings out his Skoal can. He offers it to me and I shake my head.

"I thought Yesenia made you stop dipping," I say.

"Yeah, well, I just don't do it around her."

"Oh." I'd never really thought of David as someone who'd lie, but I guess love makes people do strange things.

Dad and Mr. Thompson come out of the store, Dad carrying his boxed lights that he puts in the backseat of our truck.

Mr. Thompson calls out to David. "I'm going back for the trailer, then going to Wagoner to see if I can get the stuff we need and the posts and lights RJ wants. I want you to go with Logan and his dad and help them dig holes for the posts."

"Sure, Dad," David says. I can tell he's not thrilled with the idea. He's never minded hard work, but I bet he had plans with Yesenia today.

"How'd you feel about staying the night, helping watch their place? I thought maybe you could help tonight, then your brothers can take turns."

"Yeah, sure," David agrees, and now he really sounds disappointed.

Digging the post holes isn't so bad. Dad has a drill for the tractor because we're always fixing fences. We have about fifty holes drilled by the time Mr. Thompson shows up with a trailer loaded down with ten-foot posts, high-pressure sodium lamps, and bright-orange extension cords. Me, Dad, and David break for lunch while Mr. Thompson finishes drilling post holes around the pasture. We don't usually put the cattle in this pasture because it's where we grow alfalfa that we bail as hay to feed them in the winter, but this is an emergency. After lunch, we break into two teams, with me and David mounting the light fixtures to the posts so Dad and Mr. Thompson can plant them in the ground. We begin on the side of the pasture facing the woods, but by dinner-time we haven't even finished that side of the rectangle. Still, it's a pretty impressive line of fresh posts linked together by shiny new extension cords.

"This'll have to do for now," Dad says. He sends me to bring the gas-powered generator out, and I come back on our Kawasaki four-wheeler, pulling the generator on its trailer. Within a few minutes the lights are glowing amber.

"Mom and the girls did the milking this evening," Dad tells me. "They're holding the cattle in the pen behind the milk barn. Let's get them in here, then get some supper."

Mr. Thompson stays to help, so with the four of us, we get the cattle moved fairly quickly from the very cramped yard where they go at milking time and into the alfalfa pasture.

Supper is a buffet of leftovers and apprehension. Mom insists I check my cell phone twice to make sure it's charged up. There's an air horn and a pair of flashlights as the table center-piece. My shotgun, loaded with slugs, leans against a nearby wall with David's lever-action .30-.30 rifle and Dad's .30-.06 deer rifle.

"You and David take the first watch," Dad instructs. "I'll relieve you at about one. If you hear anything out of the ordinary, you blow that air horn long and loud. Okay?"

"All right, Dad," I promise.

"You'll need to get up at sunrise and help with the milking, like always," he tells me.

I nod.

Before we go, Mom wraps her arms around me and hugs me so tight it almost cuts off my wind. Then she steps back, still holding on to me. I notice, maybe for the first time, the wrinkles around her bright-green eyes and the silvery strands of gray that shine among the brown of her hair. "You be careful," she insists. "I'd rather lose every cow out there than you, so you get to the house if you get scared."

"Yeah, Mom, okay."

She turns from me to David and grabs him in a shorter version of the hug I got. "That goes for you, too, David Thompson."

"Okay, Mrs. Jennings," he says, obviously surprised.

We take our guns and get out to the pasture. Most of the cattle are munching grass, the white patches of their hair shining in the new lights, reminding me of the screaming calf. Some seem to be asleep standing up, and a few are nosing around the strange new posts.

Thunder is loping along beside us, sniffing the ground here and there, probably thinking we're going hunting for coons or rabbits. They'd make a racket, and I know Mom won't sleep at all anyway.

At first we feel all important, patrolling around and around the fence without talking much. That gets pretty old and tiring pretty quick, so we decide to hang around the middle of the field, closer to the lights illuminating the edge of the forest.

"You had plans with Yesenia tonight, didn't you?" I ask after a long silence.

"Yeah. We were gonna go bowling in Tahlequah. Eat some pizza. Hang out."

"Sorry, man."

"Not your fault." He pulls out his cell phone and answers a text message. From Yesenia, I'm sure.

"Well, I was pretty surprised when your dad volunteered you to stay. And your brothers," I offer.

"Why? We're neighbors. You and your dad would do the same."

"Yeah," I agree. "You really like Yesenia." I don't know if it's a question or a statement. David takes it as a question.

"Yeah. She's cool. Remember how I set her hair on fire in fifth grade?"

I laugh a little. "I remember. I think you were lucky Mrs. Hartley got to you before Yesenia put out the fire. I think she would have killed you." I remember how her big dark eyes were filled with angry tears.

"Probably," David agrees. "I never would have told her, but I thought she was cute then, too."

"That's how we flirted back then. Well, we didn't usually set them on fire, but we were mean to the girls we liked," I say. Despite the dark, it's still pretty hot outside, and humid. The air's so thick, we could almost swim in it. "We should go fly-fishing."

"Yeah. You should get a girlfriend, Logan. Maybe Christina. We could double-date." David stretches, bored.

Christina Moses is Yesenia's best friend. She's not ugly, and she's usually pretty nice, but I've never had much to say to her. I can't imagine her fishing with me, or hunting, and I have no desire to kiss her. I shrug off David's suggestion. "I don't know. Girls don't seem to like me."

"That's because you don't put yourself out there, man," he argues.

"I do," I counter, but I know he's right.

"I'll check around, see who's interested. Yesenia'll know."

"Whatever," I say.

Hours creep by. Cows sleep all around us. Once, off in the woods, a screech owl snatches up a meal, probably a rabbit, and flaps away with it. That's the only remarkable sound we hear before Dad shows up at twelve thirty. David and I go back to the house, go to different bathrooms for showers, then crash in my bedroom until my alarm sounds at four thirty. There are no monsters in my dreams, no poems, just aimless fish in a creek, swimming beneath the surface, waiting for me to catch them. I smack off the alarm with my palm and leave David sleeping on the floor to stumble out in the predawn and meet Dad in the milking barn. The cows are already gathering outside the back door, their udders full.

Later, over breakfast, Dad gets a call on his cell. "Proctor?" he says. "Yeah, I remember him." Pause. "Two of them, huh?" Pause. "All right, Sam. Thanks for letting me know." Pause. "Yeah, we got them. We'll finish planting the posts today, I guess." Pause. "All right. Let me know what you hear. Bye."

Dad puts the phone down and takes a bite of bacon, chewing it and staring blankly at the bowl of biscuits on the table in front of him. David looks from Dad to me, his eyes asking if we're going to get to find out what was said. Finally Kelsey just asks, "What was that about?"

Dad shakes off whatever he was thinking and looks around at

us. "Bob Hennessey, over by Proctor, lost two sows last night. He heard them squealing, but didn't get there in time. Nothing but blood and tracks when he got there. Whatever it was took them. No signs they'd been dragged. Carried them away, is what Sam Davis was told. Hennessey says those hogs must have been at least two hundred pounds each."

"Holy . . ." David doesn't finish the expletive, and he doesn't even see the look Mom casts in his direction.

"Hennessey and some of his neighbors got a pack of dogs together and went after it right after sunup," Dad adds.

"What did the tracks look like?" I ask.

Dad looks at me, then shakes his head. "Big," he says. "Long, with deformed toes. And long, pointed nails. Or claws. Not human, is what he said."

4

CHRYSTAL

The hotel room is easily one of the most horrible places we've ever stayed in. It's all early Salvation Army furniture. Dad drops his suitcases on one of the twin beds and stretches out his arms.

"Look, Chrystal, I can touch both walls if I spread out my arms!" He bounces up and down on his toes as his fingertips graze the walls' peeling wallpaper.

"Cool, Dad."

He scrunches up his nose. "Is that mildew?"

"I think it's the carpet." I point at the orange carpet, which is probably the source of the smell. But then I look up to where mold spots the walls. "Or maybe the ceiling."

He laughs and bounces down onto the bed, next to his suitcases, while I stand above him, hugging my bass to my chest and watching him smile.

"Do you know what?" he asks.

"What?"

"I think this is the worst hotel room we have ever had."

"What was the giveaway?" I ask, giving in to the ridiculousness of it all. "The dog poop by the front entrance?"

"That was brilliant." He looks down his beaky nose at me. "But I did like the used condom in the hall."

"You saw that?"

"Hard to miss. I think it was a Trojan Magnum. I wonder what Hector and the rest of the ancient Trojans would think to find their name is now used for prophylactics. I have to think they'd enjoy it." He laughs at the thought.

I fall onto the bed next to him. My feet hang in the air, and I laugh too. "Mom would kill if she had to stay here."

He tosses an arm around my shoulders. "Good thing she's in Europe, then."

"Yeah," I say. "Good thing."

After we've settled in and inventoried all the equipment and unpacked in our new home away from home, I go outside to call some friends back at my real home. I make laps around the parking lot while I listen to Zoe's gossip. Bugs chirp under the flickering orange lights that hang from poles above the cars. I wish they weren't here, so I could just see the stars. I click off the phone and breathe in. The air is so different here; the texture of it is deeper. I can smell the heat on the asphalt even though it's night, and then there's another smell—like berries and urine combined.

I can do this, I tell myself. I can help my dad and not be the typical resentful teen that everyone wants to make me out to be. I can be fine about my mom abandoning me for the Europe trip and me not being able to ever decide what to do with my own summer. It will be fine. Fine . . . fine . . . fine . . .

But just as I think it, something moves in the trees beyond the parking lot. It's a scuffling noise. A branch snaps hard, too hard for me to think it's the sound of a mouse or a squirrel.

I freeze and count to ten, try to be rational.

"You're freaking yourself out," I say aloud. "Just freaking yourself out."

And rationally, I know that's what I'm doing, but all my skin is suddenly goose bumps, like it's twenty-five degrees below zero, and I realize I'm walking backward toward the hotel door, away from the noise. I stare into the darkness.

"Totally fine," I murmur.

Then I can hear it, even above the hum of the parking lot lights: the sound of heavy breathing. Something sniffs the air. I step backward again. Lights swing into the parking lot. A Jeep Wrangler roars in, driving right between me and the sniffing in the darkness. Did the lights reflect in two eyes way high off the ground for just a heartbeat? I can't be sure. Lurching backward, I manage to avoid stepping in dog poop, and yank open the door.

For a second I think about running into the lobby and not looking back, but that would be wrong. Instead, I wait as two middle-aged businessmen-types haul out their suitcases and make their way safely across the parking lot. I'm like a sentinel standing watch, an ancient Trojan looking down upon the invading Mycenaean.

Once the men are only a foot away from the door, I do turn and head down the hall, my heart hammering one hundred beats a minute. When I aim the brass key at the doorknob, I have to do it three times before getting the key to fit, because my hand is shaking so badly.

Dad looks up from his laptop when I enter the room. He squints at me. "My sweet little philosopher, are you all right?"

"Yeah, I'm okay," I say, trying to convince both of us. "Just tired. Big day hunting Bigfoot tomorrow, right?"

He goes back to his computer. "Absolutely!"

"Dad?" My voice is squeaky.

"What, honey?"

"We don't have to stay in Oklahoma too long, right? If we can't find anything, we can go right to New York?"

"Of course," he says, but I can tell by the look in his eyes that he's hoping for the opposite. He's hoping for monsters.

The best thing about these trips with my dad is the diner food, *particularly* the breakfast diner food, *particularly* the home fries grilled in grease and dripping with fat and calories and salt. It is the glorious existence of such home fries at the Greasy Hog that allows me to get back to my normal, rational self and totally discount that random weird noise I heard in the parking lot last night as an auditory hallucination caused by lack of sleep.

Unlike my dad, I don't believe in bigfeet, except on ballet dancers and basketball players.

"Dad."

"Uh-oh." He sighs. "Are we going to argue?"

"I just . . . I have some problems."

"With belief? That's fine. You want proof. All good science

comes from trying to get proof." He squirts some ketchup on his plate.

"It's just - I don't believe in a Bigfoot that eats baby cows. Seriously. Why not just hop over to the Sonic and get a burger there? Why would a Bigfoot go to all that calf-ripping trouble?"

"It's a good question," he admits and then puts some egg in his mouth and chews.

I look away. Watching your parent eat isn't fun. I soldier on. "Seriously, for real this time though, why would a Bigfoot suddenly step up all his activity?"

"There have been missing cows for awhile. You saw my folder. It's full of various official county reports."

"Fine. But why so sloppy? All of a sudden it seems so sloppy? It makes no sense."

"Things don't have to make sense. Maybe what you should be wondering is more personal."

I prickle. "What do you mean? More personal?"

"Maybe you should be wondering why you refuse to believe, to even admit in the possibility that Bigfoot exists, that monsters exist?"

"Because they don't." I stab a nice hunk of home fries with the tong of my super-cheap diner fork.

"How can you be so sure?" Dad sits across from me, perusing his notes for the 190th time. His barely touched pancakes are getting cold. Fake maple syrup puddles around them. I witnessed him comb his thick brown hair this morning, but it's already completely messed up. Some of it stands on end.

He leans across the table, even more full of energy. "This is going to be the best search we've ever gone on. I can feel it, Chrystal. Are you ready for some excitement?"

His sleeve drags in the syrup. I pluck it out and say, "Then you should eat, Dad, keep up your adventurer energy."

"That's right! Have to keep up your strength when you're 'Bigfoot' hunting." He makes actual air quotes as he says "Bigfoot," and then grabs his fork and begins his pancake siege. Syrup splatters across the plastic table top. Pancake crumbs fly in arcs and land on the floor. Guilt courses through me. He loves this so much and I hate it; he's so excited and here I am being Captain Skeptic. I don't always have to throw my skepticism in his face, do I?

"So." I try not to sigh, but it's so hard. Only carbohydrates can make it better, therefore I put more potato-ie goodness on my fork before saying, "What's the plan for today?"

"We visit the boy."

"Reporting-incident boy?"

He smiles and chews. Then gulps some coffee, slapping some cash on the table.

"Dad, I still have home fries left. . . ." I protest. I'd like to stay here in town all day, really, maybe find a good place to dye my hair. I think it would like to be purple for the rest of the summer. Not really. But it would be fun to see if my dad even noticed.

"Ah!" His eyes are aghast. He rushes around to the counter, reaching behind it to grab a Styrofoam takeout container before anyone can say anything. He rushes back to the table and dumps the contents of my plate inside of it, snapping it closed. "There!"

Everyone in the whole diner is watching, and some people's mouths are actually hanging open. It only lasts a second, and then the place starts buzzing with activity again. Dad is completely oblivious, the way he gets when his mind is spinning around with the excitement of a new investigation. He motions for me to follow him and I do, but as we're passing a table that's hosting two old-ish ladies in pastel cotton tanks, he stops. I smack into his back. He doesn't even notice, just leans right over the center of the ladies' table, totally in their personal space. They start tee-heeing, because the truth is that my dad is kind of cute in an eccentric, full-haired, mismatched-clothing dad way.

"What did you lovely ladies just say?" he asks, head turning from one to the other to see who will answer and therefore who he should give his attention to.

The lady in the baggy pink tank top flushes. She's probably fifty or something. She giggles. I take a step back to watch my dad work. He is a master with older ladies, plays them like a maestro plays the bass, hits all the right notes.

"Well," she says, "up at Bob Hennessey's last night they think that the Bigfoot took two sows."

"Really! Where did you hear this?" Dad does his head-turning thing again.

The ladies are totally eating up the attention. I carefully hold my Styrofoam container away from my shirt so I don't get any of the ketchup my dad spilled on the side of it on my clothes.

"I heard it from Max Selmon's wife, Betty. They're neighbors of the Hennesseys and Betty's in my book club at church, don't you know? Anyway, she's fit to be tied, she's so scared," blue tank top lady says. She's a bit older than the other one and has that old-lady-blue-hair action going on.

The word "scared" gets all of Dad's attention. He actually scoots into the booth right next to her, which makes her giggle some more. "Why scared?"

She leans in toward him. Her friend leans across the table, too.

"Well, there weren't nothing but blood and tracks there. Two sows gone like that"—blue tank lady snaps her fingers—"and whatever it is that killed them just carried them off. That's a lot of strength."

"Indeed . . ." Dad coaxes, and waits for her to continue.

She does, so I give up and open my to-go container and start picking up home fries and eating them with my fingers. They aren't any good cold.

"So," she says, "it gets worse."

"Tell him, Darlene," her friend interrupts.

"I was, Barbara!" She smiles at her friend like this is an exchange that happens all the time. "So, anyways, once it's daybreak, Bob Hennessey gets Max Selmon and some other neighbors together and they track it and what do you think they find for tracks?"

"What?" Dad says the word like a sigh—a happy, elated sigh.

"It's two-footed like a Bigfoot, but the toes aren't fat and happy-looking like all them Bigfoot tracks, oh no. . . . They have long, kinky toes and claws, nonretractable you know, not like a cat's but more like a dog's."

"No!" My dad's so excited, I swear he jumps up and his knees knock the table, rattling the sugar shaker and Darlene's and Barbara's coffee mugs.

Darlene raises her right hand. "I swear."

For a second everyone is quiet and then Dad says, "Barbara? Darlene? What do you girls make of that?"

Barbara's eyebrows raise up toward her receding hairline and she whispers super-loudly, "It doesn't sound like a Bigfoot to me."

"What does it sound like?" my dad asks, matching her whisper.

"Why, sir, to the both of us, it sounds just like the devil."

It turns out that Dad didn't get the best directions from Barbara and Darlene. Two hours later, he hands over the paper map and says, "Okay. Program it. Here's the address."

We don't actually have the address of the Hennesseys, but we do have the address of the original sighting. I program it into the GPS. Dad prefers maps, like we're old-timey explorers, but having the GPS device is a recognized fallback plan he has to go to pretty often.

We haven't been running the air conditioning. The water in my water bottle is warmer than water in a bathtub. That's just ridiculous, yet cool, and so different from New England. On my bass case I've got all these Kierkegaard quotes and one of them—"Life is not a problem to be solved but a reality to be experienced"—seems pretty appropriate right now.

"It's like a whole different world out here," I say as the GPS says we have forty-two minutes to our destination. I give it an Aussie accent, male, because if you're going to listen to a GPS, it might as well be sexy.

"I know! How fantastic is that!" Dad says, pulling the car back onto the road. He suddenly brakes. We lurch forward. He unbuckles and jumps out of his seat. "You drive! I'm going to scan the roadside for clues."

I unclick the seat belt and fling open my door. "Deal."

The farm is down a dirt road, framed by trees and then opening up into pastures. The house is clean and sweet-looking, like something you'd see out of a movie set. There's a truck and a station wagon in the driveway, and a huge barn. A girl's on a swing in the front yard. She sees our car, waves at us, and hops off the swing when we pull into the driveway. She runs into the house, probably to announce our arrival.

"It doesn't look like a crazy kid's house, does it? But guns probably, right?" Dad asks, unbuckling. Before I can answer, he says, "Let me do the talking."

Sure thing.

The sooner the interview is over, the quicker we can determine that it's a hoax. He'll be disappointed, which is sad, but we can get on our way.

He bounces out of the car, all long-legged, quirky excitement. I can't imagine that this is going to go well. Dad can be a little overwhelming to strangers who aren't five years old. Sometimes it's up to me to make him seem more normal. It isn't easy.

Sighing, I climb out of the car and follow him up the walk. They've planted orange lilies and another plant I don't recognize all along the walkway. The air smells a bit like cut grass and cow poo and heat. I yank my hair back into a ponytail just to get it off my neck.

Dad turns around and makes big eyes at me. "I am absolutely excited. Are you excited?"

Before I can answer, he's speed walking toward the door again. The swing still moves in the trees, back and forth, slowing down. Before my dad can knock on the screen door, a woman appears. She's wearing shorts and a T-shirt. Her hair is pretty and combed back from her face. But she's not smiling.

She steps outside. "Can I help you?"

"Yes," my dad says, "I'm Matthew Lawson Smith and this is my daughter Chrystal and we—"

"You're a reporter and you brought your daughter?" The woman's body rigids up and her face is one big ole mask of disdain until she looks at me, and then it softens a bit. "I cannot believe the lengths some of you reporters will go to."

Dad starts to say something, but she holds up her hand, stopping him.

"Baby, call your father on his cell. Tell him to come up here!" she yells into the house, and then lowers her voice to talk to my dad again. "I'm sorry to be rude, Mr. Lawson Smith, but we've had enough tabloid reporters and regular old reporters around here to last a lifetime. And I don't want my son to have to be accosted by any of you anymore."

"I'm not a reporter," Dad says, holding up his hands. "I'm an investigator."

She studies him, his quirky long-sleeved shirt and trousers despite the heat, the craziness of his runaway hair. "With the police? I know all the police around here. Are you with the state?"

"No . . . no . . ." Dad blushes. "I'm not that kind of investigator. I'm a cryptozoologist."

The woman rolls her eyes.

Dad gives her his best sheepish grin. "I'm not here to bother you. I'd like to help."

For a second they are at an impasse. I move up to stand next to Dad, and when I do, some of the mommy-protector seems to seep out of her and she softens again.

"Why don't you all come inside and wait for my husband? It's hot as hell out there." She motions for us to follow her.

Dad does this little hop thing, which she fortunately does not see. He squeezes my elbow, leans in, and whispers, "Our lives are going to change. I can sense it! Can't you sense it?"

I want to tell him all I can feel is the heat, but that would be mean, so I say, "Yeah, Dad. I do."

5

LOGAN

I can't help but feel a little guilty when David and I follow Dad out to the alfalfa pasture, since Dad put his time on guard duty to use by bolting light fixtures to posts. What did we do? We talked about girls and hunting. He got a smooth two dozen posts laid out under the lights that had been burning last night. I look them over for a minute, then glance kind of sheepishly at David, then at Dad.

"I guess we could have been doing some of this last night," I admit.

Dad grunts and shrugs. He's unshaven and his face is haggard. "Don't worry about it. You had each other to keep you company. I got bored."

With the three of us working, the job of planting the posts goes pretty quick. Dad holds the posts straight while David and I shovel dirt back into the hole around each post and pat it down.

Normally you'd pour concrete in the hole to keep the posts from leaning after a while, but there just isn't time for that.

A couple hours after we get started, Mr. Thompson arrives with David's older brothers, Brian and Carl. Work really zips along then. We've just about got all of Dad's assembled posts in the ground by midmorning when Dad's cell phone suddenly blurts out a bit of Mötley Crüe's "Home Sweet Home"; that's our home phone's ringtone, obviously. In his younger days, back in the 1980s, Dad was a rocker, or so he says, which I guess explains the choice of ringtone. When Mom calls, though, his phone plays Johnny Cash's "Jackson." Weird. Dad pushes his cap back and wipes at his forehead with the back of his arm as he pulls the cell phone out of his jeans pocket with the other hand.

"Hello," he says. "Hi, Katie. What's up?" He listens, and his face turns a little hard. "I'm on my way." He pockets his phone, takes off his Oklahoma State University cap, and slaps it against his thigh. He curses. I know it's not good. Dad almost never cusses. It's another sign of just how tired and frustrated he really is.

"What's wrong, RJ?" Mr. Thompson asks.

"People up at the house," Dad answers, squinting across the field in the direction of home. "Reporters, probably. Man and a teenage girl."

"Why don't you and your boy knock off for a bit and go on up there?" Mr. Thompson suggests. "Me and mine can finish putting lights on the rest of these posts or start stringing the cords. I think we're gonna finish this job by early afternoon."

"Yeah, I think so," Dad agrees. "Still . . ." He shakes his head and wipes away more sweat. "Damn interruptions. Logan, you want to come, or not?" he asks, fixing me with his gaze.

I don't really want to. I don't care to talk to any more report- ers, but somehow the idea of Dad clumping through the pasture all alone in the heat of the day makes me feel sorry for him. "I guess I'll go," I say.

"Come on, then." Dad turns away and starts walking. I stab my shovel into the ground and catch up to him.

"This is just a story to these reporters," Dad grumbles. "It's our livelihood. Our safety. And they're out here interrupting us at our work."

There's a dusty red Subaru station wagon sitting in our driveway. The back of the wagon is crammed with boxes and sacks and pages of newspaper that look like they held nothing of interest and were simply thrown behind the front seats. Reporters don't usually carry that much stuff with them, I think. I point at the license plate on the back of the car.

"Look at that. All the way from Maine."

"Looks like your mom let them into the house," Dad mutters. I have a feeling this interview is not going to go well.

Inside, we find Mom sitting at the dining room table with a tall man who has thick hair that sort of stands up wildly, like he's been pulling at it or something. His eyes light up like Christ- mas trees when he sees me, and he jumps out of his chair and comes at me with his hand out.

"You must be Logan," he says.

"Yeah." I put out my hand too, more to stop him, but he grabs it and pumps it like my arm is an old well handle.

"I'm Matthew Lawson Smith," he exclaims. "We have traveled

down here all the way from Maine. We would love to talk to you about what you saw." He hasn't let go of my hand yet.

"You're reporters?" Dad growls.

Matthew Lawson Smith finally releases my hand and turns to my dad. "No, sir, Mr. Jennings," he says. "Cryptozoologists."

"What the hell is that?" Dad asks.

"RJ," Mom cuts in, her voice a little surprised. "Please excuse us, Mr. Lawson Smith," she says. "RJ and Logan and a neighbor boy were up most of the night watching the cattle and, like I said, they've been putting lights up in the pasture for two days now. I'm sure they're both very hot and tired."

"I'm tired *and* I still have a lot of work to do," Dad says. "We've told the reporters everything we know."

"Dad, I think cryptozoologists are kind of like monster hunters," I tell him.

"Exactly right, Logan!" Mr. Lawson Smith says, and I swear he actually jumps up in the air as he says it.

The girl at the table finally speaks. "Dad! You need to mellow." She's cute. She's got wavy black hair pulled back in a thick ponytail, a perfectly oval face, and wide-set eyes as blue as the summer sky. She looks to be about my age, too. I'm suddenly very aware of how dirty and smelly I am. The girl looks right at me and says, "Sorry. He's a kindergarten teacher most of the year, so he gets really animated when he talks. It keeps their attention."

"Oh." I don't know what else to say. Her eyes, though, seem to demand I say something else. I grasp for anything. "Y'all are from Maine?" No! Not the dreaded "y'all." That didn't really come out of my mouth, did it? Is there anything that sounds more hick than "y'all"? Other than the plural, "all y'all."

"Yes," she says. "Mount Desert. It's off the coast near Bar

Harbor, Acadia National Park. The president came there for vacation last year."

"We've never had a president come around here for vacation," I say, hoping it sounds like a joke. I think it might have succeeded, because the edges of her lips turn up a bit.

"Logan," Mr. Lawson Smith pipes up, obviously eager to be the one talking again. "Will you tell me all about your experience with the . . . with the thing you saw—"

"Look, Mr. Smith," Dad interrupts. "We have a lot of work to do. I've got a hundred and fifty head of cattle that has to be milked twice a day, a pecan grove that needs to be sprayed for bugs, and right now we're in the middle of putting up lights to keep that thing away from the cattle, which we now have to herd into a pasture where I was growing alfalfa to feed them during the winter. This is a busy, working farm. We've told the papers everything we know, and we just don't have time to repeat it. Go read the damn *National Enquirer*."

"Ronald James Jennings!" Mom says each word like she's cutting it off a loaf of bread. "These people are guests in our house and we will treat them like guests."

"We don't have time for guests," Dad barks back. "Not today. I'm sorry, Mr. Smith, but that's the way it is. Come on, Logan. Let's get back to work."

Undaunted, our guest tries again.

"We could help you," he offers. "Maybe we could talk and work at the same time."

"You ever put up light poles? Fence posts? Ever dug a hole?" Dad asks, his voice almost vicious.

"Dad," I say, trying to calm him. He gives me an angry look, so I stop.

"Well, yes, sir, I have," Mr. Lawson Smith says. "You see, I often have to—"

"The answer's no," Dad says, totally cutting him off. He stalks away toward the front door. I look after him, then back to Mom.

"I am so sorry," Mom says, shocked. "Really, my husband is never like this. It's just the stress. I'm really sorry."

"No, no, that's okay," Mr. Lawson Smith answers. "Disappointing, yes, but completely understandable. Here, let me give you my cell phone number and the number of the hotel where we're staying." He pulls a small notebook out of his back pocket and scribbles in it, then tears the page out and hands it to Mom. "Maybe when the lights are up and everyone has some good, restful sleep, you could give me a call?"

"I think that'll be fine," Mom agrees.

"I need to go back with him," I say. "It was nice to meet you, Mr. Lawson Smith."

I hold out my hand to shake with him again. He pumps it hard, like the first time.

"I look forward to hearing your story, Logan. I really do," he says, his voice as bright as the kindergarteners he teaches.

"It was nice meeting you, too," I say to the girl.

"I'm Chrystal," she says, smiling at me. She has nice straight teeth.

"I'm Logan." That's a stupid thing to say. I stare up at the ceiling before I can recover enough composure to look back down at her. "I guess you know that, though."

"I saw your picture in the paper," she says, blushing.

I cough.

"Do you really think you saw Bigfoot?"

"You say that like you don't believe me." My heart beats faster in my chest for some reason.

"I just."

"It wasn't a man."

She raises her eyebrows and waits, I think, for me to say more. I don't say more.

"There are tracks," I add.

"People can fake things," she says. "For a whole bunch of reasons. Practical jokes. Attention."

"Oh. Yeah. Well, I better get back to work." Before I go, I see Mom grinning at me, but she doesn't know what I know—that Chrystal Lawson Smith thinks I'm a liar.

Not long after we get back in the field, Kelsey rides out on the four-wheeler to deliver sandwiches and a five-gallon jug of ice-cold lemonade. As she's getting ready to leave, I step up to the green machine and put my hand on the handlebar. She gives me an annoyed look.

"It's hot out here," she complains, wiping her hair off her forehead and fixing her ponytail.

"I know. So, those people leave? Mr. Lawson Smith and his daughter?"

She looks at me like she's trying to read me. "Yes. Right after Dad told them off."

"You heard?"

"I was just in the living room." She rolls her eyes like I'm the stupidest brother on the face of this Earth.

"They seem mad?" I ask.

"No, not really. That guy was weird," she says.

"Yeah, he seemed real, I don't know, excitable."

"They left a number. Remember? You can call her," Kelsey says, then pushes the button to restart the vehicle.

"What?" I ask, trying to sound more innocent than surprised.

"I'm not as dumb as you think, Logan." She winks and sticks out her tongue, then stomps the four-wheeler into first gear. It jerks forward, making me step back, then she guns it and goes roaring back toward the house.

We finish up around two thirty and all step away from that last weather-treated wooden post to survey the rectangle of new lights and orange extension cords strung around the pasture.

"Hell of a job," Dad says.

We've worked our way back around until we're close to the big barn where we park the vehicles in winter and store all the tools. The milk barn is kind of behind it and is a little smaller. We drag our shovels and a couple extra cords into the barn and put them away, then stand around for a few minutes.

"You men are welcome to stay for dinner," Dad offers to Mr. Thompson.

"We appreciate that, RJ, but I figure we need to get back home. Beth was pretty nervous about all of us leaving her there alone. Haven't heard of anything happening during daylight hours, but I guess you never can tell. She's a good shot, though." He grins and winks. "That's how she's kept me in line all these years."

Carl, his oldest son, laughs a little at that, probably remembering last summer when his mom won the family skeet shooting competition on the Fourth of July. Carl played football in high school. I remember the university in Tahlequah was going to offer him a scholarship to play defensive end, then he blew out his knee. Sometimes he still walks with a slight limp. David keeps talking about the day Carl will finally move out so David can have a bigger bedroom, but I think Carl will probably be the one who keeps the Thompson farm running when their dad retires.

"Yeah, we should go," David says.

Mr. Thompson snorts and Brian punches David in the arm.

"That girl ain't goin' nowhere," Brian says.

"Kid's as randy as a billy goat," Mr. Thompson says. "Can't tell him how he's too young to be so serious about one girl."

"She's damn sure got him by the balls," Carl agrees.

"Can we just go?" David asks, his face reddening. I want to laugh at him, but instead I try to rescue him.

"We really appreciate you helping us, Mr. Thompson," I say. "All of you." I look at the two oldest brothers, then take my own little jab at David: "You better shower or Yesenia will think you're that forest monster."

He gives me the finger, sticking it by the side of his belt so only I can see it. I choke on a laugh.

Dad seems to shake himself out of his reverie, and extends his hand to Mr. Thompson, then all three of his sons, thanking each of them. We watch them get in their truck and drive away. Dad arches his back and it pops.

"We'll worry about those pecans later," he says. "Maybe even call Wayne Wilson and have him dust them over the weekend. I'm beat. Might sleep all day tomorrow."

I nod, then ask, "Are we going to spend the night in the pasture again?"

He puffs out his stubbly cheeks in a big sigh. "I don't know. That damn thing, whatever it is, is so unpredictable. It has a big territory. I don't have any idea if it'll be back here tonight, or where it'll be. If anywhere. It carried off four hundred pounds of pork last night. Why would it even need to hunt again tonight?"

"Could there be more than one?" I ask.

He shakes his head. "I don't even want to think about that." He pauses, then says, "I was a real ass to those folks who came out today, wasn't I?"

"Well . . ."

He smiles at my hesitation. "I was. I know it. I guess I shouldn't have been. What did you think of them? The guy seemed kind of squirrely to me."

"I don't know. He was pretty hyper, but he seemed okay. Different than any of the reporters, that's for sure." And so was his daughter, who is totally out of my league, who I shouldn't even think about, who thinks I'm lying, who I refuse to think about. . . .

"You *were* an ass, and they're staying at that filthy Cherokee Country Inn down on Highway 10." At some point Mom came outside and is now standing right behind us. I jump a little when she speaks, and I can't help but notice Dad jerks pretty good too.

"You ought to know better than to sneak up on us at a time like this," Dad says, his voice mostly joking.

"Let's have an early dinner, then me and Kels will help you with the milking," she says to Dad, but she's giving me a look.

"What?" I ask.

"Thought you might want to visit the inn," she says. "That Chrystal was cute as a bug and couldn't take her eyes off you."

"What? That's crazy." I can feel my face flushing right up to my hairline. Part of the tragedy of mothers is that they always think their own sons and daughters look like supermodels, no matter how ugly we are. "She didn't look at me at all."

"Uh-huh. Go in and shower. The chicken's already frying and Katie's shucking ears of corn," Mom tells me.

I feel like I should protest, but the heat of my face seems to have burned away the words. So I leave them and go into the house. The shower is cool and it feels really good to watch the dirt sluice off me and down the drain. Afterward, I get dressed and head for the kitchen, but the cooking is almost done and Mom shoos me to the dining table to wait for Dad to join us, which he does a few minutes later, water still dripping from his hair.

I refuse to gulp my food. But I don't participate in the conversation much, either. Is Mom really making me go talk to a monster hunter and his daughter? It's a pretty bizarre thought, but Mom talked to them more than I did, so maybe she trusts them. Obviously, she trusts them. I know she wouldn't send me to meet some guy she thought might be a serial killer or something.

I scrape up the last of my mashed potatoes and gravy, then swallow half a glass of sweet tea. I look to Mom and ask, "Do I have to go?"

She openly laughs at me. Seriously. Katie makes kissy noises. This is outrageous. I only saw the girl once, and barely spoke to her. Dad ducks his head and says to his nearly empty plate, "Please tell them I'm sorry for how I acted earlier."

"Dad'll clear your dishes," Mom says. "I want you home before dark. Way before dark."

"Logan," Dad says, raising his head, very serious now. "Bring your shotgun, just in case." That takes away all the snickering. I nod and leave the table.

The Cherokee Country Inn is just north of town. The highway twists and dips, but is pretty easy to navigate. I drive a Ford F-150 that's about ten years old. It has a granny four-speed transmission, and I can't help but remember what Mom said about it when Dad brought it home for me.

"That gear stick will keep his hands busy when he's driving," she said.

Mothers think of the weirdest things.

I pull into the parking lot of the inn and shut off my engine. The inn was built as an apartment house almost 130 years ago, back when there was more coal mining going on. It was empty for a long time, then some businessman from Tulsa bought it in the 1970s and turned it into a hotel to serve the tourists who came to the area, mostly to go boating on the Illinois River. I've never been inside it, but the outside has always seemed very dreary and depressing with its dark-red bricks, white-framed windows always in need of paint, and the sad glass front door that looks like it belongs on a five-and-dime store.

I go through the door and wait at the counter until the old man with more hair on his bare shoulders showing through his wife-beater than on his head finally looks away from the baseball game he's watching.

"You ain't old enough for a room," he says. He has at least four teeth in his mouth. His eyes appear puckered because of the fat pockets around them.

"I'm here to see Mr. Lawson Smith," I tell him. "The guy from Maine?" I suddenly realize I didn't see the red station wagon in the parking lot.

"He ain't here. Just the girl."

I don't know if this is good news or bad news. My palms are sweating like crazy. That is such a cliché that not even I would try to put it in a poem. Damn. I swallow hard, try to calm down.

"Can you tell me what room?" I ask.

He fixes me with a squinty, suspicious eye. "You ain't gonna go messin' around with that girl while her daddy's away," he warns.

"I don't even know her," I say, getting a little mad at the old guy. "They came out to my farm to talk to me, but I couldn't talk then, so I'm here to talk to them now."

"They know you're coming?"

"Are you their personal secretary?"

"Don't you sass me, boy," the man snarls.

"Sorry," I concede, holding up my hands in a show of peace. "Can you just please tell me what room number?"

"Let me see some ID. Anything happens up there and that girl's daddy needs to whup you, I wanna know who to send him after." The guy gets off the wooden stool he was perched on and shuffles toward the counter while I withhold a disgusted sigh and pull out my wallet. He copies down my name and address, then pauses. "You're the kid who saw Bigfoot."

"Yeah." I snap my wallet closed. The guy reeks of tobacco and old, greasy food.

"Was it big? They say Bigfoot has a powerful bad smell. Did it smell bad?"

"I really don't remember." Of course, I remember everything, but I'm not going to tell him about it. "What room?"

"Twelve," he says, his eyes a little wider now, like they're filled with wonder.

A minute later I'm standing outside a dull-green door with a

"12" screwed to it in flat black aluminum numerals at eye level, just above a peephole. I take a deep breath to steady myself, then wish I hadn't, as the smell of old urine and mold fills my nose.

I knock on the door.

6

CHRYSTAL

Kierkegaard said, "Faith is the highest passion in a human being. Many in every generation may not come that far, but none comes further."

Dad is full of faith.

After he left the Jennings' farm, Dad lets me rest at the hotel. Before he leaves to check out the tracks at the hog farm, he says, "I think this may be the one, Chrystal. I've got a feeling."

"I know, Dad. I hope it is."

And I do, because I like to see him happy, and sometimes since the divorce and Mom's remarriages, he gets so sad. I think he must feel all left behind, the way I feel sometimes, and so he needs to have faith in things. I have Kierkegaard and my bass guitar and he has . . . monsters.

The problem with my father is that he'll tell you he'll be back in an hour and it will end up being eight. So, I settle in for a long haul. I actually have summer homework for AP biology. It's all anatomy stuff, self-study and tests. I scoot the rickety wooden table and chair right in front of the AC and crank out some of that for an hour. The hotel doesn't have wireless; we don't have a good data plan and we use it up when we're doing the GPS, so I'll have to figure that out in the next two days, because that's when this chapter is due. But since I can't do it now, I give up and take a shower.

The bathroom is relatively clean of mold, which is a super-plus, and I put the water on lukewarm in an attempt to regulate my body temperature. I'm just toweling off with my own beach towel—I totally don't trust the hotel's—when there's a knock on the door. It takes me a second to figure out what the noise is, because it's not a forceful knock. It's timid. At first I thought it was the air conditioning breaking or something.

"One sec!" I yell.

I have no idea who could be at the door, and for a minute I'm freaked out. I should have pretended nobody was in the room, but then what if it was robbers and my lack of response made them bold enough to come inside? No . . . it's probably housekeeping. I look around the room, at the mold and dirty rugs, and wonder if they even have housekeeping here.

I swallow hard and look for a weapon. The lamp? Is that a cliché? I don't care. I unplug it, sending up a plume of dust, and get it solid in my hand before I go to the door. My heart is beating super-hard as I lean my eye toward the peephole and reel back-ward.

It's him.

Logan.

He's looking down. His hands are in his pockets and he's sort of shifting his weight back and forth.

Why would he be here?

Looking again, I verify that it's really, really him. Some guys in motorcycle leathers walk behind him. Crud. He's not safe out there. I run back and put the lamp on the table again before I fling open the door.

"Hey," I say.

He looks at me, brown eyes wide open. "Hey."

"Oh! I'm wearing a towel," I babble. "Oh my gosh. Oh my gosh!"

I run into the bathroom and slam the door, then open it again to yell out, "Excuse me for a sec."

"Uh-huh."

Cringing, I try to take a second to compose myself, but there's no hope of my heart rate slowing down at all. Instead I scoop my clothes off the door hook and slam them on. They're just green Adidas retro workout shorts and a T-shirt, but they'll have to do. I put my flip-flops on so I don't have to touch the carpet with my bare skin any more than I already have, and come back out.

Logan's eyes are still super-wide. I check to make sure my T-shirt is facing the right way. It isn't.

"Oh man," I mutter. "It's on backward. I'll be right back. I'm so sorry. Sit down."

Gesturing toward the one chair, I smash back into the bathroom and whip my shirt into the right place after I've shut the door. I quietly tap my head against the wall and chant, "Calm down, idiot. Calm down."

Why am I flipping out? Seriously. It's not like I haven't seen a cute guy before. I've dated cute people before! And it's not like he's perfect. He's a little too broad shouldered and his feet are huge. Seriously though, he has a pimple on his jaw. He's a little too country for me. Plus, he pretends to see monsters. It's his fault we're even out here.

I close my eyes and make myself breathe deeply. Swallowing hard, I open the door and make my voice as normal as possible. "So . . . um . . . hi."

He's sitting in the chair but pops back up. "Hi . . . yeah . . . my dad wanted to apologize to your dad for being a jerk today. Is your dad here?"

"Here?" I look around. There's not really any place for him to be.

He blushes. "Yeah. I didn't think so, unless he's hiding under the bed."

"I wouldn't put it past him. He'd hide anywhere if he thought it would help him gather evidence."

"He seems pretty"—he searches for a word—"obsessed."

"He is." I sit on the edge of one bed. After a second, the Logan guy sits in the chair again. "Obsessed is a nice way to put it. But he's not here. He went back out to look at some tracks. He'll be sad he missed you. I should call him."

I grab my cell and call Dad. It goes to voice mail. I leave a message.

"Sorry," I say to Logan once I'm done. "Can you stick around for a minute? Just in case he calls back?"

Logan nods. "Yeah. Of course. I can meet him tomorrow, too, you know, if he doesn't show up."

"Truth is, sometimes he's gone forever."

I smile at Logan. He smiles back. Then this ridiculous silence hangs in the air, which is stale. Then I realize my lollipop tattoo is showing. I slap my hand around it.

"You have a tattoo," he says, because I've completely drawn attention to it.

"Yeah."

Brilliant.

"Of a lollipop?"

"I like them. They're sweet and sort of innocent and I—I know—It's stupid."

His eyes crinkle up and he smiles. "No. It's cute. Kind of daring."

"My mom used to call me her little Poppie when I was a kid because I loved them so much and because I was always popping up into the air when I did gymnastics."

He nods. "Do people call you that now?"

"Oh . . . no . . . definitely not."

The silence gets awkward again. I want to shout into it, *Hey monster-seeing boy, I know I'm weird and probably not like the Oklahoma girls you're used to and I have a lollipop on my ankle, but you should tell me about this alleged monster so me and my dad can get out of here and I can get on with my life.*

I don't say that.

"I'm sorry if I seemed—um—harsh at your house. I just . . . I don't believe in monsters."

"I never did either."

"And now you do?"

"Sort of. Yes. No."

He seems like he is telling the truth. He's so earnest. That's the thing.

I ask, "You couldn't have been . . . mistaken? It couldn't have been a really big creepy guy?"

"I thought so too. I mean, I actually want to think that. But there are tracks."

"People can fake tracks." I interrupt him and feel guilty about that. "I'm so sorry it smells like cigarettes in here," I say, jumping up. "The windows don't open. And we don't smoke. . . . It's just . . . It's not the nicest hotel room."

He stands up too, and walks over to the window where I'm now standing. He's taller than me, which is not unusual, but it's still nice. He smells clean, like he maybe took a shower before he came over here, which is also nice.

He reaches past me. "Maybe it's just stuck."

"My dad tried—" I start to say, but he gets it open. "Oh . . . You're stronger than my dad."

He looks at me and smiles and then does this little half-shrug thing. I resist the urge to bang my head against the wall again.

"So, are you trapped here, waiting?" he asks.

"Yeah, just me and the TV and my bass." I point at the bass guitar case in the corner. I haven't even played it yet.

He cocks his head. "Did you eat dinner?"

I shake my head. "No. We had some Doritos for lunch. My dad forgets about food when he's on a trip like this. It's cute, but . . ."

"But you get hungry?"

"Yeah."

Wow. This is awkward.

His bottom lip curls in a tiny bit, moving toward his teeth. I wonder if he's biting it. "You want to get something?"

"To eat?"

"Yeah."

I don't know what to say. My stomach growls super-loudly. It makes us laugh. I text Dad to tell him, take the hotel key and my wallet, and follow Logan's rangy frame down the hall.

It's not until we're in his truck with the windows all the way down and buckled up that he says, "You don't think I'm a freak because of the whole. . . . *thing*, do you? I mean, back at the house, you pretty much said I was lying."

Before I *can* think about it, I reach out and touch his arm. My fingertips tingle. His skin is cool, muscled from farm work, I guess. I resist the urge to stroke it and pull my hand away.

"I meant that a lot of time people's fear make them imagine monsters because they can't understand what they see. And I also meant that you could have been joking, but then you got too caught up in the joke. But . . . I don't know. I don't believe there is a Bigfoot out there eating cows, but I also don't believe that you're a liar."

"But maybe a freak?"

I try out his name. "Logan, you met my dad."

He starts the truck. It rumbles to life. "Yeah."

"He's a little quirky, right?"

He starts laughing. "He's like someone out of a British comedy, only without the accent."

"He's not always this bad. The searches bring out his quirk. Anyway, I'm used to him, so you . . . you seem totally normal."

"*I* am totally normal? I just saw . . ." He shudders.

I touch his arm again. He seems so pained. I need to know if this is all crap or not, but I also don't want him to look like this. "Was it really that bad?"

"Yeah," he says. "It was. Topic change. Where do you want to eat?"

"Have you eaten yet?"

"Yeah." He starts moving all these spiral-bound notebooks off the seat between us and putting them in this space behind the upholstery. This reveals a tear in the fabric, where yellow foamy stuff appears. Written there are the words *I AM RIPPED*. Someone used black ink. I wonder if there are any other messages there.

"Oh!" I feel guilty. "We don't have to go. You can just tell me what happened here . . . in the hotel room of hell."

"No . . . no. I want to. I'm always hungry."

"Me too," I say just as my stomach rumbles again.

"We are going to be perfect together then," he says, and then he turns bright red because it's kind of an embarrassing thing to say. I totally like it. I want to reach out and touch his blushing skin. Instead, I sit on my hands.

I take a big risk because Kierkegaard said, "During the first period of a man's life the greatest danger is not to take the risk."

So I say, "Yeah, we are."

He coughs.

I add, "We're going to be . . . great friends . . . I think."

Awkward. It's all so awkward.

7

LOGAN

Oh. My. God.

That thing about being perfect together just popped out. I didn't even think about what it might mean. Then it was out there. Just there, like a guy who came out of a porta-potty and forgot to pull up his pants. And then . . . she agreed. And then . . . she friend-zoned me, I think.

I swallow hard and stare out the windshield for a few brutal minutes as we drive toward town. I have to say something. Something good. "There are better places to stay than the Cherokee Country Inn." No! No, stupid. Criticizing their choice of hotel is *not* the way to go. "I mean . . . well, I don't know. I didn't mean to criticize."

"It's a dump. Not at all what the website showed," she says.

"They actually have a website?"

"Just contact information and a couple pictures of a room that looks like it came from somebody else's bed-and-breakfast."

"Yeah, you hear 'country inn' and you think one thing, but that's not what it is. There's a little motel down the road that's much nicer." I pause, still thinking it's bad to criticize their room choice, even if it was an accident. "So, are you going to stay long, do you think?"

"I don't know. That depends on my dad," she answers, tucking some half-wet hair behind her ear. "The sooner we can find some resolution, the sooner we get to leave."

We enter the two blocks that make up downtown, and I see there's an empty parking spot right in front of the Greasy Hog. I wheel the truck in and kill the engine, then look at her. Man, she's pretty. Her hair is wet, but still wavy. She's not wearing any makeup, but she really, really doesn't need any. Her eyes are fixed on me, and for a second I can't talk.

"Has your dad ever found a monster before?" I finally ask.

"No," she answers. "He has pictures of lights he's sure are UFOs, and he's made plaster casts of big, deformed-looking footprints. He has one short video clip he says is Bigfoot, but a professor in Orono told him it's just a bear. Dad doesn't believe him, though. He says it's a conspiracy." She laughs a little. "He said the professor probably ran out in the woods to try to get his own video as soon as Dad left his office."

"What does he want to do? I mean, what if he found Bigfoot?"

She thinks about it for a minute. "You mean, face-to-face? Like you were in the article?"

I sigh. "It wasn't exactly face-to-face. I still don't even know if it was Bigfoot. That's what a reporter said and then everyone jumped on it. But . . . yeah."

She says, "I don't know. I think he just wants pictures. Maybe some hair. Proof that the impossible is possible."

I nod, then look at my shotgun resting upside down in the gun rack mounted over my back window. "I know what I'm doing if I see it again."

She looks at the gun in kind of a funny way and I guess she hadn't noticed it when we got in the truck.

"You'd shoot it? Kill it?" she asks. She makes a face like she's just eaten okra for the first time.

"Yeah. But whatever it is, it's killing livestock," I explain. "That costs us money. Everyone around here. Plus, well, it's just scary. It's a way of life for farmers to have guns, for people here to hunt."

She nods, but I think she doesn't believe those are good enough reasons. But hell, she didn't actually see it rip the head off a calf. Her stomach growls again and I smile at her.

"They have the best fries here," I tell her. "You get a pile of them like this." I raise my hands, keeping them about nine inches apart. "They're not the frozen kind, like at McDonald's. These are real potatoes that they peel and cut fresh every day." Her stomach growls again, and this time it embarrasses me a little. "I'm still talking instead of getting you inside to eat, huh?"

"You're making my mouth get all watery," she admits.

A few local farmers—friends of Dad's—sit around drinking coffee and talking about the only topic to matter right now, the monster. Mr. Rice waves at me with a thick hand and I wave back, then lead Chrystal to a booth in the far corner. Chelsea Newman, our waitress, arrives at the table with two glasses of water and two laminated menus.

"Hi, Logan," she says, handing out the menus. She's older than us, in her early thirties, I think. She looks at Chrystal for a minute, then says, "Hi, honey. Wasn't you here yesterday?"

"She's visiting from Maine," I say.

"Really? Maine? That's a long way away," Chelsea says. "Whatcha doin' down here? You related? I didn't know you had any relatives in Maine, Logan."

"I don't. Chrystal and her dad are here because of . . . because of what I saw. He investigates those kinds of things."

"Ooooh," she says, and nods her curly blond head. "Well, y'all can just take whatever it was right back up to Maine with you. I'm sick to death of hearing about it. Monster this and Bigfoot that and it ate this and broke that. Enough already, is what I say."

"I don't think it would fit in our Subaru," Chrystal says, and I can't help but give a quick snort of a laugh that doesn't sound very nice.

"Suburban? Oh, honey, you can fit anything in a big ole Suburban," Chelsea says.

"She said Subaru," I correct. "It's a foreign car. A station wagon, in this case."

"Oooh. Like a Honda or something?" she asks.

"Yes, like that," Chrystal says, blushing again. "I think I want a cheeseburger and some cheese fries."

The order seems to snap Chelsea back into work mode. She scribbles on her green pad, then looks at me. "How about you, Logan? The usual?"

"No, I already ate. Just an order of fries and a chocolate shake."

"You want a shake?" she asks Chrystal.

"Okay. Yeah!"

I swear Chrystal's eyes light up.

"Thanks," I say before Chelsea can start talking again. She turns and swishes away. Chrystal gives me a big-eyed look. *Country folk,* I mouth at her. She smiles, showing those perfect little teeth again.

"It's a nice place," she says, looking around. There are hand-painted pictures of chickens, ducks, cows, and pigs on pieces of weathered old wood hanging all over the place. Little wooden or wicker baskets made to look like fake nests with egg-shaped rocks in them. "In Maine it would be decorated with fish and lobsters."

"Really? That'd be nice."

"It's all in what you get used to," she says. "Have you always lived on your farm?"

"Yeah. It was my grandpa's farm, really. Him and Grandma retired and moved down to Florida before I was born, and Dad took over the farm. It was all dairy then. He planted the pecan trees. We make good money from those."

"Do you like farming?"

"Yeah, I guess. I mean, I've never really thought of doing anything else. I'm the only boy, so I'm kind of expected to take over the business."

"You shouldn't have to if you don't want to," she says.

I shrug. "I don't mind. There's always something to do and you're kind of your own boss."

"That would be good," she says. It's followed by a long pause. "Did you . . . Do you think you could tell me about what you saw?"

"Yeah. In a second. I have questions. Do you work?" I ask. "I mean, are you even old enough? Do you have to be sixteen to have a job in Maine?"

She laughs at me, but it isn't a mean laugh. "You can be fourteen with a permit. I don't work, though. Dad wants me to focus on my grades. I get an allowance."

"Oh. But, umm . . . you're old enough to work? If you wanted to?"

She laughs again. "Yes, I'm old enough."

"Good," I say, and it sounds really dumb, like I'm evaluating her as if she's a cow I'm thinking about buying for my 4-H project. "I mean . . ." I sigh and just admit it. "I haven't been out with very many girls."

She smiles and puts her hand on the table. Her hand is so small and soft-looking, with delicate, unpainted fingers. Having it so close makes me tingle even though I'm not even touching it.

"I totally can't believe that," she tells me.

"Okay." Inside, I'm saying, *Please don't pull your hand away.* And maybe a little of, *I wish David would walk in here right now.* Chrystal is ten times better looking than Yesenia. "So, have you been on a lot of these hunts? Investigations? Are you just here hanging out with me so I'll tell you what I saw?"

She taps a fork on the table.

"I'm here because I'm hungry," she teases, not missing a beat. "But how many investigations? I guess a lot. I mean, I don't know what you'd call 'a lot.' I thought I was going to spend this summer in New York with my mom, but she went to Europe with her new husband and I couldn't go. But, yes, the sooner we leave here, the sooner my dad will bring me to New York."

"Oh." That was a lot of information. I don't know what to say. Again. Talk about how my parents are still married and never even fight? No. "I don't think I'd like New York." Great. Disagreeing with her about something she obviously does like. She's looking at me like she expects me to say something else.

"Just a country boy, I guess. You know, the smog and tall buildings and noise and stuff." I shrug.

"I wouldn't want to live there all the time, but it's fun to visit. You can be anonymous. Nobody thinks your dad is crazy or that you're crazy by association," she says.

I think for a minute. Thoughts of Dad rescue me. "My dad really was sorry about how he acted. He's never like that. We were up most of the night watching over the cattle, and it took us two days to put lights around the pasture. We try to keep the cattle out of that pasture because we grow alfalfa and then bail it up for winter feed."

"Now you're talking," she teases. It embarrasses me, and she sees that. "You have a lot of cows?"

"About one-fifty."

"Do you, like, eat them?" she asks.

"Sometimes. We'll slaughter one steer a year and that'll last the family pretty well. But we're not a beef ranch. We're a dairy farm. Dairy and pecans."

"Oh, milk," she says, and nods.

"Yeah. We're part of the Double O Co-Op."

"Double O?"

"Oklahoma Ozarks is what it stands for, but people just call it the Double O," I explain. "You can find the Double O brand of milk and eggs, beef, chicken, pork, and pecans all over the eastern part of the state."

"You know your business," she says, and smiles again.

"Yeah, but now I've been talking too much and not about what you want me to talk about."

She doesn't say anything; it's just this long loaded pause before she finally clears her throat. The noise is harsh but her voice is gentle, the way Dad talks when he's trying to soothe an in-jured cow.

"So, are you sure what you saw wasn't . . . wasn't just a bear or something?" she asks. "Or a person? I mean there are some huge guys out there."

"Not rip-the-head-off-a-cow huge."

"With a weapon? A machete or something."

"Maybe. But . . . It . . ." I give up. "I want it to be human, Chrystal. Or a bear. But it wasn't a bear. The sound of it walking through the woods was bipedal. It's a different sort of noise."

"Bears can walk on two legs."

"Rarely. Short strides. Slow." I fiddle with my napkin and stop. "You really don't want this to be a Bigfoot. Why?"

Just then Chelsea reappears with our food. I can't help but grin when she puts the order of fries in front of Chrystal. Her eyes bug out and she licks her lips like a cartoon character. Her cheese-burger is a good five inches tall with meat, tomatoes, lettuce, and melted cheese hanging out on all sides. She goes after it with gusto and I try not to watch her delicate jaw as she chews, or her throat as she swallows. She pulls a few long, curling, greasy fries from the basket, dips them in ketchup, and eats them.

"Wow. Those are really good," she says, wiping at her chin.

"The best in the county," I promise.

I know she's hungry, so I shut up and let her eat for a while. When her burger is mostly gone, she asks, "So, do you want to tell me exactly what you saw on your farm, or do you want to wait and tell me and Dad? Or do you even want to talk about it?"

I pull in a deep breath and hold it for a moment, then let it out slowly. "I'll talk. Y'all—I mean, you guys came all the way down here from Maine. It'd be kind of rude for me not to talk to you."

She laughs, and for a minute I think she's going to reach over and take my hand, but instead she reaches for more fries. "You don't have to. It would really thrill my dad, though."

"I'll go ahead and tell you, then you can tell him, and if he wants to know anything else, he can ask," I offer. She nods, so I recount my adventures of that night. I add on how we heard the thing again several nights later, screaming or howling or whatever in our driveway.

"The driveway we were in today?" she asks.

I nod around a mouthful of French fries. "Yeah."

That seems to bother her, which I'm kind of glad to see because it means she believes me. I'm about ready to tell her how there was a run on posts and lights at the feedstore when my cell phone goes off. It's Mom.

"Logan? Logan, are you all right?" Her voice is frantic.

"Yeah, Mom. I'm fine."

"Where are you?"

"The Greasy Hog. Chrystal was hungry."

"You've been there the whole time?" she demands.

"Yeah. Well, I mean, I picked her up at the hotel, we talked for a few minutes, then came here. What's going on?"

"Karen Ferguson," Mom says, then she can't go on. She just bursts into sobs. A moment later Dad's voice comes on the phone.

"Logan, you need to come home," he says.

"All right, Dad, but can you tell me what happened?"

He sighs. Mom's still crying in the background. It sounds like Katie is crying too. Karen Ferguson is Dale Ferguson's sister. Dale is a year older than me and Karen a year younger. She's pretty, but shy.

"She's missing," Dad says. "Those men who went tracking that thing after it took the hogs, they found her cell phone and a shoe right by the hog carcass. One hog was stripped clean, the other barely touched, but in the weeds real close there, they found Karen's phone."

"But she's not dead, right? Just missing. You think . . . you think that thing took her?" I ask. Chrystal is watching me, her fries apparently forgotten. Her usually pale face is now absolutely white. Her big, round eyes flick to the phone pressed against my head and I realize my hand is trembling.

"Logan, come home. Come straight home right now, okay?"

"Okay, Dad. I'll be right there." I put the phone down on the table. Chelsea suddenly appears beside us.

"What was that about? What's missing?" she asks, her voice low, but loud enough that it carries across the café. Everyone is looking at us.

"That was my dad. He said Mr. Hennessey and some other men tracked that thing into the woods and they found Karen Ferguson's cell and a shoe. They think the monster thing took her."

"Oh my good lord a'mighty," Chelsea says in a gasp. "She was the sweetest girl to ever come through that door!"

"Can I get our check?" I ask. "We have to go. You want to take that with you?" I ask Chrystal.

She blinks at me a few times, then looks down at her food. She shakes her head. "No," she says, then hesitates. "Yes. Dad might want it, I guess."

Chelsea brings us the check and two Styrofoam containers. I drop money onto the table and we leave.

"Did you know her?" Chrystal asks when we're about halfway back to the hotel.

"Yeah. A little." I explain about Karen and Dale.

"They go to your school?"

"Uh-huh. I just . . ." I don't know what to say. "I just can't believe it. Karen is a good kid. I don't know what that thing might do to her."

"But they didn't find her body, right? That's a good sign," Chrystal says in a voice about one octave higher than normal. She looks so innocent and scared and hoping for the best all at once.

She's going to be alone. In a hotel room. Alone. "Do you guys have a gun? I don't know if that thing's been close to town or not. I'm kind of worried about leaving you."

"I think we'll be safer than you are. Plus, we aren't gun people," she says, and she reaches over to me again and puts her hand on my upper arm. It's comforting, but I'm way too wound up to really enjoy it. I think again about the gearshift and how Chrystal can't sit next to me because I have to shift the gears. Mom was right.

The dusty red Subaru is in the parking lot, and that's a huge relief. I don't know if I could leave her all alone. I pull in beside it and set the parking brake.

"I'll walk you in," I say.

"You don't have to," she says. "Your dad told you to come straight home, and I heard your mom crying. Go home. Dad's here, and I can get in okay."

"You sure?"

She nods.

The moment is horrible, but I can't let it go. "Can I give you my number? Or get yours? Can I call you tomorrow? You could bring your dad back to the house tomorrow and we could talk?"

"Of course. Do you want me to put my number in your phone?"

"Um . . . Ah . . . ." I do, but if she takes my phone she'll see the super embarrassing picture of Mom blowing a kiss at me. It's a family joke, but how do you explain that to a hot girl? "Maybe you could write it down?" I offer before I think that I could just put her number in my phone. Or I could just put my number in hers. It's all I can do not to hit myself in the forehead and shout, "Doh!"

She grabs one of my spiral notebooks from behind the seat and finds a pen in my glove compartment. She writes down her number and puts the notebook over the rip in my seat. She's written her number under one of my absolute worst poems. I don't stare at it because I don't want her to notice what I've written on the page. I flip to the back, to a blank page, tear it out and write my number on it for her.

"Thanks for dinner. It was really nice of you to pay and take me and everything," she says. "You must be one of the best new friends I've ever had."

Friends?

She squeezes my arm, then scoots out the door of my pickup and jogs up to glass door of the Cherokee Country Inn. She tosses a final wave back at me, then goes inside.

"Bye," I say, though she's already gone.

Friend.

I drive home as fast as I can.

8

CHRYSTAL

The news about that girl Karen being missing sends my father into an absolute tizzy. He'd already been excited about a new plaster cast and a digital photo. So now he's basically resonating with purpose.

"This. Is. Horrific," he says. "We must find her! Are there search parties?"

"Yeah." I imagine Logan in a search party, roaming around with some serial killer lurking in the woods. I cross my arms over my stomach and try not to throw up. Meanwhile, the parental unit is rummaging through the big red duffel bag that holds some of his favorite books and several files in folders. He pulls a couple books out, flips through them.

He points his finger at me. "We have to stop it. We can't let it hurt people."

"I know, Dad, but I'm sure the police are—"

"The police! Brilliant! You are brilliant, Chrystal!" He interrupts me and starts pulling his shoes onto the wrong feet. "I'm going to the police. I have to tell them about this. This is a whole new ball of wax."

"Ball of wax?" I ask.

He ignores me. Instead, he realizes his mistake and shoves his shoes onto the appropriate feet. "I need to offer them my assistance."

"You want me to come?" I can't imagine what the police are going to think about him. People tend to trust him a little bit more when I'm there. Mom calls me a "normalizing influence."

"No . . . no . . . Cops can be rough." He hugs me quickly and kisses the top of my head. "You man the fort here."

Then he's gone. I don't get a chance to tell him about what Logan said at the diner or anything else. Sitting on the bed, I text him as much information as I can, hoping he'll actually check his phone. I wonder if he even knows where the police station is, or if it's local police or state or county that's doing the investigation. Well, he's a smart—if scattered—man. He'll figure it out.

I pick up my bass case and unzip it because there's nothing else to do. Then I hesitate and text Logan: HOPE U R OK. THANKS 4 DINNER.

He's awkward, but in a totally different way from my dad. He seems so solid somehow, with his sweet parents who obviously still love each other since they give each other those looks even when his dad was being a jerk, and the big, old American farm life. He's a farm boy.

It makes me smile to think about him, which is much better than the queasy feeling I get whenever I think of Karen, the missing girl. She was close to my age, and that's just wrong.

I stare at my guitar for a second. The whole point of the bass is to lay down the rhythmic framework and sort of hold the harmony together. It's like an anchor when you're playing with a band. People don't think of bassists as ever soloing, but we do, especially for Latin and funk. Mine has no frets so I can do glissandos and stuff. I start one now, just pushing the notes around with my fingers. I get into a zone when I play, and it takes a lot to snap me out of that zone, but something does.

I smell it first: urine, berries, copper, a weird mix of animal and man. It's the same smell from the parking lot last night.

Holy crap.

Putting the bass down, I look to the window. Whatever is making that smell has to be outside. It's so strong that the window must still be open behind the big, moldy curtains. Holy crap. If the window's open, then whatever is out there . . . It could smell me, too. It could get in. Assuming it's even the monster thing, but do I want to take that chance? No, I do not. Tiptoeing back to where I was sitting, I tuck my bass under the bed for safekeeping and slip my cell into the pocket of my shorts. Swallowing hard, I creep toward the window. The smell wafts through again. It's so pungent, it makes me want to vomit. Seriously.

I don't know what to do. My stomach is squinched up like I've ripped all my abdominal muscles in a back twist that's gone horribly wrong. I try to think out the sequence of what I have to do, like my actions are notes meant to be played, and if I play them in just the right order, all will be safe.

I have to shut the window. That requires reaching behind the curtain. There's a screen, but if some crazy guy is out there, is a screen really going to stop him? Is a window? I don't know. I don't know anything, but it seems logical to shut the window, right?

People break into hotel rooms all the time. They look for easy-access things like ground-floor open windows. I can't believe I left it open.

One more step gets me close enough to reach it. I slip my hand behind the curtain, grab the wooden edge of the window, and pull. It thunders down.

There. Good.

I'm not going to lock it, because I'm too much of a wimp to risk looking out the window. I'm honestly that freaked out that I—

Something bumps against the glass. I let out a little shriek and jump away, clapping a hand over my mouth. I can see a dark, thick shape, just a shadow behind the thin curtain. It seems to be pressing its face against the window. Then I hear . . . snuffling.

A bear? Bears snuffle. Maybe it's a rabid bear that's doing this—no matter what Logan said about it walking away. A bear actually makes sense.

I run out of the room and into the hallway, pulling the door closed behind me. I stand there for a minute, my back pressed against the opposite wall, not sure what to do next. Finally I run down the hall to the registration desk. A strongly-built woman with bleached hair is sitting at the desk, reading a romance novel. She looks up at me and I wonder why she's wearing so much turquoise eye shadow.

"Umm, someone was just outside my window," I tell her.

"Those damn peeping toms," she says, slamming her book face-down onto the counter and jumping up. She pulls a baseball bat from somewhere down below and comes around the counter, her cotton dress swooshing as she heads for the door.

"I don't think—" She's out before I can tell her a baseball bat might not be enough. Not if that thing is what I think it was. I can't let her just go out there and die. I hurry after her and catch up as she rounds a corner of the building. There's nobody there.

"Move it, hon," the woman says, pushing past me and hurrying back toward the front of the building. I jog after her and catch up to her again in the parking lot. She's got the bat resting on her shoulder now. There's nobody at the front of the building. She looks up and down the street.

"Darn kids," she says. "The Roper boys live up the road a ways. We catch them peeking in the windows sometimes. A pretty girl like you probably got them all worked up."

We watch as an old SUV passes along the street. The driver wears a straw hat and dark glasses and is looking back at us as he passes.

"I hope they didn't scare you," the woman says. "They don't mean no harm. Probably just hoping to catch you changing clothes. I'll call their dad and tell him I'll send the law if they do it again." Despite the horrid makeup, she has kind eyes. "You okay?"

"Yeah," I tell her. "I'm fine. Do you ever get bears around here?"

"All the time. They go dumpster diving, but this would be early for one. You never know though."

I watch as she trudges back to the hotel door, her bat still over her shoulder and her feet bare despite the gravel. She pauses at the door and looks back at me.

"Coming in?" she asks.

"In a sec," I answer.

She goes inside. I look around for a minute, then go back around the building.

The back side of the Cherokee Country Inn faces pretty dense woods that seem to loom all dark and secretive about thirty feet from the brick building. Nothing's moving, though. I think of what my dad would do in this situation. He probably wouldn't think twice about something being in the trees. What about Logan? He would be holding that huge gun that was in his truck.

I am not them.

I am me.

And I step forward. Another step, then another. I'm holding my breath. I let it out. Nothing is moving around me. I keep walking. Then I'm standing outside the window that I know is the one to our room. It's in the right place in the building. And . . .

I stare down at the ground. There is no grass in this shaded place between the building and the woods. There is only dirt. Loose, dusty dirt. And there in the dirt is a very clear set of very inhuman footprints. There are claw marks beyond the toes. It's like an elongated bear paw maybe?

A hoax.

It's got to be a really clever hoax. Right? But that poor Karen girl is missing. And Logan saw something out there. . . . Maybe a hoax by a sick serial killer, then. A deadly kind of crazy where the person doing it doesn't just get off on the killing, but also on the fear.

I'd almost prefer a monster.

But either way, it's dangerous and we need to stop it.

My hand shakes as I pull my phone out of my pocket and snap a couple pictures of the prints. They don't come out very clearly, but I send them to Dad anyway, then I head back for the door of the hotel, keeping my back to the building and my eyes on the dark forest that's too quiet to be safe.

9

LOGAN

Mom's waiting on me in the yard when I pull up. She comes rushing at my truck even before I get the engine turned off, and yanks open the door. She kind of lunges into the cab and throws her arms around me. Her voice trembles a little as she says, "Thank God, you're home safe."

"I'm fine, Mom," I say, sitting patiently and waiting for the relief I know she feels to subside a little and for her to let me go.

"Come on, let's get in the house," she says, pulling at me.

I take my shotgun off the rack and walk beside her toward the house. Dad and the girls are standing on the porch. My sisters are watching us, but Dad's eyes are roaming around the farm as twilight reaches out with weak gray fingers. Dusk and dawn have always been among my favorite topics for bad poetry.

On the porch, Dad stops me and sends the women inside.

"Seriously?" Kelsey says, hands on her hips.

"Seriously," Dad says.

We watch them close the door on us. Dad's still looking pretty haggard from worry and lack of sleep. "Your mom told you about the Ferguson girl?"

"Yeah. Karen," I say. The numbness and disbelief have made my stomach hurt. "I . . . I don't know what to say."

"We're doing search parties. Tonight. Now." My dad's voice is clipped and almost military. He doesn't sound like himself. "One of us needs to help search. One of us needs to stay here with the girls."

My cell phone goes off, telling me I have a text. I reach into my pocket and silence my phone.

"Now that there's a human involved, the police are more interested. The sheriff is asking for volunteers to start a manhunt tomorrow. Manhunt." He snorts. "Whatever. A hunt. I'm going along for that one definitely."

"I'll come—"

"No, Logan. I know you want to, and I know you'd do fine, but I need you to stay here. We have three women of our own to take care of," he says.

"That's sexist!" Kelsey yells.

Dad groans, rubbing his hands across his eyes, and mutters, "Probably is."

I'm disappointed. I'd much rather go out and hunt that thing tomorrow, and go out tonight and look for Karen, but at the same time I can't bear the thought of Mom, Kelsey, and Katie being home alone. "Okay. I'll stay with them."

Dad drops a hand onto my shoulder and squeezes. "You're a good son, Logan. I couldn't have asked for better. Thank you."

I was looking him in the eye just fine until he said that, but now I can't. My chest gets all tight and my eyes almost water up. I duck my head, but say, "Thanks, Dad. I do my best."

"That's all anybody's got a right to ask of you," he says, giving my shoulder one last squeeze before dropping his hand away and heading down the stairs, asking, "How were our visitors?"

There's a moment of silence as I think about how to tell Dad what I did. Finally I just come out with it. "I told Chrystal they could come back out tomorrow morning and I'd talk to her dad then. Is that okay?"

"That's fine," Dad says without looking at me. He's squinting off toward the pasture, where we can hear the faint lowing of cattle. The herd sounds content. He puts his hand on the door to the truck. "Let your mom know. I'm sure she'll want to feed them lunch."

"I will."

"They sound okay out there. Be strong, Logan," he says, opening the door now and slinging his gun onto the seat next to him instead of putting it in the gun rack in the back.

"Stay safe, Dad."

He nods, honks the horn, and backs out of the drive.

I go inside and talk to Mom and the girls and then I feel restless, just full of energy and thoughts, and I go back on the front porch with my gun. Mom follows me, her lips pressed tightly together.

"I think I'll sit out here for a little bit, if that's okay."

She nods and heads back inside. My feet on the wooden steps rouses the dogs sleeping under the porch. All three of them follow me back up to the front door. Our porch stretches across the front of the house and wraps around the south side to overlook

Mom's flower garden. I take a seat in a wooden chair not far from the crook where the porch turns, propping my shotgun against the rail.

Galahad tries to jump up in my lap as soon as I'm settled. I push him down and he prances around me while Daisy crawls under the chair and lies down. Thunder sits patiently beside me. I'm afraid Galahad will knock over the shotgun, so I lay it down on the porch in front of me and tell him to calm down. Instead he brings me his tennis ball. I throw it out in the yard, then scratch Thunder's head as we watch Galahad run for the ball.

"Does he ever get tired?" I ask Thunder. He doesn't answer, just rolls his sad brown eyes up to look at me. I throw the ball for Galahad three times before I remember my phone. I pull it out of my pocket and unlock it. At first I don't recognize the strange number with its 207 area code, but when I read the actual message, I feel my pulse pick up a little. I text Chrystal back, YOU'RE WELCOME. SEE YOU TOMORROW.

I wait a few minutes, hoping she'll respond, but she doesn't. Well, there wasn't really anything to answer. I think about her, how she touched me, the tone of her voice, the earnest light in her eyes, and how she touched me. Yeah, I said that twice. If I concentrate, I can almost feel her delicate fingers on my arm still. That's crazy. Or is it?

I text David. DID YOU HEAR ABOUT KAREN?

He texts back. I AM SEARCHING NOW. NO SIGN. THIS IS SOME WHACKED CRAP BRO.

I reply. YEP.

I'd really rather be out there looking. But what if something happened again here? No. It's good. I fetch a notebook from my truck and return to the porch, writing and marking out lines. After a half hour I have a few lines I don't hate, though they are free verse, which always feels like cheating to me.

> *I wasn't born until you touched me.*
> *I existed in limbo*
> > *Going through*
> > > *The motions of life*
> *Without realizing I was flesh without a heart.*

It isn't great. It's a little corny, I suppose, but at the same time I kind of like it, especially the indents that show motion. I copy the lines to a fresh page, then turn back to the one I'd been scribbling on and make a few notes about Chrystal's hair. Wavy. Dark. Thick and mysterious. How does it smell? That stops me. How would it smell? It's a good question. I ponder it as I watch the sun sink below the trees.

After coming in from the morning milking and taking my shower, I see the screen light up on my cell phone. I check it and my heart does a quick double beat when I see I have a message from Chrystal. Then I read it and my heart thumps even harder. I THINK IT WAS OUTSIDE MY WINDOW YESTERDAY.

I call her immediately. She answers on the third ring.

"Chrystal?" I blurt. "Are you okay? It's Logan."

"Hi, Logan. Yes, I'm okay. You got my text?"

"Yeah. It was outside your window? At the hotel?" I ask.

"Yes. Well, I mean, I think so. I smelled something, and something was definitely out there. When I went to check, there were huge footprints."

"You went outside?"

"Yes. With the hotel lady. She had a baseball bat. Whatever it was was gone, though," she says. There's something in her voice. Not really fear, not now, but I can tell she had been afraid. "I'm okay. It was gone."

"That was pretty brave of you, I guess." I want to yell that it was a pretty dumb thing to do, going outside with a woman with a bat to look for a monster that can tear the head off a calf. But that would be mean, and maybe just me being an overprotective guy telling a girl what she should and shouldn't do. Kelsey would say I'm being sexist. She's probably right.

"So, umm, can Dad and I still come out to talk to you today? He's pretty excited about it," she says.

"Sure. Anytime you want," I tell her. "You can come right now."

"Okay. Actually, we're kind of on our way. Sorry," she says. I laugh and tell her it's fine. "Dad was wondering if he could put motion cameras on some trees on your farm. Out by where you first saw the thing."

"Cameras?"

"Yes. They take a picture whenever something moves in front of them," she explains. "Usually we only get deer and stuff."

"Oh. Yeah, I guess. I don't think Dad will mind that."

"Okay. Well, we should be there pretty soon. I'll see you then."

We hang up and I go down to breakfast. Chrystal and her dad arrive just as we're finishing, and I can't help but notice how Chrystal looks from the living room to the dining room where Mom and my sisters are clearing the table. I ask if they're hungry. "There's still some bacon and biscuits and gravy," I say.

"I couldn't eat a bite," Mr. Lawson Smith says, standing there rocking back and forth on his heels.

"I could," Chrystal says.

"Oh. Oh yes, I guess I haven't fed you, have I?" her dad says, and his voice shows he's surprised he's forgotten. I lead them into the dining room and Mom brings them plates.

Mr. Lawson Smith has me repeat my entire story, then asks if I'll take him out to the place where the thing ripped off the calf's head. I do it, leading him and Chrystal through the yard and into the woods above the house, carrying my shotgun. Mr. Lawson Smith chatters the whole time, but I'm thinking mostly about Chrystal, who walks on the other side of me. I can smell her perfume, and sometimes, as we move around trees and rocks, our arms almost touch.

"This is it," I say, pointing to the small clearing. The calf's head is gone, of course, taken by the wildlife people for examination. The blood is gone too, probably licked up by coyotes or some omnivorous creatures of the forest. I show them where the monster was, where I was, how the dogs were acting . . . everything about that night.

"Excellent! Excellent!" Mr. Lawson Smith says, then unslings a tan backpack and starts unloading equipment. He takes an army-green rectangular box with canvas straps to a nearby tree and is examining angles.

"One of his motion cameras," Chrystal explains.

I nod and we watch him. I ask her, "Were you scared?"

"Yes." She moves a step closer to me. "The scariest part was after, though. When I was in the room alone and I knew that thing had been out there. Dad was gone." She whispers the last part.

"I have an extra gun. It's just a .22 rifle, but it's better than a hotel woman with a baseball bat," I offer.

She shakes her head. We're both still watching her dad as he fastens his camera to the tree. "I've never shot a gun. I wouldn't know how. And wouldn't want to."

"Oh." There's a long, awkward silence over the low sound of her dad humming happily. "What are you doing this afternoon?"

"Searching for Karen."

"I hate that I can't go."

"Yeah. I would too," she says, and now we look at each other.

"I promised Dad I'd stay here. He's out hunting that thing. Most of the men around here are. I told him I'd stay home with Mom and the girls."

"I'm a girl," she says, like I need any reminder of that.

"A girl willing to face down Bigfoot outside her hotel room," I say.

She coughs. "Not Bigfoot. A bear. I'm pretty positive it was a bear."

10

CHRYSTAL

The police search for the "creature," and since my father and I are able-bodied, they let us join.

"We want everyone we can get," says this tall blond sheriff's deputy person. "I don't care who you are as long as you are mobile and breathing and have two eyes in your head."

"And a cell phone," another cop says. This one is short, dark, and looks like an ex–high school soccer player.

"That's right."

They give us numbers, assign us to groups, give us areas to search. Dad and I are with a boy named David and a couple other older people, two police deputies, and a waitress from the diner. We head out to some road named after a number and enter the woods, fanning out, looking for clues and signs. We have maps. We do not have a dog, like some of the other groups do.

"Imagine if we find it," Dad says.

"Cool," I say because he wants me to say it, but I seriously do not want to be the person who finds an alleged monster unless it's a dead monster. "You stay safe."

He doesn't say anything back, just heads into trees, personal GPS in hand. The deputy looks at me. His eyes squinting from the sun, sweat rolling down the side of his face. I don't know how he can stand wearing that uniform with a bulletproof vest in this heat, poor guy.

"It will be okay," he tells me. "We don't have a hot area. Plus, I'm pretty sure that we're not looking for a creature."

"You aren't?" I ask.

"Nah. We're looking for a psycho. And even if it was a creature? It seems nocturnal. We're in broad daylight. We're safe."

Dad starts to say something, but I elbow him to be quiet. I also decide that I like the way this deputy thinks.

To the left or the east or something a mile away is a farm where some pigs were taken three months ago. They don't even know for sure the monster took them. The trail is cold, really cold, which is probably why we were assigned here.

David and I walk together, which is nice because it gives me a break from my dad. No offense to him. David tells me that he's best friends with Logan. I'm not sure why he's telling me this.

"Yeah?" I try to make my heart rate steady, but it doesn't work.

"He mentioned you," David says all casual as we step around a big tree toward a patch of dirt.

"Yeah?"

"Yeah."

"What did he mention?"

"Stuff."

Sigh. Oklahoma boys are not wordy when you want them to be.

"Look at this." David squats down and points at some tiny marks in the dirt. I squat down too, but I can barely make out anything.

"See this?" he continues. "This is from a squirrel. Squirrels hop like hare. But there are two paired track sets. The bigger ones from the hind feet are actually in front. There are four toes in each of the rear footprints."

I have no idea what he's saying.

"A squirrel was here," he concludes.

"Uh-huh."

"You don't talk much, do you?" He cocks his head and squints at me. "No wonder Logan thinks you're hot."

I raise my eyebrows and stand up. "He thinks I'm hot?"

David stands up too. He doesn't answer my question. "You like him?"

I don't answer *his* question.

"You have calluses on your fingers," David observes. "That from guitar?"

"Bass," I correct him, smiling. "You have dirt on your nose. That from picking it?"

He stares a second, laughs, and shakes his head. "You're okay. I like you. No wonder he does, too."

We stand there a second. "So a squirrel was here, huh? But no monster? No psycho guy?"

"No monster. No psycho guy."

I groan and rub my hands over my face, which is so hot and sticky. It's like living in a sauna here. "I want to find whoever is doing this. I mean, I don't—because I'm scared of him, but I do because . . ."

"Because it's hurting people now."

"Exactly. It isn't just cows. It's getting more daring. Like it's . . . like it's taunting us or it's bored, which is why I don't think it's a monster."

"It's not human."

I groan. "It doesn't matter. What matters is that the violence is escalating. And it will escalate more, I bet."

"Damn, I hope not." David's eyes are wide and scared.

"Yeah, me too." I sigh. "Kierkegaard says that 'Purity of heart is to will one thing.'"

"That means this monster's pretty pure of heart, huh?"

"Yep."

"So, this Kierkegaard, your boyfriend?" he asks.

It's all I can do not to laugh. "Closest thing I have to one right now."

Something catches my eye, just off to the left. Something that doesn't fit.

I step toward it, off our path.

"Chrystal?" David's voice is a flat note in the chittering noises of the woods and I only barely notice it. I'm too focused on not losing what I see. I don't want to blink. I don't want to lose what I think I'm seeing.

One step.

A twig breaks beneath my foot.

Another step.

I move through some underbrush and reach up to the branch of a tree. Pink. Cotton. A piece of something bigger.

Looking down, I see it. A bone.

A bone.

The world around me stills.

I part the twigs of the bush, trying to see it better, and I'm almost gentle trying to move them, trying to figure out what it is, how to do this, how to see what I think I'm seeing.

"Chrystal?" David's behind me now. Close, so close.

The hairs on my arm prickle and stand up. Tiny little sentinels telling me what my brain refuses to accept.

I've found Karen.

Or someone.

Or what's left of someone.

"Ah, mother of God." The deputy has moved David aside and he breathes over the top of me. He smells of pizza and soda. He smells of fear. His hand lands on my shoulder while his other hand keys his radio, calling for backup, calling for help when help is obviously way too late.

In the distance, among the thudding footsteps of the searchers, the chatter of the police officer's radio, the shrill of birds, I think I hear it. A laugh.

Dad's standing at the end of the driveway, squinting up at the Jenningses' farmhouse like it's some sort of big puzzle. I bring him some water and stand next to him as he sips it absentmindedly. All his focus is on the house and not on me or the fact that I just found pieces of a dead person who is probably Karen.

"What is it?" I ask.

"A woman has been taken."

"Right, Dad. I just found her."

"No. Another one. He's getting more violent and risky."

Another one.

"You make it sound like it's a deliberate choice, like he's choosing to escalate the violence," I say all calmly, but in my head I'm thinking, *Another one. Another one. Another one.* I recycle the thought over and over like it's going to eventually be comprehended. "I don't get this. I don't understand what's happening."

He makes some sort of humphing noise. "People like to think they can understand evil."

"And . . . ?"

"They want to understand motivations, causes. We think . . . We think if we understand the monsters, then we have a defense against them. We think, *Oh, the mass murderer was bullied. Or the killer had a bad childhood or was unhinged or misguided.*"

I shudder. "Dad. You going somewhere with this?"

"I'm not sure if we can understand it." He clears his throat, takes another sip of water.

I don't have an answer. He swings toward me. His thin face changes expression and he seems determined. "I'm going to visit my professor friend. The one who sent me the files."

I try not to twitch. I hate visiting professors, but I don't want to be alone right now and I want my dad to feel—to feel loved. "Okay. Let's go."

His eyes twinkle. "Really?"

I loop my arm through his. "We're a team, Dad. When all of this is over, it's still going to be you and me, right? We'll stop this guy. Maybe we'll even understand him, but either way, we have to stop it, and the best way to do that is to gather the data, the information, right?"

He hops on his toes. "Right."

"It's not a monster, Dad. It's a man."

"Sometimes men can be monsters."

Dr. Martin Borgess is a smaller man, sort of my size, and he's not tweedy at all, but wearing a short-sleeved button-down shirt tucked into some dad jeans. He pulls my father into a big hug and then pulls me into one, too.

"Chrystal! It's so nice to finally meet you." He lets go of me and smiles into my face. He smells of mint toothpaste and has a faint accent, maybe somewhere from Eastern Europe? "Sit down! Sit down!"

He motions to chairs opposite a desk. Unlike my dad, his papers aren't anywhere to be seen. There are no random book stacks, no signs of mad genius.

"Your desk is so neat," I say as Dad and I settle into chairs. Dr. Borgess remains behind us somewhere.

"Ha!" he laughs. "Neat space. Neat mind."

Dad coughs. Dad's desk is five thousand books, crayons, teaching books, and random hair samples stacked on top of one another. My friends always tease him about it.

"Your father isn't so neat, Chrystal?" Dr. Borgess asks. He's in my space all of a sudden, far too close to me.

"Not really," I admit.

"Do you take offense at my insult?"

For a second I have to figure out what he means. "About neat space, neat mind, so therefore my dad's not neat-minded?" I raise an eyebrow because I like to do that when people are annoying me. "No. It takes a lot more to offend me."

"Like what?" he asks.

Dad's blowing us off. I swear he isn't even listening.

"I don't like being ignored."

"I can't imagine you get ignored often."

"I don't like people hurting other people on purpose," I add. "Or scaring them."

"You think this is a hoax?" he says, backing away from me towards his desk.

"Potentially," I say.

Dad has stopped leafing through a book he's picked up off a shelf. "Chrystal is a strong-willed human being with a well-activated suspicion response, which helps with her self-preservation. Always good for teenagers."

"That's almost offensive," I announce, and smile in an attempt to ratchet down the tension. "How about you, Dr. Borgess? What offends you?"

"Being ignored." His answer is snappy and quick even as his body language is casual. He leans on the desk. "Being underestimated. Doubted. People who don't like to inquire. Now, what can I do for you two today?"

"The situation is escalating," Dad says. He sits in an oversized chair, tilts forward, and tells the professor what's going on. "It began, as you know, with the boy's suspected Bigfoot sighting."

"He seems a credible witness," Dr. Borgess says.

"He is, but people try to make truths out of things they don't understand. Weather balloons become UFOs, smudges and shadows become ghostly reflections," I say.

They both stare at me for a second.

"There is nothing wrong with chasing down possibilities," Dr. Borgess says to me, and then goes and sits behind his desk before saying to Dad, "Continue."

"There were footprints. Nothing like a Bigfoot's. More canine, but elongated."

"People think it's the devil," I scoff.

Dr. Borgess clears his throat. "What do you think it is?"

"A prank. Someone without a lot of cryptozoology experience pranking everyone."

"So the killing was a prank?" Dr. Borgess taps his fingers on his desk.

"No," I say. "But we don't know they're connected. The killings could be one thing. The footprints another."

"That would make no sense." Dr. Borgess sits up straighter. His voice is a bit higher. "All logic would link those two events."

"The world doesn't run solely on logic. I would think that someone who studies the things you do would know that."

Dad starts talking again, doling out the details. I refute a couple, saying things could be a man not a monster, and then I tune out a bit and scan the office, which is sort of Pinterest perfect, dark leather-bound books in neat rows on shelves. Plants, leafy and green, make their homes by the windows that overlook the campus. Dad and Dr. Borgess start debating what the monster could possibly be. Werewolf? Bigfoot? Devil? Chicken man? Deerman? The Lawton Werewolf from the 1970s?

"It's a person," I say.

They ignore me.

"It could be deliberately misleading us," Dad says, standing up. He strides to the window and looks out.

"That would suppose that this is a sentient monster capable of preplanning," Dr. Borgess says after a moment. "Which points to a werewolf or a devil. Not Bigfoot."

Dad doesn't respond. He's so deep in thought that I'm not sure if he even heard. I get up and join him at the window, gently touching his arm. He startles a bit. "I think it *is* a werewolf."

"It's not a Bigfoot. It's not a werewolf. It's not a monster at all," I insist. "It's a person. An evil person."

"A person can't rip the head off a cow." Dr. Borgess stands up, too.

"A strong person with a weapon could," I say.

"You are struggling too hard to make this fit your world view, Chrystal." Dr. Borgess asks, "Why is that?"

I say, "Kierkegaard said that 'There are two ways to be fooled. One is to believe what isn't true; the other is to refuse to believe what is true.'"

Dr. Borgess suddenly grabs my wrist. His hand is thick for a small man, and strong. "Do you like mysteries? Or just philosophy, Chrystal?"

"Philosophy is a delving into mystery," I say, resisting the urge to rip my wrist out of his grip.

"Oh! She's so quick. So quick." He lets go of me. Leaning forward, he says to Dad and Dad alone, as if I'm not even here, "Is her mother so strong?"

Dad clears his throat awkwardly. He's paying attention again, but not answering.

"Mom's not strong," I answer, demanding that they listen to me. "You know that this could be a man. You two just want it to be a monster because it would prove that monsters exist."

The professor's eyes twinkle. "Oklahoma is a state that seems dead or dying to a lot of people. The strip malls are destitute. The cars that go to the auto body shops never seem to leave."

I glare at him. "Do you have a point?"

"Chrystal!" Dad warns.

Dad never warns.

"I'm just saying that we're here trying to find out about some sort of killer that has taken cows and now women. And our best source of information is talking about the plight of the Oklahoma economy? Which is important, yes . . . but . . ." I say and lose track of my sentence.

"It doesn't seem relevant," the professor says. He frames my face with his hands like I'm a portrait. "You're an interesting girl, Chrystal. Very interesting." His hands shake the tiniest of bits. He closes his eyes for a second and whispers something to himself. While Dad and I are exchanging a look, he opens his eyes again and announces, "I don't think it's a Bigfoot. The feet don't match."

"People say it looked like cloven feet. Then they said like a dog's," Dad says. "There's no uniformity in the accounts."

"Maybe it *is* a hoax?" the professor says. "But I don't think so. No . . . I don't . . ."

He goes back to his desk and sits in his chair like he's done with us.

"What do you think it is?" Dad asks.

"I'm not sure. If I were you, I'd look into creatures that enjoy vengeance."

"It's not a vampire," Dad says.

"Seriously?" I throw up my hands in disgust and turn to Dr. Borgess. "If you think it's a monster, then you need to help us. More women could die."

"And cows," Dad adds.

The professor smiles. "I'll help you."

"How?" I ask. "Do you know what it is? Do you know how to stop it?"

"I don't, but I do think . . . vengeance . . . that's the key."

"So, he's angry at cows and random women?" I ask.

"Maybe, he's much smarter than you think he is." Dr. Borgess smiles in such a calm way that I don't quite know what to make of it. "It never pays to underestimate your enemies. Monster or human."

He promises Dad that he will look for some more resources, do some more research, blah-blah-blah, but we leave there no better off than when we entered his office. Honestly, I don't know what I was expecting from one of Dad's friends. They're all weird and almost uniformly non-helpful.

When we get back in the car, I announce, "I don't like him. Also, please put on the air conditioning. Damn, Dad."

Dad turns on the car. I turn on the AC.

"He's a bit peculiar," Dad says as he backs out of the parking lot. "And disappointing. I expected him to be more excited by the events. But he did tell us to think about vengeance. That is interesting. We do tend to think of monsters as lacking the skill to plan, particularly Bigfoot."

"Dad, *you're* a bit peculiar. That guy's just an all-out butt face."

Dad starts laughing like this is the best phrase ever. And after a second I start laughing, too. Because sometimes you can't do anything but laugh.

I take careful aim, lining up my shot, try not to think about how I do some kind of weird little prancing skip-step on my approach, then release the ball. The black-and-red bowling ball glistens under the fluorescent lights as it rolls down the shiny blond lane toward the innocent pins. It hits the headpin just to the right. There is a clatter we can hear all the way back at the score machine, and all the pins are swept away. I turn away to see little Katie jumping up and down and cheering for me.

"Yay, Chrystal!" she shouts, her doggy-ears hair flopping crazily around her face. Before we started the game, Katie had declared I was on her team against Logan and Kelsey.

Kelsey gives me a high five and Logan shakes his head, grinning, as I slap Katie's hand and we bump hips twice, twirl, bump one more time, then say "Hunph!" in a deep grunt. It's a victory dance she made up for us. I slide onto the plastic seat beside Logan.

"You didn't tell me you're a hustler," he teases.

"I didn't say I've never bowled before, just that it's been a while." I watch as Kelsey hefts her pink ball and steps onto the lane. This is my fourth non-parent encounter with Logan in the past two weeks. If you can call an afternoon of bowling with him and his sisters an encounter. Nobody will let us go out at night. Most of our time together has been him picking me up at the dreadful hotel to play board games at his house or eat at the Greasy Hog. It's soooo much better than following my dad around while he talks to people, measures footprints, looks for hair samples, or whatever.

Today Dad is at the university to meet up with the creepy professor again, hoping to get him to be more helpful without my skeptical presence. There will be a lot of excited murmurings, outbursts of explanations, and happy dancing intermixed with the scholarly perusing of old texts. Let's just say I'm glad to be bowling.

Kelsey knocks over four pins and turns around with a disgusted look on her face.

"You can pick them up," I call to her.

"Chrystal!" Katie says, giving me a stern look. "She's on Logan's team."

"Oh yeah. We can still be nice, though. Can't we? We want her to do well."

"As long as we do better," Katie says, then turns to watch her sister. Kelsey only gets three more pins. Katie looks at me. She doesn't say anything mean to Kelsey.

"You're up," I tell Logan. "Don't be self-conscious about people looking at your butt."

He stops at the ball return and looks back at me, grinning. He has a really nice grin. "Who? Who would look at my butt? Tell me. Who?"

"Look, Katie, someone let an owl in," I tease.

Together, Kelsey and I start saying, "Who? Who?" and then we break up laughing.

Logan still gets a strike. He really does have a very cute butt. I would like to pack up that butt and bring it to Maine with me.

After three games of bowling, Logan buys us lunch in the bowling alley restaurant, then sends Katie and Kelsey with a roll of quarters to the arcade.

"Kind of a lame day, huh?" he says.

"I'm having fun."

"I wish I could take you to a movie tonight. Or something. Something interesting. You must think we're all pretty backward if the best we can do is an afternoon of Monopoly or bowling with my little sisters," he says as he plays with a burnt piece of French fry, dipping it into a glob of ketchup and drawing stick figures on his plate.

"I understand what's going on," I tell him. "It isn't safe to be out after dark. And I like your sisters. Maybe when this is all settled, people can feel safe enough to go out at night again. That's what I want."

"If it ever gets settled. Has your dad found anything yet?"

"No, not really," I say. "Witnesses. He's looked at the animals that were killed and found. He tried to look at . . . at that girl, at Karen, but the police wouldn't let him. I'm glad. I didn't want to go in there."

Logan nods. "Nothing's happened much since then. At least, nothing around here. Just a couple missing sheep and that runaway girl—and who knows if that's from that thing or not. Maybe it moved on, or went back where it came from, or whatever."

"Maybe." I sip my soda. My gut is telling me that the killer hasn't moved on, but I don't explain that to Logan. I'm too busy trying to figure out why he'd want to go to a movie with me. Maybe he really *does* like me that way. My palms feel super-itchy suddenly. I look at him and say, "Thanks for lunch."

He smiles at me. "Mom gave me the money for lunch. It's her way of paying me back for bringing the girls."

Then he clears his throat, looks down, and looks back up at me. "I'm paying for the games, though."

His sisters go through the roll of quarters in about a half hour, then Katie says she's ready to go home. Logan drops me off at the hotel. He's driving his mother's sedan because we couldn't all fit in his truck. He walks me to the door of the hotel and we can feel his sisters watching us.

"Thanks for going with us," he says. "I really like hanging out with you."

The air is awkward again. I hate awkward. But I like Logan, and his cutie family. They all try so hard to be nice and good. I want that kind of family. I love my dad, but . . . There is still awkward silence. I sort of bluster into it. "I like it, too. It was fun."

"You were amazing. Your dad's car isn't here," he says, looking around.

"He could be talking shop with that professor for hours. It'll be okay. I can spend some time with my bass," I tell him.

"Yeah. When do I get to hear you play more of that?"

"Next time you come alone," I promise. He nods and starts to turn away. I stop him with his name. He looks at me and I step into him and put my arms around him. It isn't a real hug. Not a boyfriend/girlfriend hug, just a friendly hug, but I know it'll make his sisters tease him all the way home. He hugs me back, kind of hard, but good, then leaves me at the door of the smelly hotel.

"You are amazing, Chrystal." He says this so quietly I almost think I didn't hear it, but I did. He said I was amazing. Logan Jennings thinks I'm amazing.

We hugged.

We hugged each other.

That doesn't mean anything.

I try not to jump into the air.

He is such a good hugger.

In my room, I check my phone. There's a message from my dad. He sent it almost two hours ago, but I guess I couldn't hear my phone in the bowling alley. DR BORGESS OUT TODAY. AT UNIVERSITY LIBRARY. LOVE YOU! I put the phone on the table between the hotel beds, sit on my bed, and slip my bass out of its carrying case.

After about an hour, I pause mid-riff. Something isn't right. I listen, but don't hear anything unusual. I look around the room, but can't see anything out of place. It's a smell. The same awful bear smell. My eyes slide down the wall to the window.

I shut the window. I checked that it was locked before I even sat down to play. Still, everything inside of me feels adrenalized, like right before an audition. The fear pulls my stomach into knots and paralyzes me.

Listening as hard as I can, I lean forward. The smell isn't as strong as the other time. Because the window is closed. If the window is closed and locked, I'm safe. Still, I slide my bass beneath the bed. I creep backward toward the wall opposite the window and closer to the bathroom and grab my cell phone. I hit the lights off so it seems like nobody's here, and I tap out 9-1-1 but don't push the send button that will connect the call.

Nothing.

The window has to be closed.

"If it's closed, I'm safe," I mumble into the darkness.

The glass shatters. An arm rips through the drape.

Screaming, I run into the closest place, the bathroom, and slam the door shut. I lock it, but the door's not super-heavy. Someone that can rip a calf's head off can bash through that door. I push send.

"Cherokee County Sheriff's Department. Please state your location and the nature of your emergency."

"I'm at the Cherokee Country Inn. Room twelve. Someone just broke into my room!"

"Miss, can you calm down and repeat what you said?"

I do, but I don't know if she can understand me. I shout out the name of the hotel again and beg, "Come! Come now!"

I toss the phone onto the floor but keep the call connected. That way the dispatcher will be able to hear but my hands will be free to fight whatever is at my window. How am I going to fight it? Something thumps in the bedroom, just past the door. Something else is thrown against the wall.

There's no window in here. I'm totally trapped. If he figures out I'm in here and comes through the door . . .

I need a weapon. Razor? No good. The blade is too little and all encased in plastic. Toilet? No good. Bolted to the floor. Air freshener? Okay . . . Okay . . . I grab the air freshener. It's a spray can. I'll spray him in the eyes if he comes in here. Maybe I can blind him, slip past, run into the hallway . . .

The door rattles. Five long rips appear at head level and I think of fingers dragged across a chalkboard.

I'm going to die.

I'm going to die in the bathroom of a cheap hotel room in Oklahoma.

The thing howls. It's long and high and an A-flat pitch that shudders all the way down to a G_7.

Switching off the light, I press myself backward and step into the bathtub. There's a curtain, but there's no point. If it's a bear, I bet it can smell me. And if it's a man? This is such an obvious place to hide. The curtain will do nothing to hide me from an animal, a predator, a monster.

The door shudders again.

I will not die. I will not die. I will not die.

I hold the air freshener in front of me. Its scent is called Spring Rain. I need a match. I wish I had a match. At home, Dad lights candles in the bathroom to hide odors. If I had a match, then the air freshener could become like a torch.

That's when I make it out, thanks to the glow of my cell phone: above the sink, there's a long, plastic candle-lighter thing my dad always uses because he's useless with matches. I stretch out and grab it just as the door breaks in half. Wood shards fly everywhere. The smell is overpowering. My hands shake like hell, but I hold the air freshener and lighter in front of me.

He bursts in, huge and brown-haired. From what I can tell, his ears point up like a dog's, and his hands . . . His hands have pieces of wood in them. He is definitely a boy.

My dad—my loopy, quirky dad—was right. There *are* monsters. Monsters that aren't men.

This is not a good time for him to be right.

I can barely hold the spray can. I press my back against the wall.

He howls again and the room shakes with it. His eyes meet mine, shining in the dim light. His teeth are more fangs and his eyes . . . his eyes glint.

He steps forward, tearing through the rest of the door, fully entering the bathroom.

I can't help it. I scream. A high C.

He growls, low and primal. A low F-flat.

The cell phone light disappears.

If he takes just one more step, then he'll be able to reach me. I press the lighter on. Hold it up. Then I push the spray. It strikes the flame of the lighter and blows out a blast of fire. It hits his neck, I think. He roars and rocks backward, batting at his neck with his claws.

I keep spraying. The flames could get sucked into the can, making it a bomb in my hand, but I can't let go.

"Get out!" I scream at him. "Get out! Get out! Get out!"

I step out of the tub, move forward, closer to him. Fur burns and smells terrible. He roars again and backs up, pushing back into the darkness of the bedroom. He smacks his hand against the fur on his shoulder—I think it's his shoulder—trying to stop the burning.

"Get the hell out!" I scream, following him.

Someone's pounding on the door.

"Police! Open up!"

"Go!" I screech. *"Go!"*

The beast continues to swat at the fire. The can fizzles out just as the hotel room door breaks open, bringing in the light of the hallway. A sheriff's deputy busts inside, swears, then whips out his gun as the monster sees him. He lunges at the deputy and slashes his chest, ripping through the vest. The deputy goes down and the sizzling creature stands over him, roaring.

Another cop enters the room and yells, "Hands up! Get them up!" which would be kind of funny if everything wasn't so scary.

The beast turns toward him and the cop shoots. The bullet goes wide. He shoots again. It nicks the monster's arm. The thing roars again and flees, jumping back out the window on all fours, howling.

I sink to the floor, still clutching the air freshener can. I must have dropped the lighter. The room is totally trashed. The laptop is on the floor, along with half the mattress. The pillows have been ripped apart. The table is cut in half. Hoping that my bass is okay, but not checking, I crawl toward the injured deputy as the other cop talks frantically on his radio, stepping over us and going to the window.

The fallen deputy's gone white in the face. I pull off his shirt, which has a zipper behind pretend buttons. His bulletproof vest is harder to remove.

"It's okay. You're going to be okay," I murmur when I finally see his wounds. They are slash marks, but not too horribly deep. Still, blood drips from them. "I'm going to get some towels and water."

The other cop has stepped through the window. I'm assuming he's chasing after the monster. I'm not sure that's a good idea.

"What was that thing?" the wounded deputy asks. He's dark skinned, brown eyed.

"I don't know." I press the towel against his wounds, five long scratch marks.

People are standing out in the hallway, peering into my room. Their voices get louder and louder as they're asking questions and spouting theories and panicking. Sirens wail in the distance.

"Everyone stay back," I say. "Someone please call 9-1-1 and make sure an ambulance is coming."

The deputy cringes beneath my hands. Blood starts soaking through the towel.

"You're going to be okay," I murmur again.

He nods really quickly like he's trying to convince both of us that what I just said is true. His eyes take in the mess of the room, the broken window, the splintered bathroom door.

"I thought it was supposed to be Bigfoot," he says.

"I don't think we're that lucky." My voice shakes just like his does. He's some stranger, some hero man with a job that makes him face the horrible every day, and now he's bleeding beneath my hands. I wonder if he has a family. I wonder if he has a dog or a cat or dreams. I hate that thing for doing this to him. I hate it.

"First the cow, then the pigs, then that girl, maybe another girl." He lifts his head so our eyes meet. "And then almost you."

"And you." I grab his hand in mine.

His grip is not so strong, which worries me. His head goes back to the floor and I use my free hand to make sure it touches down smoothly. He's so tired, so hurt, but still he says, "But he came in here. He wanted you."

The horror of it is too much to think about. The eyes of it. The teeth. But still I make myself movie-heroine tough and say, "Well, he won't get me."

"Nobody else." The deputy shudders and lets go of my fingers one at a time.

I think he might be going into shock. I yank the ripped bedcovers from under a chair and wrap them around him before repeating his words, "No, sir. Nobody else."

11

LOGAN

I'm working on one of my poems—a new one, and a real stinker, where I'm trying to make a piece of quartz crystal a metaphor for Chrystal's soul. I'm about to give it up and tear the page out when my cell phone rings. I swipe the screen to answer. The screen glows pretty bright, making me realize it's later than I thought. It's Chrystal's number. "Hello?"

"Logan? Umm, this is Logan, right?" Her voice isn't calm and sweet like the bubbling brook I was going to compare it to. The words are high and shrill, terrified. Something is obviously wrong. She'd know it was me. My name is programmed into her phone.

"Yeah. What's wrong?" I ask, sitting up straight.

"He was here, Logan. He was *right here* in my room," she says, then she's crying.

"Who was—" Then it hits me. "Oh my God, Chrystal. Are you okay? What happened? Are you okay?"

I hear her taking several deep breaths, trying to get herself under control. In the background I can hear men talking. Calmer, Chrystal says, "He was outside the hotel. I smelled him. God, Logan, he smelled horrible. I was so scared. He just smashed out the window. I ran to the bathroom, and he came in. He was in the room." She pauses, and I know she's fighting to stay calm. "I hid in the bathroom, but after he trashed the main room, he ripped the bathroom door apart and was coming for me. I sprayed him with fire and the cops came in and he finally ran away."

I listen in awe. Sprayed it with fire? I have no idea what she means, but I'm not about to make her explain it to me now.

"I think he was after me, Logan," she says, almost in a whisper. Behind her, the men are still talking. One of the voices is her dad's.

"It sounds like it," I agree. "You're okay?"

"I'm fine, but I mean it: I think he was after me. Specifically me. Why my room instead of one of the others?"

"I . . . I don't know." Maybe 'cause she's a girl? It seems to like girls. I don't say that, though.

"I'm afraid he's hunting me," she says, her voice still low. She cracks on the last two words and they come out as a sob. "Dr. Borgess said that the monster seemed vengeful. Maybe my dad did something. Maybe it doesn't like bass guitar. I don't know . . . I can't think of anything that I've done that would make a monster come after me. Or maybe it's just girls. Karen was a girl."

"Chrystal, who are you talking to?" It's her dad. His voice is louder now, and I know he's come to stand next to her.

"It's Logan," she says.

"We're moving to another room," he says. "We need to gather up everything we can salvage."

"Another room?" she asks. "Here?"

The last word is so full of fear, I can't stand it.

"Chrystal," I call, hoping she'll hear me above everything else. "Chrystal?"

"What?" she asks. "Just a minute, Dad."

"You can't stay there. Not if it's looking for you. No way. You can come here. Stay here with us." That's bad. I shouldn't do that without checking with Mom and Dad. I jump up and hurry for the front door. "I mean, I better ask, but I'm sure they'll be okay with it." I move quickly into the house. Mom's sitting in the living room with a book of word searches while the girls watch *Wizards of Waverly Place* reruns. I can hear Chrystal explaining to her dad what I'm offering.

"Mom, we've got to help them," I start. She looks up at me, obviously perplexed. I spill Chrystal's story as fast as I can, watching Mom's face slacken in horror as I talk. "They can't stay in that hotel. Not if that thing knows she's there. We have to help them. Can they stay here?"

Mom's mouth finally snaps closed. She looks up at the ceiling, and I know she's thinking she should consult Dad before making a decision, but then her face hardens like it always does when she's made up her mind about something. She looks back at me and says, "You tell them to get right over here. Mr. Lawson Smith can sleep on the couch, and Chrystal can either share with Kelsey or I'll put the girls together."

"Thanks, Mom." I tell Chrystal what Mom said and listen to her relate the information to her dad.

"Is it safe?" he asks. "Shouldn't we stay in town, closer to the police station?"

"They have guns," Chrystal tells him. "I don't want to stay in town. It isn't much of a town, anyway."

"Okay. Okay. We still have to save my books and everything," he says.

"Logan, my dad says yes. We have to pack up some things, then we'll be there. Thank you so much!"

I nod at Mom, who immediately goes into motion. She heads for the stairs, probably to tell Dad we're having guests, then to get sheets and blankets for the hide-a-bed in the couch.

"We can't let you stay there," I tell Chrystal. "You don't really know anybody else here, so we have to help you."

"Is that the only reason?" she asks after this incredibly long pause.

"No," I answer quickly because it sounds like I might have hurt her feelings. "Just, you know . . . Well, I think I'll like having you here." My face flushes because my sisters are watching me closely.

"Oooooo," Katie says from her spot on the floor. She makes hugely exaggerated kissy faces while Kelsey laughs at her. I turn my back on them.

"Thanks, Logan," Chrystal says. "We'll see you soon."

"Okay. Call me when you're close and I'll meet you outside with a flashlight and my gun."

She promises to do that, then we hang up.

"You didn't say 'I love you,'" Kelsey teases.

"Shut up. I barely know her." My face reddens even more, though. I go outside to grab my notebook and gun. When I come back in, Mom has put a stack of linens on one end of the sofa and is telling my sisters they better behave.

"She's a pretty girl, and nice. You can't blame Logan if—" She suddenly realizes I'm standing, like, three feet from her, and stops. She looks at me and smiles, but she's a little embarrassed to be caught in the act of talking about me.

"If what?" I say.

"Well, it's just a shame she lives so far away," Mom says, and that somehow hits me really hard.

Chrystal does live halfway across the country. She'll go home when her dad is finished with this monster investigation, if she even survives this monster investigation. I will not think that, or about her leaving, or . . .

Mom sees that she's hurt me. She takes me by the arm and says, "You just have to enjoy every day you have, one at a time, and trust God to work things out."

"Yeah," I say, but I'm not at all sure I'm going to like this Sunday school lesson. Mom doesn't usually bring up God, but when something goes wrong, she'll always say it was God's will. "Why'd you say they could stay here, Mom? I mean . . ."

I'm not sure what I mean.

My mom brushes dandruff or something off my shoulder. It's probably nothing. It's usually nothing. I think she just needs to touch and think I might consider myself too old for a random hug. "It's the right thing to do, Logan. I'd want people to take care of my family in a time like this . . . and . . . well, I like that girl. I feel for her. Her father's a lovely man, I'm sure, but she needs some mothering and . . . it's just right. That's all."

I lean my gun against the front doorframe and sit in a chair in the living room to wait. I wanted to work on my poem some more, but it seems pointless now. I stare vacantly at the TV as Selena Gomez's character causes more trouble in her parents' restaurant.

Midway through the third episode in what seems to be a marathon of the Disney show, my phone rings again.

12

CHRYSTAL

Why do you think the creature was stalking you, Chrystal?" All of my dad's quirkiness seems to have drained away and been replaced by something I've never seen. It's almost like fear. Maybe it is fear. His voice is tight and tired-sounding.

The blacktop back road rolls by, monotonous under the Subaru's tires.

"Today wasn't the first time he's been there," I say. "I smelled him the day we checked into the hotel. In the parking lot. But then a Jeep pulled in. I might have seen his eyes in the woods. I'm not sure. Then, another time, I smelled him again and he bumped into the wall. Remember, I sent you a picture of the footprints in the dirt?"

"That was outside our hotel room?" he asks, looking at me. The Subaru drifts over the dotted yellow line. No other cars are around, but I still reach over and take the wheel, helping my dad ease back into our lane.

"Yeah, it was," I tell him. "Plus, Dr. Borgess said all that weird stuff about it being about vengeance, maybe. Remember?"

He hangs his head and I have to grip the steering wheel hard to keep us going straight.

"I'm sorry," he says. "I never should have brought you here. I should have stood up to your mom."

He looks so sad. Sad and beaten. "It's okay, Dad. It'll be okay. We'll be safer with Logan and his family. Now, please pay attention to your driving."

Our hotel room is a crime scene now. So is my head—it's full of images of violence and gore, blood and horror.

I'm pretty sure that I never really truly believed in monsters before. All the evidence? The unexplaineds my dad collects? I figured that they could one day be explained. Now, though, the reality of a monster is too big to push away again.

There's this theory that we see monsters all the time, but our brains choose to ignore them. A dark, hulking form by the side of the kitchen, we turn into a shadow. A large, troll-like creature on the side of the road, standing by a mailbox, we turn into a homeless woman or a tree or something—anything—that our mind can accept and so that we can go on living.

I can't do that anymore.

There are no streetlights on the 720 Road. Everything is dark. Anything could be hiding in that darkness. Monsters. Creatures. Wolfmen. Hell. I think about the deputy in the hotel room, wonder if he's still alive. My cell phone vibrates with a text. It's my friend Zoe. I ignore it. I can't deal with positive affirmations or plans right now—I just can't. I wonder if that makes me a bad friend.

Dad keeps talking. "This one is too dangerous for you. It isn't like Brazil."

"We didn't find any monsters in Brazil." My seat belt is on, but my knees are pushed into my chest and I hold them there with my arms. "I could have died. That sheriff's deputy was really hurt."

A little sob escapes his throat. His hand goes around my shoulders and he drives with just his left hand.

For a moment, neither of us speaks. Then he sort of chokes out, "I couldn't live with myself if anything ever happened to you, Chrystal."

"I'm okay, Dad."

"But . . . but . . . I put you in danger by bringing you here. You didn't even want to come. I should send you home. You could stay with Zoe, maybe."

This is all true, but saying it isn't going to make either of us feel any better, really. So I resist the urge to do the five-year-old temper tantrum where I say he loves his crazy quests more than he loves me, because:

1. I don't think this is really true.
2. It wouldn't change anything.
3. Having a temper tantrum isn't going to help save anyone.

"Who wants a life without danger?" I say instead, trying to make my voice very jolly and rah-rah team. It almost works. "Plus, I didn't die, and I did see a monster. I'm sure I'll think that's cool as soon as I stop being so freaked out about it. But first—"

"But first?"

"We have to find a way to keep these people safe, Dad. That thing—he was evil."

We drive a little more and eventually I get my breathing back to normal. He pulls his arm away just as we turn into the driveway of the farmhouse. I take out my phone to call Logan, but before I do, my dad puts his hand on my arm.

"I'm so proud of you," he says. "You were a warrior in that hotel room. You must get that from your mother."

Thinking about how devastated he was about the divorce, about how he insists that there are things unknown in the darkness and how he stands up to ridicule as he tries to prove that his beliefs are real, I shake my head.

"No, Dad," I say. "I actually think I get that from you."

As soon as I call Logan, he and his dad rush onto the porch with their guns. They each take a side, eyes scanning the darkness, ready to provide us cover from the monster that could be waiting in the night. The three dogs come out from hiding under the porch and bark at the car until Logan and his dad call them back. Reluctantly, the dogs back off. I know all their names now, thanks to Katie showing me photos at the bowling alley. Thunder goes up onto the porch and sits next to Logan. Galahad sits on the ground in front of the porch, and it's easy to see he's just itching to prance and bark at us. Daisy, the older hound, disappears back under the porch. I feel kind of sorry for Daisy, and make sure I give her extra petting whenever I can.

"Do you think I should tell them that we aren't sure it's a Bigfoot?" my father whispers, leaning over.

"Not yet," I say, patting his knee. "Let's try to keep the monster talk to a minimum tonight. Everyone's a bit spooked."

"All the more reason to give them as much information as possible," he insists.

"Dad . . . trust me . . . people can take only so much in a twenty-four-hour period." I unlock the car door.

"True," he says, looking like he's in deep thought as he pulls the keys out of the ignition. "I wonder if—"

"They're signaling for us to come," I interrupt. "We have to run, okay?"

"Should I bring my books?" he asks.

I grab the bag of toiletries and my bass, which survived the attack because of its nice safe place under the bed. My clothes were all ripped apart. "Just one bag, Dad. And your stuff for sleeping. We'll come back out to the car when it's light. Okay?"

"Okay."

We run toward the house, past the flowers, over the thick grass, and up the steps in record time. Still, I swear I can smell the monster despite the odor of cow and manure and night woods, and I swear I can hear something snort in the darkness, almost a laugh but not quite.

"In the house. In the house," Logan's dad says as he motions us forward and we rush inside. Logan and his dad follow us. Mr. Jennings locks the door behind us, leaving the porch light on, and mumbles, "Not sure what good that's going to do."

"We find safety in routines," Dad says. Then he clears his throat and extends his hand. "I can't thank you enough for helping us, for letting us stay in your house. It's really exceptionally kind."

Tears sprout in Dad's eyes.

Logan's father shoos the words away. "It's nothing. Anyone would do it."

Logan and I make eye contact as he leans his giant gun against the wall. He smiles just the tiniest bit, but his eyes fill with worry. I keep staring at him even as his mom rushes forward and starts hugging me.

"You poor, poor girl!" she exclaims. "You're so lucky you survived. Don't you worry about a thing. We'll take good, good care of you."

She's soft to hug and she smells good, like dinner and dish soap and kindness. Tears spring to my eyes now. I haven't cried about this, though. I refuse to cry.

"Logan," she says, letting go of me but rubbing my arms and looking into my face. "You show Chrystal upstairs. Honey? Do you want your own room or to share with one of the girls?"

"I'll share with her!" Katie pipes up. She rubs her hands together like she has evil things in store.

"Oh, no, you won't," Mrs. Jennings says. "How about you stay alone tonight, Chrystal, see how that goes? If you get too scared, you tell one of us and I'll send Kelsey in to sleep with you."

"Thank you," I murmur as she lets go of my arms. Logan takes me up the stairs. I pad after him, trying not to stare at his butt, which looks really cute in his shorts. He turns around, grabs my bag and bass, smiles at me, and keeps walking, past the stacks of books and ponies that are crammed onto the edges of the stairs.

"Smoochie, smoochie," Katie murmurs.

Everyone starts laughing and then her mom scolds her.

They are so nice. I can't believe people are so nice, but I'm really glad they are. It's funny, really, how I can now believe in monsters, but I still have a hard time believing in nice.

The room must be Kelsey's, because there are pictures of sparkly vampires on the walls and a lot of middle-grade and teen books on the bookshelves. The walls are light yellow and she's put giant flowers all over them. The flowers are cut from construction paper and have glitter-glue designs. It's really cute and really homey.

"Here you go," Logan says. "Is this all you brought?"

He leans my bass up against the desk and puts my bag on a pink flower rug that covers part of the floor.

"Yeah. He—I— The—he—he ripped apart most of my clothes. All my clothes," I say, trying to find the words while not actually remembering the sounds of him tearing things up while he tried to find me.

"So that's all the clothes you have?" His eyes go wide.

"Yeah."

"I'll get you some. You can borrow some of my T-shirts. My mom's pants would be too big for you, and my sisters' are probably too small. Maybe there are some shorts?"

"I'll be okay," I say. "I can probably go shopping tomorrow or something. Clothes aren't important. Trying to figure out how to get this thing. That's important."

I plop down on the bed. The world suddenly seems very dangerous and very difficult. Logan sits down beside me. The bed moves from his weight. He grabs my hand in his and holds it tight. I stare at our entwined fingers. There are a couple blisters on the tops of two of my fingers, and the side of my index finger, from the fire. That's going to make it so hard to play bass. The blisters are tiny, though, so nobody will notice them, which is good, because I don't want anyone to make a fuss. I still haven't texted Zoe back. Guilt pulls inside me and makes it so I can't even really enjoy the fact that Logan is holding my hand for a super-extended amount of time. He has such nice hands. They aren't furry. They are so human.

I stop thinking.

"I feel like I'm losing it," I whisper.

"I felt the same way . . . after . . . you know . . ."

"I'm really sorry I doubted you."

"Sometimes even I doubted me."

The digital clock on the bookcase flashes the wrong time. There must have been a power outage before or something. I look away from it. The flashing wrong numbers remind me too much of my head—how I seem to have what happened in the hotel stuck on repeat and it's a wrong image. Any image that involves a cop bleeding, a monster howling, burning fur . . . That's got to be wrong.

"We've both seen him," he says really slowly. "I figure that binds us together somehow, you know? We've both seen him and survived him."

I nod really quickly and turn toward Logan so I can see his face. His eyes make little sad circles in his rugged, sunburned face. The hand that isn't holding mine reaches up and tucks some hair behind my ears.

"You must have been so scared," he says. "I know I was, but I wasn't trapped in a room and I had the dogs, and you . . . You were just so brave. You know that, right?"

I shrug. "I don't feel brave. Now I just feel scared. I just keep seeing him in my head, smelling him . . . What if he finds me here? What if my being here puts you and your sisters and your parents in danger, Logan?"

It's too horrible to think about.

"We'll handle him. We've got guns and lights. He'd have to be pretty fast to get all the way here tonight, unless, you know, he drives a motorcycle or something."

He lifts his eyebrows, which is so endearingly cute that it makes me want to laugh.

"I can totally see him on a scooter," I say.

"No . . . a Segway."

We both start laughing really hard.

"A skateboard."

"A unicycle."

"Skis."

"Tricycle."

"Sow."

"No. He'd eat it halfway here."

We crack up even more. It's not even actually that funny. It's more just absurd, trying to imagine the hairy, evil, clawed thing traveling on all these different transportation devices. I start hiccupping from laughing so hard and this makes Logan snort, which makes me laugh harder.

Right then Katie appears in the bedroom and screams at the top of her lungs, "THEY ARE KISSING! THEY ARE KISSING ON THE BED!!"

I leap away from Logan and flatten myself against the wall. He jumps up and starts walking in a frantic little circle.

Katie makes smooching noises while I hide my face in my hands.

"Stop it," Logan orders.

This inspires her to just giggle more.

"Katie, go to bed, or something."

I peek out from behind my fingers. Logan's face is all fire-engine red. Katie runs, still giggling, out of the room.

"I'm so sorry," he says, turning toward me.

"It's okay. It's kind of funny. We need funny." Out the window, the field with the cows is lit up like a Walmart parking lot or something. "Do you think lights will scare him away? Because my hotel room and the parking lot was lit and it wasn't . . . It didn't keep him from coming in."

"Honestly?" He stands behind me. We aren't touching, but I can feel his body just inches away from my back.

"Yeah. Honestly."

The voice that answers isn't Logan's. It's my dad's, and he's standing at the door. "Nothing will."

13

LOGAN

I stiffen at the sound of Mr. Lawson Smith's voice. After what Katie was yelling, I'm more than a little worried he's going to be mad at me when I didn't even do anything. What if he tells Chrystal they're leaving right now and then the monster gets her? What if he thinks my offer to let them stay here was just so I could get with his daughter? I don't want him to think that. I don't want Chrystal to think that either. I don't think she does. I turn to face Mr. Lawson Smith.

"The lights won't keep him out," he says.

He doesn't mention Chrystal. He doesn't look at me like I'm the devil. I let myself breathe.

"No, sir," I agree. "We were guarding the cattle and we thought the lights might at least help us get a good shot at him."

He nods. "That they might do."

He seems different. Kind of lifeless, like all his energy has been drained out of him. I guess he's pretending not to have heard Katie screaming about kissing.

"You're tired, Dad," Chrystal says. "You should get some rest."

"I will," he promises. "I just wanted to be sure you're okay up here." There's some implication in that line and I redden a little. Something knots up inside my stomach and someone behind Mr. Lawson Smith clears his throat.

In the hall, my dad stops in the doorway and looks in at us. "Everything all right up here?"

"Yeah, we're fine," I tell him.

"Logan, you behave yourself," he warns. So, obviously, he heard Katie too.

I insist, "Dad, we're fine. We're not doing anything."

"Let Chrystal get to sleep. She's had a big day. I'm going to bed," he says, then moves on down the hall. I hear my parents' bedroom door close.

"Well, all right. I'm going back downstairs," Mr. Lawson Smith says. Before he goes, though, he comes over to Chrystal, and there's a little of his old bounce in his step as he reaches for her and hugs her real tight. "Good night," he tells her, then nods at me. "Thank you again for having us."

"We're glad to do it, Mr. Lawson Smith," I say.

He leaves the room and almost bumps into Mom.

"You're all set up, Mr. Lawson Smith," she says after they laugh a little over the near collision.

"Please, call me Matt," he says. "Thank you again. Really, I can't tell you how much it means to us to be invited into your home."

Mom waves his words away like they're mosquitoes. "Go get

some rest, Matt. You look beat." She peers into the room. "Logan, you come out of there and let Chrystal get to sleep, too."

"She needs some clothes, Mom. The thing tore up all of hers. I'm going to give her one of my T-shirts to wear."

Mom nods, then says, "I think I have some shorts you can wear, Chrystal." She disappears and Mr. Lawson Smith also moves away. His feet thump against the wood as he goes down the stairs.

"Here you go." Mom reappears and offers Chrystal a pair of blue terry-cloth shorts. "They're old. I guess nobody wears shorts like this anymore. I had them when I was about your age. And size. I kept them, always hoping I'd get back to that size, but after three kids . . ." She lets her words trail away. "Go get the shirt, Logan. I'll stay with Chrystal."

She waves me away, so I go to my room and find my newest Forest Road Consolidated High School 4-H Club T-shirt. I've only worn it a couple times, so it shouldn't have any manure stains on it, but I give it a quick check just to be sure. It's good.

Outside the bedroom, I hear Chrystal and Mom talking about me.

"Logan's a good Christian boy," Mom says. "He's never really had a girlfriend, so he probably doesn't know how to treat a girl he's interested in. He should know better, but if he gets out of line, you just let me know."

I step into the room. "Yeah, Mom, he is," I say, and try to smile like I think the whole thing is funny and not horribly humiliating.

"I know, Logan," Mom says. "I know. It's just that this is a pretty unusual circumstance. Oh, I know you'll behave." She comes over and hugs me, then pulls my head down to her level so she can kiss my forehead.

"Mom," I whine. "Come on. You'll be showing her the naked baby pictures next."

"I have to save something for tomorrow," she teases.

Chrystal looks like she's about to bust up laughing again. Her eyes have an extra sparkle. As soon as Mom leaves the room, Chrystal puts a hand over her mouth to smother the giggles.

"I found you a shirt," I say, offering it to her.

She takes the shirt and whispers, "Your mom is really nice."

"She's not usually so embarrassing," I promise.

We still stand there, like two chocolate Easter bunnies that have melted and fused together after being left in a hot car. I can smell her hair now. It's very . . . girly. Like a field of flowers after a light rain.

"You smell so good," I whisper.

"You too," she says.

"I have to go."

"Umm-hmm," she agrees.

It's a huge effort of will, but I finally pull myself away from her. Our hands connect and cling as I back toward the door until finally they fall away from each other.

"Good night," I tell her.

"Good night."

Sleep is a long time coming and full of questions about monsters and missing women.

I'm up before dawn, like usual, and helping Dad with the milking. Kelsey comes to join us about halfway through. She looks sleepy.

"What are you doing up so early, pumpkin?" Dad asks.

"Katie's bed is too small. She kept kicking me and I couldn't sleep," Kelsey answers.

"Well, tell ya what," Dad says. "Logan here'll go up in the attic today and bring down a couple camping cots and we'll see if we can't make everyone more comfortable tonight."

"Thanks for giving up your room," I add.

"For your girlfriend," Kelsey teases, then laughs. "She's really nice."

"Yeah." Girlfriend . . .

"Mom's going to make a huge breakfast," Kelsey says.

"Then let's get these girls out of here, so we can help her." Dad slaps the rump of a Holstein he's just taken the electric milker off and backs her up.

Dad and I milk, while Kelsey shuffles the cows in and out of the milking barn. The job isn't so hard. The cows eat grain from a trough while me and Dad slip the teat cups onto the udders. By the time we've attached the cups to the last cow, the first one is about finished, her milk sucked out and sent to the bulk tank via big yellow hoses. The bulk tank is in the next room and holds the milk until Nate Saul arrives in the Double O truck to take it to be pasteurized.

"After what happened yesterday with Chrystal and the deputy, the men in town are going out hunting that thing again today," Dad says.

"Are you taking Mr. Lawson Smith?" I ask as we wait for the last few cows to be finished.

Dad sighs. "I don't know. I guess I should ask him if he wants to. Handing him a gun makes me a little nervous, though."

"You never know. He could be a crack shot," I say.

Dad grunts. "Maybe."

"He seemed really sad last night," Kelsey adds.

"His daughter was almost the latest victim of that thing," Dad reminds us. "Any father is going to be sad. And mad."

Conversation is pretty much dead after that. We run the last cow out of the barn and watch her trot along the worn trail up the hill and into the trees where I first saw the monster. There are two man-made ponds on the other side of the rise, and the cattle usually go up there for water after the milking. I wonder how many cow pictures there are on Mr. Lawson Smith's tree cameras up there.

"Who's going to wash it down?" Dad asks.

We all look back inside at the floor of the milk barn. Cows don't mind pooping while they eat and get milked. Dark-green cow flops, most with deep hoofprints in them, dot the floor behind where the animals had been standing.

"I'll do it," Kelsey says reluctantly.

"I'll help," I say. "I'll shovel and you wash."

"I appreciate that, Logan," Dad says. "It's daylight and we're right here in the barn, but I don't want your sister out here alone. I don't want you out here alone. I don't want anyone out here alone."

Dad's just full of cheer this morning.

I get the wheelbarrow and a shovel. For the next ten minutes, I scoop up cow pies and haul them around back to add to a pile in a corner of the yard well out of sight of the house. Not much of anything goes to waste on a farm. Not even waste. The manure is mixed with straw and Dad sells it as compost to other farmers with vegetable crops. Once I have the patties scooped up, Kelsey washes the concrete floor, directing the small bits I missed into a grated drain where it runs out of the barn. Naturally she sprays me with water several times . . . after I toss a couple fresh pies toward her feet. It's all good farm fun.

Inside the house, Dad has cleaned up and is already wearing the bright-orange vest he always wears when he's going hunting. I can see the rectangular shapes of shell boxes in the pockets of the vest. His face is set and grim. I know he's worried about the hunt, about the danger of hunting something unknown, and of leaving the house and his family.

Mr. Lawson Smith isn't on the couch. I ask Mom about him and learn that he's taking a shower. Pretty soon the seven of us are crowded around the long dining table. Mom put the leaf in to make it longer. We pass around a platter of biscuits, a bowl of gravy, another platter of bacon, and scrambled eggs. After a while, Dad breaks the silence.

"Matt," he says to Mr. Lawson Smith, "do you want to go out with me and some of the other men today to hunt for that thing? Or do you have your own plans?"

Mr. Lawson Smith's old enthusiasm seems to have come back in the night. "Oh, thank you. Thank you. But no. You see, I'm not good at all with a gun. No good at all." He waves his fork as he talks. "A camera, that's what I usually hunt with. No, I'm going to go back to our hotel room to see what evidence I can gather. That's first on my agenda, then I hope to talk to the policeman who was injured."

Dad stabs a chunk of gravy-covered biscuit. "The cops might not let you back in that room."

"Oh, I'm sure they'll let me in. Tell me: How will you hunt the . . . the monster?"

"Sam Davis, over at the feedstore, made some calls and got the best dogs in the county over here. We're going to start at your hotel room. The trail will be a little cold now, and I'm not sure the dogs will even know what scent it is they're supposed to track, but that's where we're starting." Dad gulps his coffee.

"You be careful, Ron," Mom says. I finally notice she's barely touched her food.

"I will," Dad says, then looks at me. "Logan, keep your gun with you. Stay out of the woods. Keep close to the house." He points at Kelsey and Katie with his fork. "You two stay right around the house. I mean it. Don't leave the yard, and I want you to have Logan or one of the dogs with you anytime you're outside. Understand?" They both nod. "All right. Well, I need to get out of here."

Dad gets up and kisses Mom where she sits at the table. We all watch as he walks to the front door and picks up his rifle from next to a bookshelf. He gives a final wave, then leaves us. The house is quiet for a long while.

"He's going to be okay." Other than a brief greeting, it's the first thing Chrystal's said since coming downstairs. I watch Mom smile at her.

"I know," Mom says. "Still, this whole situation is just strange. Makes me think of when I was a little girl and saw that movie about the monster over in Fouke, Arkansas. That scared me to death, especially the scene where the man was sitting on the toilet and the monster reached through the window. But . . . I guess I never believed monsters were real until now."

14

CHRYSTAL

'm really not sure how I feel about guns," I say as Logan hops onto the back of this four-wheeled ATV. "I'm sort of against violence."

"Spraying that thing with fire wasn't violent?" Logan raises an eyebrow.

"True." I stand there looking down at him. There's a bit of wind today, and it blows his hair around. At his side, Galahad, who is the goofiest dog ever, wags his tail at me. I bend down and scratch behind his cutie-pie ear. "Who is the cutest doggy ever? Who is?"

"You're going to spoil him." Logan smiles at us and then goes right back on topic. "And you wouldn't have shot him—the creature, not Galahad—if you'd had a gun?"

I think about it for less than a second because I can't delude myself about it for that long, even. "Oh, I would have shot it."

His lips are grim and set. "Exactly."

"My father would rather keep him alive. He thinks of him

more as an endangered animal or something. He thinks it's wrong to kill another life-form just because we don't understand it, or because it has the potential to hurt us."

"So he's never killed a mosquito or a tick?"

"Well, those aren't exactly endangered, are they?"

Kelsey yells something in the house. We hear Katie yell back, but I can't make out the words. Logan motions for me to hop on the ATV. I climb on behind him and wrap my arms around his chest, trying to be careful of my blisters. He's not super-big, but he's solid and strong, wiry. The cotton of his T-shirt doesn't hide the fact that he's got this sexy-guy thing going on underneath. I give in to the urge and rest the side of my head against his back as he starts up the engine. I've never actually been on an ATV before, but it's beyond loud and beyond bumpy. I lift my head to watch the fields and cows as we gallop/wheel/bump over the terrain. Galahad runs after us, still wagging his tail.

"Can you make it go faster?" I yell in Logan's ear. His hair smells like coconut.

His head tips upward and back as he laughs. "Oh yeah . . ."

And then we're *really* hauling across the field. I scream, but it's a totally happy scream, not like my screams last night. Riding this is like zipping on a roller-coaster ride. I reach my hands up above my head and whoop like a cowgirl, which cracks Logan up so much that he starts to slow down. Then he must think better of it and we're off again.

He brings me past pecan trees to a smaller field filled with some sort of waist-high plant. Hopping off, he points to the targets right by the tree line. Two are just bull's-eyes painted on plywood. Then there's one that's the silhouette of a bear, and another of a wolf or a coyote. The last is the outline of a man.

I must make a face, because Logan bumps me with his hip.

"Yeah, we're just outlaws," he says. "Total hicks."

"You're not hicks," I say.

"You're so nice, Chrystal. I can't believe how nice you are."

I'm about to protest that I'm not really exceptionally nice, I'm just me, but something seems to shift in him. His hands go into his hair, and he sort of runs them through it before he gets off the ATV and grabs the guns off the back. He stands there for a second and swallows so hard that I can actually see him do it.

Galahad catches up with us and his happy doggy face leaves him. His tail droops and he whines as he stares at Logan. Wow. He must really love his master.

I step toward Logan even though he's holding guns and I'm not exactly sure what the etiquette is on that sort of thing. Logan looks so sad. I reach up to touch his shoulder just as a crow caws, and say, "What is it?"

"It's just . . ." He looks away, and then it's like he's willing himself to man up and meet my eyes. I almost wish he hadn't, because his eyes are full of hurt. "It's my fault, you know?"

"What's your fault?"

"The monster thing . . . the attacks . . ." His chin tilts up and he breaks our gaze. His eyes go to the sky.

My heart lurches in my chest, pounding. "Why? It's not you, is it?"

"What?" He steps back. His mouth drops open. And I realize how stupid I'm being. He doesn't even know Dad's werewolf theory.

"How could it possibly be your fault?" I ask.

"Because I didn't kill that thing when I saw him." His voice is flat, dead. "If I'd had my gun that night . . . If I had killed him, you wouldn't have almost died, Karen wouldn't be dead, that deputy wouldn't be hurt. Our fathers wouldn't be hunting the thing down. Everyone's at risk now because I didn't kill it."

"Oh . . ." I can't think of what to say. I grab for him again and he snuffs like he might cry. I pull him into a hug. "It's not your fault, Logan Jennings. It couldn't possibly be your fault."

He hiccups and says some more, but I can't make out the words. We stand there and I rock him back and forth, wishing I could magically take all his guilt away.

"You don't always carry your gun with you, do you?" I ask.

I feel him shake his head against my shoulder as he mumbles, "No."

"You didn't have any reason to have it that night. You couldn't have known what you were going to see. It's not your fault," I tell him.

Galahad whimpers and nudges at us with his head. He goes for my calf and then Logan's, one and then the other, over and over again.

"He wants in on the hug," I say, and pull Logan down so that we're both squatting in the grass with Galahad by our knees. The dog takes the opportunity to start licking Logan's cheek. Logan almost smiles and sort of waves Galahad away, but Galahad won't stop. I lean forward and lick Logan's other cheek, which makes Logan's eyes go wide with surprise.

"Hey!" He laughs.

Him laughing is so much better than him crying, so I lay my hands on his chest and push him over, knocking him onto his back. He stretches his arm out and lets go of the guns. I climb up and lick the other side of his face again, hoping it's not too sloppy. His face tastes like salt and sadness, tears and sun. He cracks up.

"Stop! Stop!" he begs.

"Are you ticklish, too?" I tease as my fingers do their wiggle magic at his sides, just above his waistband.

"No! No!" He pants and cringes. "You're killing me."

Galahad and I halt our attack for a second. "Then no more blaming yourself, got it?"

He nods quickly. "Got it."

I flop onto the ground next to him. Little rocks stick into my back. The sky above us is blue and flat. Another crow caws in the distance. A crow friend answers him. It's really super-hot. A bead of sweat trickles over my scalp. Galahad pants so hard, I think he might make the earth shake, and then he puts his head on Logan's stomach and sighs, resting too.

"The world can be so beautiful and so scary all at the same time," I say. "How is that?"

Logan grabs my hand in his. "I don't know. But it is."

We stand up after a couple minutes. Galahad runs off to explore the woods.

"He sounds like he found something," Logan says, and whistles to make him come back.

"He's definitely got something."

There's a piece of blue denim in his mouth. He rushes up to us.

"Drop it, Galahad," Logan commands.

Fear hits me before I consciously recognize the smell. My hand covers my nose.

"L-Logan . . ." I sputter.

Galahad drops the fabric. It's a man's shirt, ripped, with no buttons on it anymore. Urine and berries smell up the air.

"H-holy . . ." Now it's Logan's turn to sputter. "That's the smell, isn't it?"

I nod vigorously, looking all around me at the trees that line the field. Anything could be lurking there. I wish we'd finished the stupid lesson.

"Is he here?" I whisper. "Grab your gun."

He grabs it, but then he says, "Galahad would be going crazy if that thing were here."

It makes sense, but my heart is still pounding eight hundred beats a minute. I manage to stop looking at the woods and focus on the shirt instead. Squatting down, I search for blood or marks.

"There's no blood on the fabric," I say. "The buttons are all popped off, or they were never on there at all. The seams are pulled away too. See? Look at the stitches."

Logan squats down with me to look. He's still holding the gun even though he said Galahad would be freaking out if we were in danger.

"Weird," he says. "It reminds me of that old TV show *The Incredible Hulk*."

"Uh-huh," I say, "like the Marvel movies, right?"

He doesn't quite answer. "When Bruce Banner turns into the Hulk, his shirt rips off."

This sinks in for me, but Logan is confused.

"Why would a monster wear clothes? Unless . . ."

"Unless what?" I ask.

"These aren't his clothes? Maybe . . ." He looks in the direction where Galahad found the torn fabric. "Maybe these are from a body lying over there."

"Maybe," I say, but he feels the doubt in my voice and looks at me, asking without words. "My dad has a theory."

"What?" he asks, but his eyes go back to the field.

"That it might be a werewolf. Not Bigfoot. He think it's a man who transforms into a beast."

He looks at me again. "A werewolf?"

I nod. "Yeah."

"I don't know. I don't know," he says, his voice confused and defeated. "Bigfoot seems more, I don't know, more real. A werewolf?"

"It's a theory. It would explain the missing buttons," I offer.

"We have to go over there and look for a body," he says. He stands and pulls me to my feet. Both of us carrying guns, even though my lesson was incomplete, we walk in the direction where Galahad found the cloth.

There is no body. But under a lone tree there are more pieces of torn denim shirt. And ripped khaki pants, torn socks, and, what seems weirdest of all, a pair of dark-brown loafers, size ten, polished but flecked with dirt.

Logan squats down and looks at the clothes. He turns the waistband of the pants inside out. "Look at this." He points to a ring of dark hair stuck to the waistband. The smell under the tree, clinging to the clothes, is nauseating.

I look at the hair—the fur—and nod. "We need to show my dad," I say, and get out my phone to call him. It rings forever. I leave a message. While I'm doing that, Logan's phone rings. His face goes white with shock.

"What is it?" I ask the moment he ends the call.

"We have to go back to the house," he says. "*Now.*"

15

LOGAN

What did your mom say? Logan? What is it?" Chrystal's voice is sharp and agitated. "Is it there?"

"No. It's . . . She said some weird men are outside, making a lot of noise. Snooping around." I quickly tie the guns down on the rack of the four-wheeler, then jump on.

"Reporters?"

"No. Worse than that, I think."

Chrystal gets on behind me and wraps her arms around my chest. That feels so good, and I wish I could savor it, but there's no time. Mom said that the dogs are barking at the house and that Kelsey is scared. I gun the Kawasaki and we roar toward the house with Galahad running hard behind us, his tongue hanging out the side of his silly mouth.

We fly out of the pecan grove and I can see Thunder and Daisy standing between the house and the barn, barking their heads off, looking beyond the barn to the wooded hill. I can't hear them over the sound of the four-wheeler yet. Mom's face appears in the kitchen window for a moment, then disappears. A minute later she's standing in the back doorway with Dad's shotgun in her hands.

I park at the corner of the house and we jump off the machine. Galahad has already raced over to be with Thunder and Daisy, but being Galahad, he isn't content to stand with them and bark. He runs for the fence, but the gate is closed, so he stands there and barks instead. I untie the guns and hand Chrystal the .22.

"Go on inside," I tell her. "Stay with Mom." She gives me a look that says she wants to stay with me, but no way I can let her do that. "Please—" I begin, but am cut off by a very human whoop coming from somewhere behind the barn.

"What was that?" Chrystal asks.

"It sounded like a whoop. Like you do when you're encouraging your hunting dogs." I scan the trees, looking for movement, but I don't see any. "It's probably hunters. Go on inside and I'll check it out."

"Are you sure?"

"Pretty sure. I'll go check it out."

"Logan, you be careful," Mom calls. "You're not wearing a hunting vest. Make sure they know you're coming."

"I will."

"I'm coming with you," Chrystal announces.

I think about it. I can hear the men whooping closer now. I don't hear any dogs other than our own, though. I nod at Chrystal and start off at a fast walk. Thunder falls in beside me. I have to push Galahad back into the yard with the butt of my shotgun to keep him from coming with us.

"You take Thunder, but not Galahad?" Chrystal asks.

"Thunder will behave and do what I tell him," I explain and then we're silent, listening.

We enter the trees. I stop us. I can't hear anything now, but Thunder seems to know where the problem is. He whimpers and starts off to our right, then stops and looks back at us.

"Good boy, Thunder, but stay with us," I say as I fall in after him. Chrystal is behind me.

"Thunder is smarter than Galahad?" Chrystal asks, whispering.

"Yeah. He's a great hunter, too. We've tracked down hundreds of coons, possums, squirrels. . . . You name it and we've hunted it."

"You kill them?"

"Not always," I say. I stop suddenly because the hair is standing up on Thunder's back and he's growling deep in his chest.

"What's wrong?" Chrystal asks.

"What is it, boy?" I whisper.

Thunder keeps growling, then I hear it.

Someone is hurrying away from us through the dry leaves.

"Who's there?" I yell. "This is private property. The Jennings farm. Who's out there?"

A moment later a big, burly man in jeans and a black T-shirt steps out of the trees ahead of us. He's got long, curly hair and a short, scraggly beard. What bothers me, though, is that he has a rifle in one hand and an open bottle of beer in the other. Then two more men, with two more guns and one more bottle of beer, appear behind him. I don't recognize any of them.

"We're huntin' Bigfoot," the first man says, then takes a swig from his Rolling Rock. His eyes move from me to Chrystal, and he grins the kind of grin that makes you queasy. I step to the side to block his view, and his grin just gets bigger. "We heard he likes to hang out back in these woods."

"These woods are on private property and you're trespassing," I tell him. "You're going to have to leave."

"You telling me that your skinny self, that pretty girl, and that mangy hound's gonna make us?" he asks. His friends snicker behind him.

"My mom's already called the sheriff," I tell him.

"Ooooh, the sheriff," he says, turning to look at his companions. "Well, I heard he took a bunch of men hunting over by Scraper."

All this time, Thunder continues to growl. He's not looking at the three men in front of us, though. His eyes are fixed on something to our left. I glance that way and see another, smaller man trying to hide behind a thick sycamore. There's something wrong with him, but I don't get time to study it. I don't think Chrystal sees him at all.

"Let's go, Logan," Chrystal says. Her hand is on my arm. "We'll just let the sheriff deal with this."

"She's smart *and* pretty. Smells good too, I bet," the redneck says. This is the kind of trash that gives country people a bad reputation. "That your sister?"

"You guys are going to have to leave," I repeat. "That thing hasn't been back here since that first night I saw him."

"You sure about that, boy?" one of the other guys asks. This one has long, thick red hair. "We saw some tracks back there that looked like they might belong to a Bigfoot. Maybe it was your mama, though." He snorts at his own joke.

My hands tighten on the stock of my shotgun. Chrystal's hand on my arm seems to shake. Thunder's growl becomes a short bark, then a louder growl. The smaller man hiding behind the tree is moving, hurrying away from us.

I can't make out any of his features, just a general size.

The first guy to speak drains his beer and casually tosses the empty bottle aside. He belches at us, then winks. "You're wanting to use that shotgun, ain't ya, boy? Maybe prove yourself to the honey there?"

I don't answer. I just glare at him. I've never even thought about shooting a person before. I've never even had to point a gun in the general direction of a human, but I'm suddenly very scared of these three men. If one of them swings his gun in our direction, what do I do? Would they just shoot me outright, then hurt Chrystal? Would they just shoot us both? Or do they just want the fun of scaring us?

"Let's go, Logan," Chrystal says. "Let's just go."

Her hand pulls at my arm.

Thunder wants to go after the man who has already retreated. That seems pretty strange to me, considering the real threat stands right in front of us. Three of them.

"Thunder," I say, my voice stern. "Let's go, boy."

He turns his head and looks at me, then back the way the man went, and growls again.

"Let's go!" I tell him. I nudge him with my shin. Behind me, Chrystal is backing away. I do the same. The three men watch us, grinning, but not making any move to come after us, or to follow their companion. Thunder isn't liking it, but he's beside me, ready to go, though he keeps looking behind him. Finally I turn around and start walking, but listen for footsteps behind me.

"Maybe we'll see ya around again," one of the men calls after us.

"Ignore him, Logan," Chrystal whispers. "Just keep walking with me."

I do. Thunder does too. He calms down about the time we come in sight of the gate letting us back into the yard where Galahad is still pacing and barking. Up by the house, Daisy is sitting and barking intermittently. I push Galahad back and let Chrystal and Thunder in, then close the gate behind us.

"Let's go inside," I say when Chrystal starts to say something.

Inside, Mom starts talking, but I cut her off too. I don't want those men to get away. I pick up our house phone and dial the number for the sheriff's office that's posted with other important numbers on the wall above the kitchen phone.

"I want to report four trespassers," I tell the woman who answers. I explain who I am and where I live, then add, "They had guns and refused to leave when I told them to."

She asks if they pointed their weapons at me or threatened me with them in any way.

"Well, not exactly," I answer. Mom looks to Chrystal, who shakes her head. The woman asks if I know the men and I tell her no.

"There is a county-wide search on for the person or animal that has been killing livestock and the Ferguson girl," the dispatcher tells me. "It could be that those men were part of a search party."

"There wasn't a deputy with them," I tell her.

"Well, I wouldn't worry about it too much if they didn't point their guns at you," she says. "But I will make a note that you called and give it to the sheriff when he comes back to the office. Will that be all?"

"They were drinking and carrying guns," I argue. "They're here, on our land, which is private property, and my dad is out in the hunting party with the sheriff."

"I understand, sir," she says. "I'll radio the sheriff and let him know, but I don't think he's going to be able to respond, or even send a deputy today."

"Okay, fine. Whatever." I hang up the phone.

"I would like details about what happened," Mom demands.

I tell her while Chrystal heads to her Dad's computer and starts fiddling with it.

"Stupid white-trash rednecks," she says. Behind her, Kelsey and Katie both gasp. Mom doesn't usually say bad things about people. "Probably some hicks with a pot farm who thought this was a good opportunity to trespass on other people's land and shoot things up. We've got the dogs in the yard to warn us if they come around here. We'll just stay in the house, at least until milking time."

"I guess that's all we can do," I agree.

"The girls were about to play a game of Monopoly," Mom says. "Why don't you and Chrystal join them?"

I look to Chrystal and she shakes her head. "No, thanks, Mrs. Jennings. I'm not very good at it."

"Me neither," I say. "I really suck at the money games. I like the war games."

"Don't say 'suck,' Logan," Mom scolds.

"Sorry."

"Logan, could I talk to you?" Chrystal asks. She makes big eyes at me and barely moves her head, which I think indicates she wants to talk in private.

"All right. Want a drink?" I open the fridge and grab two bottles of water. Chrystal ignores the offer and walks away. I follow her up the stairs.

"Which room is yours?" she asks.

I point and then go into my room. "This one. Come on in. It's a mess." It really is. There are clothes all over my desk, my bed isn't made, and books are scattered everywhere.

"Can we close the door?" she asks.

"Sure." I close it and offer her one of the waters. She takes it but doesn't open it. Instead she starts pacing around the room, kind of wringing the bottle between her hands.

"I'm scared," she says.

I sit down on my bed. "Of those guys? I think they'll go away."

"Did you see that one? The one who wasn't with the others? The one Thunder kept growling at?" she asks, stopping and fixing me with a really intense look.

"A little, yeah. I was more worried about the three facing us with guns."

"The other one . . . ," she begins, then gives the unopened bottle a good wrenching. "Did you see his face?"

"Not really."

"Me either, but I have this weird image I just uploaded from my dad's computer. I took a picture of it because I don't want your Mom and the girls to know." She holds out her phone and there's a photo of her dad's computer and a timestamp from early this morning. There's a figure in it—blurry, but you can tell it's a half-naked man holding his hand up towards his neck.

At first I don't get it. I really don't. I just stare back at her, wondering what she means. Then it hits me. "Ooooh. Oh man. Burned? Are you sure? You think this guy is burned?"

"I'm not sure," she says. She opens the water bottle and takes a drink. Her hands are trembling. "Look. There's a naked guy on your property. That guy who was hiding was obviously hiding.

Why? Maybe because he's hurt? Maybe those other guys were protecting him and distracting us so he could get out of here? I don't know. I just know that there shouldn't be men hiding in your woods. There shouldn't be this image on Dad's camera."

"Oh God." I reach for her, catch her by the shirt, and pull her onto the bed beside me. "You're really sure? I mean, it couldn't have been him. The monster. He was too small. That thing is huge."

"All I know is that I burned the monster's face and shoulder when he attacked me. This image—I can't make anything out because it's so pixelated, but the man looks like he's injured. He's sort of leaning and his hand is up like he's protecting a wound. Of course that would mean that the monster—that he actually shifts his shape between a person and a monster. . . ." She breaks down suddenly and buries her face against my neck. I wrap my arms around her and hold her tight.

I stroke her hair with one hand while pressing her tight against me with the other. She keeps crying for a while. I say dumb things like, "It'll be okay. We'll figure this out. I'll protect you," but they sound pretty lame. Finally she snuffles real big and raises her face. I reach for my nightstand and grab some blue tissues from a box. She wipes at her eyes, cheeks, and nose.

"Are you okay?" I ask.

"I guess. I'm scared."

"Yeah. Me too."

"You didn't seem scared out there when you were facing those three idiots with their guns," she says. "That was very brave of you."

"Well, you know, it's our land. We've got the cattle and all, and there have been people before who would shoot cattle from the road, just to be mean. They were trespassing," I say. "Any farmer would have done the same thing."

"Still, it was very brave. There were three of them, plus . . . that other."

"I wonder why they were here. Why were those men with the . . . God, can I really say I wonder why they were with the monster?"

"Maybe they don't know?" she suggests.

"Maybe." I don't want to say it, but I feel like I owe it to her to say what I'm thinking. "Maybe they're looking to cover up his tracks. You know, revisit where he's been and remove evidence?"

She puts a hand over her hip pocket where she put the piece of shirt we found earlier. "Could be," she says. "You didn't recognize any of them?"

"No. They don't live anywhere close by."

"We have to find out who they are," Chrystal says. I agree. "How can we do that?"

I think about it for a minute, then say, "Sam Davis might know. He runs the feedstore. He seems to know everybody around here. I wonder if he went on the hunt. I'll go call him. His number is posted with the sheriff's on the wall downstairs."

"I'll stay here," Chrystal says. "I want to call my dad again."

I go downstairs and call the feedstore, but there's no answer. Mom asks about lunch while I stop off at the dining room table. When Kelsey looks up to say she wants chicken nuggets, I slip a Monopoly fifty-dollar bill out of the bank box and add it to Katie's stack of cash.

"Thanks, Logan," Katie says.

"Mom, he's cheating again!" Kelsey whines.

"You have to be quiet about it," I whisper to Katie as I take the money and put it back in the box. "Nuggets are fine with me. I'll ask Chrystal. If she's okay with it, just make enough for all of us. If not, I'll let you know."

"Is she okay?" Mom asks. "She looked like she had a pretty bad scare out there."

I have to think about it before I answer. Tell Mom what Chrystal thinks? No, not yet. "Yeah, she's okay. She's not used to seeing people with guns. She didn't even know how to hold my .22."

"Oh, well, I was like that when your dad met me too," she says.

"You're still like that, Mom." I dash up the stairs to avoid the dish towel she throws at me. Mom's actually almost as good a shot as me.

Chrystal's still on the phone. "You're almost here?" she asks, then pauses. "Ten minutes? Twenty?" Another pause. "Okay. I'll see you then. Yes, I'll ask." She puts her phone down.

"He's on his way back?" I ask.

"Yes. He's almost here. He found something he's all excited about. He wants to know if he can set up his microscope and stuff somewhere."

"Yeah, we can find a place for that," I say. "Would a table in the corner of the living room be enough, do you think?"

"I don't know. . . ." she says. "He, umm, really gets into his work. It might be distracting to anyone around him."

"Oh. Well, I'll ask Mom. Are chicken nuggets all right with you for lunch?"

Outside, the dogs start barking and we hear the honk of a car horn. It used to be that hearing a car horn in the driveway made me happy, but now—now, it's like an interruption of Chrystal. Chrystal leaps off the bed.

"I think it's my dad," she says, and she's out the door before I even move.

16

CHRYSTAL

I honestly don't know what to think about that guy who was hiding in the bushes, but it all makes a twisted sort of sense that he was on their property, right? I mean, we're only here because Logan saw him. Maybe he has something against the Jennings. Dr. Borgess was talking about vengeance. I try to logic out what I know.

1. He was hiding, but the other guys knew he was there. That means they knew he had a reason to hide.
2. He was hiding, and small, but the other creeps totally waited for his orders, for him to move.
3. The man my dad's camera caught this morning looked injured even though I couldn't make out his face or anything about him really because it was such a bad image.

I know it's jumping to conclusions, but it's just . . . It felt like the monster. The moment I saw him, everything in my stomach sort of twisted up, and the hair on my arms (not that there's a lot of hair on my arms) stood on end. And if I'm right, that means he's here, and it means he knows we're here. And it means he has scumbag friends.

I'm thinking all this while I mash potatoes for Mrs. Jennings. Everybody is getting ready for dinner, except Mr. Jennings, who isn't home yet, and my dad, who is all set up at a folding table in the corner of the kitchen. He's murmuring to himself and looking through his microscope.

I push on the masher, squashing the potato chunks into smooth bits, changing the pieces into one solid mass. I add more butter.

The question is: Is it a coincidence that he's here, where I am? Could he have tracked me here? Or . . . since he was here already—this *was* his first sighting—maybe there is some other connection. He likes fresh beef? Were they looking for evidence and trying to get rid of it? Maybe his shirt? Maybe it is all about vengeance? I keep going around and around in my head with these same thoughts and questions, but I don't feel like I'm getting any cloer to the answers.

My hand shakes as it grabs the salt. I put only a little in. I'm not sure how salty the Jennings like their potatoes, and somebody could have high blood pressure. I don't know. I don't know anything about this family, really. Katie starts happy dancing across the kitchen floor, twirling in circles. Mrs. Jennings starts laughing. Okay. I know that this family is cute. That's one thing, right?

I look to Dad, think about telling him my theory, but he's in "data mode" right now, not "information gathering/theories mode." I could tell Logan, but he's already looking like he's stressed to his maximum capacity. Mrs. Jennings? Probably a good idea.

I say in a ridiculously loud voice, "Mrs. Jennings, can you come help me with this?"

"Of course!" she says, sliding some aluminum foil over a chicken that's been roasting all day. "What do you need? Are they runny? That's okay, Chrystal. Potatoes are hard to master. Oh! They look great!"

I put my finger over my lips and then start murmuring my theories to her. I know we weren't going to tell everyone about the extent of the trespassers, but I'm not cool with that idea anymore. When I'm done, I expect Mrs. Jennings to do something wimpy like put her hand to her forehead or her heart or say, "I have to sit down." Instead she just straightens up, standing to her full height.

"Good to know. I'll tell Mr. Jennings, Chrystal." She puts oven mitts on. "You're a smart girl." She raises her voice a little to get my dad's attention. "You raised a smart girl, Mr. Lawson Smith!"

Dad doesn't even look up.

Mr. Jennings gets home just before dinner. He's covered in dirt and grass stains and sweat, but Kelsey and Katie rush over to him anyways, throwing their arms around him like he's a hero returning from war, which in a way, I guess he is. After he takes care of them and hugs Logan in the man-hug way (quick pat on the back while breaking apart), he gives Mrs. Jennings a really long hug and relaxes a little bit in her arms. Then he smiles at me and says, "I'm glad you're here, Chrystal."

"Thanks," I say. "I'm glad to be here."

I'm thinking that we covered this last night and kind of wondering why he's talking about it again. He shoots a look at his girls and says, "Kelsey. Katie. Can you get your old man a beer?"

"Both of us?" Katie asks.

He nods. "I need one for each hand."

Kelsey rolls her eyes, but she and Katie head to the kitchen and Mr. Jennings says, "Your dad in there?"

I tell him he is. Logan explains that my dad's a bit distracted at the moment, doing something. We're not sure what. I haven't even been able to talk to him about the man his camera caught.

Mr. Jennings pulls off his baseball hat and uses it to wipe at the sweat on his forehead. His hair is soaked, darkened with it. "It's big. We know that much. Easily three hundred pounds. It has big strides, so it's tall. And it seems to cover a huge area in one night— literally miles."

"But you didn't find it?" Logan asks.

"No." He puts his hat back on and focuses his next words at me. "And that's why I'm glad you're staying here again tonight. I don't know how you fought off that thing, Chrystal, but I'm glad you did. They found another woman."

"Found her?" I ask.

His face folds inward somehow. "'Found' isn't the right word. Well, she's missing. An older woman. We found her. Plus, another woman is missing. She's about just the other side of twenty. It looks like it dragged her out of her car. There was blood on the road and . . ."

It's like a sucker punch. I whirl away toward the kitchen so I don't have to hear. I can't hear. I can't stand not doing anything about this, can't stand hiding here.

Kelsey comes out of the kitchen with a beer.

"I'm only a year younger than you," she says.

"I know."

"And they won't tell me anything."

I stare at her. "They want to protect you."

"They aren't."

"I know," I say again, and I pull her off toward the stairs to the basement. Whispering quickly, I tell her everything I know. She takes it all in without panicking. Her eyes harden just the same way her mom's did when I told her my theory. Finally I finish and Kelsey goes, "I can shoot, you know."

"Yeah? Are you good?"

She smiles. "Nah. I'm brilliant."

I smile back.

"Let's sleep together tonight," she says. "If you're okay with that. You can have my bed still and I'll take the cot. That way, if it's coming after one of us, we'll be together. . . ."

"But what if it's targeting me?" I protest.

"It started before you were even here, Chrystal. You were alone when it went after you. I bet those other ladies were alone, too. I bet Karen was. So, we stick together."

"Okay, but you should have your bed."

She rolls her eyes. "Fine."

"Girls! Where's my beer?" Mr. Jennings yells, but it's not a grumpy yell, more goofy.

Katie rushes past us, mashed potato on her cheek, and yells, "Right here, Daddy! Right here!"

Despite all the fear and all the weirdness these past days, dinner goes really well. People talk and tease. The food is amazing and it's almost perfect. It's like I've stepped into some 1970s family drama. Everyone loves one another. Nobody is on drugs. The parents don't glare. The only problem is that Dad refuses to join us. He's too busy. He can get like this, forgetting to eat for days if you don't push him. So I make up a plate for him and put it on the table, right near his microscope.

He still hasn't touched a bite by the time we've cleaned everything up, the dogs have mooched off a billion scraps, and Mr. Jennings goes out to take watch on the porch. The dogs go with him, except Galahad, who Mr. Jennings thinks is a nuisance. Galahad stands by the trash can, keeping watch over that while Mrs. Jennings boils down the chicken carcass to make stock for gravies and soups. I helped her add celery and onions and carrots, and now I'm watching the stock to make sure it doesn't boil over while she and the kids set up a game of Sorry! in the dining room.

"Dad, you need to eat."

He doesn't answer.

"Dad . . ." I cross my arms over my chest and lean against the doorframe between the dining room and the kitchen. "Have some water at least. It's hot. You'll dehydrate."

"I'm working, Chrystal!" His eyes flash up at me for a second, impatient, but at least he's acknowledging my existence, which is a pretty big deal for him when he's in a mood like this.

Pivoting away, I bump into Mrs. Jennings. There's pity in her eyes, which I really just can't stand.

"Thanks for helping with dinner, Chrystal," she says. "Those potatoes were far better than any I've ever made."

"Oh gosh . . . Thanks . . ." I struggle to find a way to accept the compliment. "It's just the onion powder. I think you're an amazing cook."

She smiles and smooths her hands over her hair, tucking it into place. "You do a lot for your dad, don't you?"

I shrug. It's not really something I think about. "He gets distracted sometimes."

She nods. Her lips purse. Something lodges in my throat. Swallowing hard, I try to push it away, even though it's obviously not something physical. It's not a hairball, I mean. It's an emotion, a bad emotion. It's like sadness or guilt or just a big clump of half-solidified tears or something.

"It's hard when you have to be the parent," she says.

Behind her, in the living room, everyone's playing Sorry! Mr. Jennings is taking his shift out on the porch. Every once in a while someone will go to the window and watch him pace, or join him and talk. It's funny that he's gone from protecting his livestock to protecting us.

"I love my dad." I don't know how else to answer her.

She reaches out in a total mom move, touching my cheek. "I know, sweetie."

"My mom was worse," I blurt. Then I close my eyes because I can't believe I just said that and because I don't want to see any more pity.

"She's okay now," I rattle on, "but she used to drink and she'd forget things. She wasn't mean, but she'd leave food in the oven, or leave the car running in the garage, or she'd forget to shut off the bathtub water, and . . . my dad couldn't handle it. He started studying the science of the weird even more, just retreating. . . ."

"And you were left taking care of things," she says.

I open my eyes back up.

"Mr. Jennings's dad had issues like that," she says, straightening her back like there's some sort of awful crick in there. "I could tell you that it makes you strong, but that's not going to do you much good. You already know that, right?"

"Mom!" Logan's voice interrupts us. He's still sitting at the table, playing. "Are you giving Chrystal a hard time about something?"

"No," I answer for Mrs. Jennings, and move toward the table. "She's being nice."

Logan's mouth opens, and just at that moment there's a long, howling noise that barges in through the open windows. The haunting echo of it drifts through the house, silencing all of us.

"What was that?" Kelsey whispers. She's got her arm around my waist.

"Coyote?" I ask, hoping against hope. I head towards the computer to check the camera feed.

Logan springs up from the table and races to the front porch. The rest of his family hurries after him.

Katie's clinging to her mom's side as we all stare out into the darkness.

Dad appears in the doorway. He has shotgun shells in his hands and he starts towards the front porch.

"Dad!" I yell.

He keeps walking.

"Dad! Come look at this."

I point at the camera and there it is—a dark, huge beast, shuffling across the view screen. It's too close to make out, but then . . .

but then . . . the camera jerks and the image vibrates and changes. Suddenly, it's a view of tree limbs and sky.

"Well," Dad says, enthusiastically "That is absolutely fantastic."

17

LOGAN

I grab my shotgun and throw open the front door to join Dad on the porch. Dumb ole Galahad almost knocks me over in the doorway as he races outside, hair bristling while he barks non-stop. He's off the porch and standing on the lawn ahead of Thunder and Daisy, barking and jumping around as I come to stand beside Dad.

"Toward the cattle?" I ask.

Dad shakes his head. "Across the road. Hadley place. I think. I'm not sure. It's hard to tell."

Roger Hadley and his family have 360 acres, with their house on the south end and their back pasture meeting up with the road across from us. Using the mile-section roads, their house is almost three miles from us.

"Should we go?" I ask.

"No," Dad says, his voice stiff, angry. "Damn it. We can't. But we can't just leave them." He glances over his shoulder at the front of the house. Mom and the girls are standing in the doorway, the screen door closed, but they seem to be listening to Mr. Lawson Smith, who I can just see behind them.

Chrystal rushes out. "It was here. It pulled Dad's camera down. It's . . . That proves it's smart. But . . . it's here."

"Did you see which way it went?" Dad asks.

"No . . . it's . . . The camera is just pointing up at the sky." She stares at us. "I'm going back inside to check on my dad."

As soon as she's gone, my dad says, "I saw one of those women, Sarah Fields, just the other day, Logan."

"Sarah Fields?" I ask, not recognizing the name.

"First-grade teacher," he says.

"Mrs. Fields?" She's a short, perky woman with real light reddish-blond hair. She's probably in her early thirties. Kind of pretty for a teacher. "She's dead?"

He nods. "Yes. That's three they blame on this thing."

"Three?"

Dad sighs, his gaze still focused on the darkness over the Hadley farm. "Alison King. She works up at the Walmart. About twenty-two. They found Mrs. Fields's body during the searches today. They are assuming it was the monster."

The thing out in the dark howls again. I can tell now that it's not on our property, but our cattle begin to snort and shift, their sounds carrying clearly through the otherwise still night. Dad's mouth tightens as we hear the thunder of hooves pounding the earth in the Hadley pasture. Something is chasing the cattle.

"What that thing did to her . . ." Dad says. "I don't understand it. No animal would do it. The sheriff called the coroner out. Just an estimate, but he said it looked like she'd died a week ago. Her husband thought she'd run off with a guy he suspected she'd been seeing. That was two weeks ago. That thing kept her alive for a week, then killed her. Something just ain't right about it. Animals don't do that. People do that."

A line of headlights appears on the road and turns into our driveway. Dogs in the backs of two of the trucks approaching the house begin baying.

"How'd they know?" I ask.

"I called as soon as I heard the howl. We set up a network—a phone tree is what Sam called it. I called him, he called others, and here they are."

Men with guns start jumping out of the trucks. I see Mr. Thompson, with David and Carl, plus about a dozen others. The dogs are unloaded as me and Dad join the men.

"Logan, you and David stay here, watch the house," Dad calls. "Go inside!"

"Let's go get that son of a bitch!" someone else calls. The mass of men and dogs race off toward the road.

"Left behind again," David says as he comes to stand with me, his rifle held loosely in his hand.

"Yep," I agree. I almost want to say *Now you know how it feels* because of him always taking off with Yesenia, but it doesn't matter much anymore really. Seems stupid and petty. Turning around, I stare at my home. Chrystal's standing at the bedroom window with Kelsey, both of them peeking out. That's what matters.

Dad and the other men don't find anything. Nothing but a herd of tired cattle and one dead steer, partially eaten. The hounds track the killer's scent to another road, then lose it. Dad comes home tired.

The incident is repeated the next two nights, except then it's Dad getting the call and rushing into the night to chase the monster across someone else's farm farther away.

Another woman goes missing. This one is the waitress from that first time Chrystal and I ate together.

Another woman is found mauled and dead. This one was apparently a student at the college Dr. Borgess works at. What she was doing in town? Who knows? But they found her car. And then they found her.

Even saying 'another woman' sounds wrong. Like they are disposable bodies, or statistics, when they are anything but.

Then there is a pause. It's a pause of days.

But nobody's nerves get any less frayed. We are raw people, ready to jump, to scream, to fight for our lives and our families.

Inside the house, the phone rings. A few minutes later Dad comes onto the porch with his rifle in his hand. He looks at us, then toward the road.

"It's started again," he says. "It just killed a hog over at the Benson place. Chased it out of the pen and killed it right under the kitchen window. Liberty Benson looked out and saw a huge, hairy thing loping away with the carcass."

"At least it was just a pig this time," Chrystal says.

Dad grunts, his eyes on the driveway. "Bill Thompson and his boys are coming to pick me up. David will stay here with you."

Beside me, Chrystal clasps my arm. She knows how I feel about being left behind. She's letting me know she needs me, and

I understand that. Mom needs me. Kelsey and Katie need me. But I'd rather be out there hunting that monster.

"Is my dad going?" Chrystal asks.

"I asked," Dad answers, and he doesn't do a real good job of hiding his scorn. He has a hard time figuring out Mr. Lawson Smith, I think. "He started talking about flowers again. Said he wasn't ready. He was on the phone with someone—Burgess? Burguest?"

"Oh. Borgess. He's a professor friend," Chrystal says. I catch her hand and squeeze it reassuringly.

Mr. Thompson's truck turns into the driveway and approaches the house. Dad goes to meet it. David joins us on the porch.

"Together again," he jokes, his rifle held in the crook of his arm.

"You all go inside and lock up," Dad calls as Mr. Thompson turns the truck around and drives away.

About a half hour after Dad leaves, Daisy barks outside. Just once. Then Thunder barks twice. Inside the house, Galahad jumps up and rips off a series of his short, choppy barks. Then the house is still. Galahad goes to the front door and scratches at it. I let him out, look around quickly, then close the door.

"Logan, I'm going upstairs for more guns," Mom announces.

I see Chrystal give Mom a surprised look and wonder what she thinks of a country woman always so willing to grab a gun.

And then our back door bursts open.

Kelsey and Katie shriek. One of the guys points at Kelsey.

David and I turn toward the kitchen and raise our guns. But we hesitate. We don't shoot when the three men Chrystal and I saw in the woods charge through the doorway from our kitchen to the dining room. We don't shoot as they look from the dining room to the living room. They have guns too. One points a heavy-looking black revolver at me. The one who'd pointed at Kelsey aims a shotgun in David's direction while the third points a rifle at Mr. Lawson Smith.

David and I could have shot them. We had the angle from the moment they entered the kitchen doorway. We could have shot them in the dining room before they locked onto us. We could have, but we didn't.

"Put those guns down, boys," orders the big guy who'd done most of the talking the last time we saw him. He looks over his shoulder at his friends and says, "We want the older girls. Don't hurt that one."

"Fine. Take me." Chrystal steps forward.

"Not just you. Her too." He nods at Kelsey.

My blood seems to go cold when I hear that. What do they want? What are their plans? An image of Kelsey hurt, bloody, dead like those other women flashes across my mind and my throat goes dry."

"We should have shot them," I whisper to David.

"Who are they?" he asks.

"Friends of that thing out there," I answer.

"Put them guns down," the brute says again.

Chrystal's face is deathly pale. Kelsey and Katie are clinging to each other and Katie is crying hysterically. Mr. Lawson Smith seems completely dumbstruck by the turn of events. He stands with his mouth open, staring from the three men to where David and I face them with our own guns pointed at them.

The leader of the trio cocks the hammer of his revolver.

"Damn." I lower the barrel of my shotgun, then carefully lay it on the floor by my feet. David puts his rifle down too.

"Very good," the man says. The three come into the living room, still holding their guns on us. The leader motions to his companions and they step forward to pick up the guns David and I just put on the floor.

That's when I see Mom raising the rifle on the landing of the stairs. My mouth goes dry, then a single, sharp crack rings out in the house. The man in front of David grunts and crumples to the floor, a red stain blooming around a hole in his back.

I suddenly find my spine and shove the redneck intruder who was reaching for my shotgun. He staggers backward but doesn't fall. Instead he raises his handgun even as he's trying to keep his balance and I'm going for my shotgun.

Mom fires again. The man's grinning head explodes, the left side flying away in gooey red pieces.

The third man turns and runs for the kitchen.

Me and David both grab our guns and run after him, but he's out of the house by the time we get to the kitchen.

"Help me with the door," I say. We close it. The lock is shattered, as are two of the glass windowpanes. We haul a wood-and-metal baker's rack over to block the door, then go back to the living room.

"I just can't believe it. I can't believe what I just witnessed," Mr. Lawson Smith is jabbering.

Mom is on the phone, telling someone she just shot two men who broke into her house. "There were three. The other one got away." She looks to me and David for confirmation. I nod at her even as she's so calm, so quietly calm. "No, they're dead. I told you: they're in my living room." She listens for a minute, then says,

"Okay. Fine." She hangs up the phone. "They're sending a deputy. And an ambulance," she says to us.

"I just can't believe this," Mr. Lawson Smith says again. "It's . . . oh—ah . . . I'm so sorry. So sorry that all of this is happening to your sweet family."

Chrystal pulls her dad into a hug, hushing him.

Mom turns to Chrystal and asks, "Are these the men you two confronted when I called you that day? The same men who were trespassing?"

Chrystal nods. Her face is still so pale. Her eyes are big and round and scared and I feel really bad for her.

"They pointed their guns at us," she says. "At me and Kelsey. They were going to take us. Take us to him. And they have been casing out this house, your house, your farm, for days. Obviously. This is big. This is bigger even than some monster killing people. It's . . . How can anything even be bigger than a monster killing people? But these guys . . . these guys must be helping him."

Nobody can say anything for a minute. Outside, our dogs are quiet. Why? Why didn't they go after the three men who came through the back door?

I rush to the front door and throw it open. All three dogs are lying there, happily tearing off huge chunks of meat from bones. Pork, from the looks of it. Galahad ignores me. Daisy and Thunder raise their heads, still chewing.

"With all the commotion out front, they probably never even heard or smelled them," David says behind me.

"Yeah," I agree. "Pretty scary, though."

"Man, that whole thing was scary," he says. Then he adds in a low voice, "Your mom just shot two men. She's being super calm about it."

"She's probably still in Mom shock or emergency mode." I nod, thinking of that, but refusing to process it just yet. I'm still holding my gun. "All our dogs bought off with chunks of meat. Let's take them around back, see if they can pick up anything from the one that got away."

"No, Logan, you're not going out there," Mom calls.

There are dead people on our carpet. I have to catch myself to keep from swearing. I'm already sweating up a storm and I just—I want to be away from the dead men. "I think you can handle things in here, Mom. We should make sure that guy isn't still hiding out back. He could be in the barn or something."

"The deputy is on his way. That's his job."

"It's our farm, Mom. It's our job."

"Logan, please," Chrystal says. That ends it. Her wide, scared eyes and shaky voice are not to be denied.

Mom looks around at Mr. Lawson Smith, Chrystal, and Katie and Kelsey, who are still holding each other. Katie's crying, though she's not hysterical anymore. Kelsey looks about like Chrystal, except she has wet tracks where tears have escaped and run down her face. I probably look just as freaked out as all of them.

"Come on," Mom says. "Everyone out of this room. Kelsey, please take Katie upstairs. Read her a book. Play some music. Try to get your minds off what happened. These two are dead and that other one won't be coming back."

"I'll go with them," Chrystal says. She gets up and moves toward my sisters, then stops and hurries over to Mom. She throws her arms around Mom's neck and hugs her tight. I see that she's whispering something to her, but can't hear it.

Mom pats Chrystal on the back and says, "Thank you. It's going to be all right."

We watch as Chrystal ushers my sisters up the stairs and into Kelsey's room.

Then something happens to Mom. She falls into a chair, buries her face in her hands, and breaks down crying.

"Mom?" I hurry over to her, pull out a chair, and sit beside her.

"Will you help me in here, Mr. Lawson Smith?" David asks, leading Chrystal's dad out of the room.

"Mom? You . . . You okay?"

She raises her face and she suddenly looks so much older than I've ever seen her look. Her hands are trembling and her face is wet with tears. "I shot two men, Logan. I killed them. I . . ." She begins sobbing again.

I put my arms around her and pull her tight against me, but I don't know how much good that does, because I'm trembling too. "You had to, Mom. You had to. You knew that they were going to do terrible things to Kelsey and Chrystal. Maybe even little Katie. You had to do it. I wish I'd done it."

"No, Logan, no, you don't," she says, pushing herself away from me. She puts her hands on my shoulders and squeezes so tight it hurts a little. "Don't say that. It's a horrible feeling. I know it had to be done. I know that. I know it, Logan. I know it, but killing is a bad thing. I feel . . . I feel like something inside me has died."

Convincing me of this has brought back some of her strength. The tears are gone. Her face is set again.

I nod my understanding. "Okay, Mom. But you did the right thing. And, well, I'm proud of you. I'm sorry you feel so bad about it, but you just did what you had to do."

"Fine. That's fine. Thank you," she says, and smiles at me just a little.

David and Mr. Lawson Smith come back into the room, each carrying a tablecloth.

"Not that one!" Mom jumps up and takes the white cloth from David's hands. "My grandmother made that one. I don't want that man's blood on it." She returns to the kitchen while me and David stare after her. Mr. Lawson Smith goes about the task of covering one of the bodies with the hideous striped cloth he has.

"She cries over killing men who are worse than animals, but straightens right up when her best tablecloth is in danger," I whisper to David.

The home phone rings. I answer it and am greeted by Sam Davis from the feedstore.

"Logan, is your mom there?" he asks.

"Well, she's kind of busy," I say. "Dad's out with the hunt and we had three guys break into the house. We're waiting on the police right now."

"I see. Is everyone all right?" he asks.

"Except the guys Mom shot."

"Uh-huh. Logan, I hate to say this, but there've been some injuries. Your dad's hurt. That thing got him pretty bad."

18

CHRYSTAL

What you never realize in TV shows or books or movies is how loud gunshots are. Here's more: What you never realize in TV shows or books or movies or even in real life is how fear isn't just an emotion. It's tangible but changeable. Sometimes it's a straitjacket that pushes your arms to your sides, keeps you from moving, keeps you from saving yourself. That's the way it was when those guys came in the house. Sometimes it's a hand pushing at your back, whispering for you to run. That's how it is for Katie upstairs.

"We have to go," she says, scratching behind her ear. "We all have to just get in the car and go as fast as we can."

She's sitting on Kelsey's bed, rocking back and forth, as if motion is the only safety. I try to soothe her by rubbing little circles on her thin back. Her shoulder blades are like tiny wings.

"We have to go," she repeats. "Cars drive fast. They drive . . .

We have to go. Maybe we could go live with you, Chrystal. In Maine. Maine's far."

Her eyes look up at mine, pleading. There are some thumps downstairs. Kelsey goes to the bedroom door, almost steps out, and then changes her mind.

"I would love to have you all live with me," I say into Katie's hair. It smells of chicken dinner and coconut, like Logan's. "You're all invited anytime."

"Mommy killed them," Katie says, totally switching gears in that little-kid way she has.

My stomach clenches, but I manage to say, "Yes, she did."

"Mommy's a total badass." She blusters the words out.

"Katie!" Kelsey admonishes from the door, but she also giggles. It's just enough humor to break her shell of fear. That's another way fear manifests itself. Sometimes it's like three chugs of booze. It numbs you as it gnaws away at your insides. I think that's the way it is for Kelsey.

And for me? The fear is a foreboding. It's a monster with a burned face waiting for me. I can feel him under my skin, ready to strike.

"'Badass' is not a swear word," Katie mumbles. She starts scratching at the skin behind her ear again. It's a raw line. I move her fingers away. She jumps up and starts pacing. "And we should all just totally leave. Go far away. Like, to Disney. We never get to go to Disney. And they're always promising. We should just go. You could come too, Chrystal."

I watch her go to the window. She stands there for a second before she gasps.

Kelsey and I both rush over to stand behind her. Kelsey puts her hand on Katie's shoulder. "What is it?"

"Someone's hurt."

There's a black pickup truck on the road with about five men sitting in the back. They've all got rifles and there's another man, convulsing in pain, flat on his back until the pain strikes and then he curls up. There's blood all over his shirt, which is ripped and soaked into some unrecognizable color. There's a white tourniquet wrapped around his arm. Blood's soaking that, too.

Logan and Mrs. Jennings and the dogs are running across the front lawn, followed by my dad and David. Mrs. Jennings is leaping into the back of the truck, which means . . .

"Oh no . . ." Kelsey whispers. Her hand goes to her mouth.

"Daddy!" Katie screams. Then I recognize him too. It's Mr. Jennings, who is so terribly hurt. Katie whirls away and heads out of the room. We follow her down the stairs, past the dead men and onto the lawn. Katie bolts right into the truck, yelling for her dad. Then her face goes white and she's silent.

He's trying to hold Mrs. Jennings's hand. There are five massive claw marks across his stomach. The lowest looks like it cut clear down to his intestines.

"Somebody needs to put pressure on those wounds," Logan orders, jumping into the truck and doing it himself.

Fear and concern fill all the men's faces. Their mouths and eyes are hard and bright. I catch only snippets of the conversation.

"Can't wait for the ambulance."

"Too much blood loss."

"I'm coming with him."

"The police are headed this way."

The snippets all swirl around in my head as the men waste time figuring out what to do. Logan, poor Logan, he is so sweet and tries to be so strong. My heart breaks for him.

"You need to go now," I say in my loudest, most commanding voice. "Mrs. Jennings, you go with him. You too, Katie and Kelsey and Logan. The police can interview you at the hospital."

"Someone has to stay here, keep the farm safe," Logan says.

"We will," one of the men says, jumping out of the truck. "We won't go chasing him anymore tonight, but we'll patrol the farm. I expect some deputies will too."

Two men stay in the truck. Three get out of the back and two leave the front, which is where Katie and Kelsey go to sit. The truck flies off into the darkness, dirt swirling behind its back wheels. We all stare at it, watching it retreat.

"Holy crap," one of the men says. "Holy crap."

Dad puts his hand on my shoulder. I'd forgotten he was there, but right now his words echo the other men's. "Holy crap is absolutely right."

The police come without an ambulance. They met Mr. Jennings on the road and transferred him into the ambulance right there so that they could transport him the rest of the way to the hospital.

The officers in uniform and some men in plainclothes tape off the living room, dust the back door for prints, take pictures of the bodies. The living room is starting to smell like feces and rotten eggs and cabbage mixed with mothballs. They ask us questions, making my dad, David, and me go alone with them one by one to Katie's bedroom, which is now police headquarters, I guess. After what seems like hours of this, the coroner's truck comes and takes the bodies away.

The house phone rings and David gets it. When he hangs up,

he says, "He's in the intensive care ward. He's lost a lot of blood, but they think if he holds on tonight, he'll make it through."

Relief seems to rush out of everyone.

"Logan, Kelsey, and Katie are coming back with Sam, but Mrs. Jennings is staying there for the rest of the night," he adds.

There isn't much left of the night, not really. Looking for something useful to do, I straighten up Katie's bed and turn down her sheets, and then I do the same with Kelsey's and Logan's. The police investigators and the coroner truck have finally left, but there is still a patrol car parked in the driveway. It'll be here until morning. I try not to worry about the officer being a sitting duck out there.

Dad has gone back to his table of experiments. His food would have been untouched except that Galahad stole the chicken off the plate when he thought nobody was looking. I guess evil men, dead bodies, injured masters, and a monster don't affect that dog's stomach, but it really has affected mine.

I drift around Logan's room. It's so *guy*. There are books about war, knights, and zombies in a pile by his bed. A picture of him and David with a monster fish is tacked to the wall. They're both smiling super-huge. They look so innocent and unworried, pre-monster. On the wall above his desk is a gun rack with one rifle in the wooden notches. The other set of notches is empty. Beside the gun rack, one of those compound bow thingies hangs on a hook in the wall. But what catches my attention is an open notebook on his desk. I glance at it. The lines are short and the writing is neat. Each letter looks as if it was thought out. I resist the urge to read what he wrote, because that would be too snoopy. Instead I go and smell his shirt, which is almost creepy. It smells like grass and coconut and boy deodorant. It smells ridiculously good.

I put it back. Poor Logan. I can't even imagine how he must be feeling. Or Kelsey or Katie. Or Mrs. Jennings. They're so nice and they're being terrorized by this thing, and those men . . . Those awful men with the guns. I play bass for a while, picking away at it. My fingers are totally healed now. I can play again, but it doesn't help. I don't lose myself, don't make anything beautiful or interesting, don't feel more skilled.

Headlights swing up the road and stop in the driveway. I rush downstairs to meet Logan, Katie, and Kelsey. They have to come in through the kitchen because the police want to preserve the crime scene/living room for another day or so.

Logan comes in first, carrying the sleeping form of Katie. I want to rush into his arms and tell him it'll be okay, comfort him, but instead I have to make do with a look that passes between us.

"I'm going to bring her upstairs," he whispers as Thunder sniffs at his ankles and thumps his tail a couple times.

Kelsey comes in next and she looks from me to David, as if trying to decide who to hug first. She goes to me because I'm closer, I think.

"It's all so awful," she sobs. "He looks so awful."

I do my best to comfort her and then motion for David to help since he's known her longer. He sort of awkwardly comes over and starts patting her back. She turns and throws her arms around him, sobbing. He looks surprised but returns the hug.

"It'll be okay," he says, using the same words I used. "It'll be okay."

Dad watches this all with interest but doesn't say anything. He does, however, actually take a sip of his water, which has been sitting there all night. Logan comes back down the stairs.

"Mr. Davis is outside," he says, "talking to the cop."

He updates us on what happened. Kelsey and I sit on the counter and listen. She holds my hand. David leans by the back door, watching outside but listening. Dad stays in his chair but he also listens. Logan paces from stove to refrigerator, telling us all what happened.

"The police are going to arrange another hunt tomorrow, focusing on our property," he says, "because so much activity happened here. They aren't charging Mom with anything . . ."

Kelsey snorts. "Like they could."

". . . since it's self-defense," Logan finishes. "And they're going to look for that third guy based on our descriptions."

"I don't think you understand how urgent it is that we find this man," Dad says, finally speaking. He looks at Logan and then at Kelsey and then at David and then, finally, at me.

"Dad . . ."

"We know it's urgent, Mr. Lawson Smith. He hurt our dad," Kelsey says. Her hand squeezes mine. "He's killing people and eating them."

"Yes, yes . . . That's part of it, but . . ." He looks into my eyes, as if asking permission to speak the unspeakable. I nod. "It bit your father, Logan. Kelsey. It didn't just maul him. It bit him, and that means that if we do not find the beast and a potential antidote, that he, too, will become a monster."

Logan staggers back and bumps his butt into the counter so hard that the silverware in the dish rack actually shakes. "What? You mean . . ."

Dad nods even as Logan's words trail off. "Yes, I mean your father will become a werewolf."

19

LOGAN

Werewolf?

I look at them, all these people staring back at me, and it's like they're there but not really there. They're fake. They're those big cardboard cutouts of people like they have outside movie theaters. Except they're not. They are looking at me and their faces are worried and expectant and I don't know what to say. How can this be? Then Kelsey hiccups a huge sob and I focus in on her.

"This is so not fair," Kelsey says. She hunches over and her shoulders shake. Chrystal goes to her, wraps her arms around her, and holds her.

"What—" My mouth moves, but I can't push any air through my throat. I take a deep breath, lick my lips, and try again. "What can we do about it?"

"We have to find the werewolf," Mr. Lawson Smith says. "That's the first thing."

"Why do you keep calling it a werewolf?" David asks. "I thought it was Bigfoot."

Mr. Lawson Smith's eyes light up in the way only a teacher who's about to deliver a favorite lesson can.

"A common misconception," he says. "I have a theory. I've written it up, but all the journals have rejected it so far. This is my chance to prove it's true." He pauses and looks at me and Kelsey. A little of his enthusiasm drains away, but only for a moment. "I'm just very sorry it's at your family's expense."

"What's your theory?" I ask.

"No one has ever found a Bigfoot," he says. "No one has ever captured one. No one has ever produced a corpse. Not even a partial corpse. Fingers, arms, whatever. No skeletons. Think about that." He's really wound up now. "Why? You have to ask yourself why that is. All these supposed sightings, tracks, even bad video footage, and yet no body. Why not?

"Some say it's because they take care of their dead, like we do," he continued. "They bury them, some supposed experts say. Because there aren't very many of them, in relation to humans, it's easy for them to do this in the deep woods where no human eyes can see. And yet, not one single Bigfoot grave has ever been found. Ever!"

I glance at Chrystal and Kelsey. They are both looking at Chrystal's dad. Kelsey's tears have stopped for the moment as she listens, but I know she could start up again at any moment. Chrystal gives me kind of a helpless look, as if to say her dad will continue like this, slowly leading up to where he's going before he gets to his point. He *is* a teacher, after all, and he's driving his lesson home.

"Burying their dead," he says sarcastically. "Why would they do that? Are they so intelligent that they know they have to hide even their dead from us humans? Do they have religion? I say no!"

"Then why?" David finally asks. He's never been very patient in class.

"Aha! Because"—Mr. Lawson Smith makes a long, dramatic pause before saying—"because there is no such thing as Bigfoot."

We all stare at him.

"The alleged Bigfoot sightings are really werewolves," he confides, as if he's telling us the mystery of creation.

"I don't get it," David says.

"No Bigfoot bodies are ever found," Mr. Lawson Smith explains. "But human bodies are found in the forest all the time. You see—"

Kelsey beats me to it. "They turn back into men when they die," she says.

"Bingo!" Mr. Lawson Smith claps his hands, and for a second I think he's going to jump into the air with his excitement. "Something happens to kill them. They die and become human again. Some hunter stumbles across the body later and it's reported as a human, when in truth it was a werewolf, which would have been mistaken for Bigfoot if it had been seen before it died."

"What kills a werewolf? Silver bullets?" David asks.

"Yes, silver does it." Mr. Lawson Smith looks at me, nodding.

"So we just have to shoot that thing full of silver bullets?" I ask, not at all sure I believe this line of reasoning.

"Ah, if only it were that easy," Mr. Lawson Smith says, ignoring my skepticism. "However, there are other ways. Werewolves are highly susceptible to rabies, hydrophobia."

"Why?" I ask.

"I'm not sure," he answers. "But they are likely to come into contact with raccoons, skunks, and other animals that have it. I believe a lot of the bodies found in the forest—those not dumped by a completely human murderer or simply lost hikers—the ones who were werewolves, died of rabies."

"Mr. Lawson Smith," I finally say, "I don't want to be disrespectful. I'm tired. My mom killed two men and my dad is in the hospital with really bad wounds. Our living room is a mess. I don't want to sound mean, but, really, what are you basing all of this on? The silver bullets, the rabies? Is it the movies? Comic books? Where do you go to find facts on something that isn't supposed to exist?"

"The research is out there, Logan. It's just hard to find. You have to read between the lines in ancient texts a lot of times. The government, too, doesn't want it out there. Some say various governments know about the werewolves and are trying to use them for military purposes. There's a professor at a local university here who—"

"Government conspiracies?" David asks, and he snorts a little. "Isn't that a right-wing craziness thing?"

Mr. Lawson Smith shrugs. "I'm not necessarily saying I believe that part, but the references to werewolves, or lycanthropy, is there in various forms if you know where to look."

"Dad, everyone's really tired. Can we finish this in the morning?" Chrystal asks. She looks to me and says, "It really is a lot to take in, especially after all that's gone on today." Then she turns back to her dad. "They're hearing this for the first time. Let them sleep on what you've said so far, then you can tell us the rest in the morning."

"I want to hear the rest," I say. "But those cows are going to be lining up for milking in just a few hours. If that thing, your werewolf, didn't scare them so bad that they won't milk. Kelsey, are you going to be up to help me?"

She nods, and I'm suddenly very proud of my little sister. Would I have blamed her if she'd broken down crying again and said she just couldn't do it? I don't know. Maybe. But I don't have to answer that, because she knows the responsibilities that come with running a farm. Something in my face must give away what I'm thinking, because suddenly Chrystal smiles at me.

"How about you, David?" I ask. "Want to help?"

"Sure," he says.

I'd ask Mr. Lawson Smith, but he's already seemingly sunk back into himself. His eyes have that distant, distracted look they did earlier, when he was sitting at his microscope and makeshift desk.

"I can help," Chrystal offers. "I mean, I've never done it, but I can learn."

"It's no fun," David warns.

"The thing is," I say, "Katie needs to sleep in. She'll probably sleep through the whole thing, but if she doesn't, and she wakes up and can't find anyone, it will scare her pretty bad."

"Especially if she goes in the living room and sees the bloodstains on the carpet and has to relive it all again," Kelsey adds. "I really don't want her to see that. Mom wouldn't either."

"Okay, I'll stay for her," Chrystal says. "But I'm going to do something useful. I can make breakfast while you guys work."

We leave Mr. Lawson Smith at his table. I'm not sure where he'll sleep now that the living room is a crime scene, but he brushes me off with a "Have no worries for me, young fellow" when I try to mention it. The girls take blankets and pillows into Katie's room to make pallets on the floor. David does the same in my room. I linger in the hallway, waiting for Chrystal to notice me. Eventually she does and comes out to join me. I lead her into my parents' bedroom, then catch her hands in mine.

"I'm so glad you're here," I tell her.

"Me too." She leans into me, resting her head against my chest. She's warm and solid but also so soft and feminine.

"Thank you for everything you're doing. All the help," I say.

"Ummm," she says, and kind of nuzzles me in a sleepy way. "You've really taken charge of a bad situation."

"It doesn't feel like it. It feels like that thing out there is in charge."

"We'll win," she says. "My dad may sound crazy, but I think he knows what he's talking about."

"He seems to be the only option we have." I reach up and stroke her hair and it seems so natural. I can't help it. I don't want to *not* touch her. "My dad . . . ," I begin. "He'd kill himself before he becomes like that thing."

"I know. He's a good man. Like his son."

We hold each other for a few minutes and it feels so good. It feels right and comforting and like something I want to do forever. Forever . . . "Chrystal?"

"Hmm?"

"What about when this is over? When it's time, you know, for you to leave? I . . . I don't know. I like having you here. I like . . . Well, I like you. A lot."

Her smile flickers, but only for a second. "I like you too, Logan. We'll worry about the rest when it happens, okay? Right now we have other things to worry about. Get to sleep. Those cows won't wait. Remember? Good night."

She leaves me standing there in my parents' bedroom, missing her.

In the morning, as we're stumbling out the back door, I notice that Mr. Lawson Smith isn't sitting at his table. Kelsey notices too.

"Where do you think he is?" she asks as we cross the dark yard.

"Asleep, probably," David answers.

"Where?" she persists.

"On the . . ." I trail off. He can't sleep on the couch. It's part of the crime scene. I shrug. "Maybe he went up to Mom and Dad's room."

"His car's gone," Kelsey says.

We all stop and look at the driveway. An older green Dodge pickup sits empty. It belongs to Mike Dooley, one of the men who volunteered to stay and watch over the cattle last night. In front of the truck is the sheriff's patrol car with a dozing deputy inside. The red Subaru is nowhere to be seen.

"I'll ask," I say, heading for the cop car. I knock on the window, which is halfway down. My knock scares the young deputy inside. He jumps and I see his hand jerk to the gun holstered at his hip before he realizes I'm probably not a threat. He turns the key in the ignition and lowers the window the rest of the way. The heat is overwhelming and I almost burn myself on the door handle.

"Sorry," he says. "Nothing else happened, so I guess I slept a little. You guys doing the milking?"

"Yeah. We were wondering, though, if you saw Mr. Lawson Smith leave?" I ask.

He gives me a blank look.

"That red station wagon that was pulled up close to the house last night," I remind him. "That was his car. Did you see him get in it and leave?"

"Oh, him," the deputy says, nodding. "Yeah. He came out of the house at about two in the morning. He was talking to himself. Pulled up some of your flowers and was getting in his car when I stopped him and asked what he was doing. All he'd tell me was that he'd discovered something and he had to test it out. He's an odd guy."

"That's him, all right," David says.

I give him a harsh look.

"Sorry," he offers, putting up his hands.

"He didn't say anything else? Didn't say where he was going?" I ask.

"Nope. Really odd guy. Just kept excusing himself. It was like he was talking to himself more than me. I was just in his way. I didn't have any instructions about not letting anybody leave, so I let him go," the deputy explains. "I radioed in that he was leaving, and dispatch said it was fine. Is everything okay? He wasn't, like, mentally handicapped and not supposed to be driving, was he?"

David laughs. When I glare at him, he turns around and starts for the milk barn, but he's still laughing.

"No, nothing like that. He just gets wrapped up in his work," I say.

"His work? What's his work?"

"Cryptozoology," Kelsey answers before I can.

"I have no idea what that is," the deputy says. "Animal graves?"

"He studies Bigfoot and stuff like that," I explain.

"Oooh. One of those guys." The deputy nods knowingly, like I've given him a code that means Mr. Lawson Smith *is* a little mentally handicapped, but in a funny, harmless way.

"Come on, Logan," Kelsey says. "I'm sure he'll be back pretty soon. Look. Mr. Dooley is already pushing cows out of the barn."

I look over and, sure enough, our neighbor from a mile section over is slapping a cow on the rump and ushering another one inside. He's a burly, older guy with red cheeks and happy eyes. He waves at us, then claps David on the back.

"Yeah. I suppose so," I say to Kelsey. I look back to the deputy. "Thanks for staying. How long will you be here?"

"Until dispatch says I can leave," he answers.

His car is gone by the time we're finished milking the cows.

20

CHRYSTAL

The day moves slowly. Katie, Kelsey, and Logan go to visit Mr. Jennings in the hospital, and this nice feedstore guy, Sam, stays behind, watching the cows. He's rounded up some of Logan's friends and one of his own grown sons to help do the chores and watch the property with him. I'm kind of amazed by how everyone is helping the Jennings family. I stay at the house to wait for my dad and for the police wearing blazers instead of uniforms, who come once again to do intake on the crime scene, taking pictures, processing more evidence in the daytime, I guess. Their efficient movements, the way they try to figure out what has happened, seeing if evidence corroborates what we've told them—it reminds me of how my dad works a case, only more organized, with more profanity and less jumping up and down and pacing.

I've called my dad over and over again. And texted. And called more. I don't get any response. Logan texts me though, even though cell phones aren't allowed in the ICU. They can only go in to see his dad two at a time. He looks horrible, I guess. He's not really speaking yet. Some sort of toxin seems to be working its way through his body.

IT DOESN'T LOOK GOOD, Logan texts.

STAY STRONG, I text back. WE'LL FIGURE IT OUT.

And I hope my words are true.

I call Dr. Borgess's number. He answers and I tell him that my dad was supposed to see him, but I haven't been able to contact him.

"That must be worrying," he says. "He has not appeared here today. Can I help you with something?"

My breath whooshes out in one horrible rush.

"Are you worried? I am sure he is fine. He does become a bit—absentmindedly focused," he says.

"I know. That's true. It's true. Would you mind letting me know if you see him or hear from him?"

"Of course not, my dear," he says.

While the police work, I clean up the remnants of breakfast, feed the dogs again, give them more water. They are always thirsty and hungry, but they're good company. The police officers' voices make a comforting background noise. Every once in a while their radios go off and they talk in ten-codes. It makes me feel so much safer to have them in the other room. Eventually I go on the laptop that the family shares and start googling WEREWOLVES and HOW TO STOP TURNING INTO A WEREWOLF.

And I get?

Pretty much nothing. There's a lot about how to turn into a werewolf, but even that is mostly about turning into a "spiritual werewolf," where you believe you're the wolf, and you're "at one" with the wolf spirit, but you aren't actually, physically a wolf. Not very helpful, really. There are some sites that talk about the wolves' need to protect its family and pack and how it will track down threats.

This shakes me. Dr. Borgess talked about vengeance. But seriously? How could any of us be a threat to—to such a horrible, strong creature? It seems ridiculous. And those three guys? Who are they? Are they his family? If so, he's going to be even more hyped up to hurt people.

Thunder the wonder dog pushes up against my legs. I reach down to pat him and try different search words. I type REVERSE WEREWOLF CURSE just as Thunder Butt proves why his name is appropriate.

I wave the air in front of my face, hoping for relief. "Doggy, that is nasty."

He flops onto the floor and wags his tail.

"No, seriously," I tell him. "That could be classified as a chemical weapon."

This time the hits are a bit better, but the cures seem silly:

1. Rolling around in the dew
2. Hitting yourself on the head with a knife three times
3. Being blessed with the holy cross
4. Having someone say the cursed werewolf's baptismal name three times
5. Plunging into water

It all seems like superstition, not like something real. I mean, if you get it because you're bitten, it seems more like a virus, like HIV or something. And the hospital people said there seemed to be a toxin in Mr. Jennings's blood, so maybe if they could isolate that somehow, they could find an antidote.

I don't know. It seems impossible. Seriously, how long have they been trying to find a cure for cancer? And there're all those resources for that, and I want them to magically find a cure for Mr. Jennings's lycanthropy in what . . . ? By the next full moon, I guess, because that's what all the sources say. According to them, the person who is bitten transforms at the first full moon after the bite. Although, to be fair, that sounds pretty superstitious to me too.

A police officer pokes his head into the kitchen. "We're done now. If you and Mrs. Jennings want to clean this up, you can go right ahead."

"Really?" I stand up and walk to where the officer is standing. I have to look up at him because he's so tall, maybe six foot six. He looks like Shrek with a crew cut.

"Yep." He sighs. "I can give you a card for a cleaning service, but that's going to run you about 2 to 3 thousand. I'd recommend you rip up the carpet, bleach the walls, repaint them with something darker to cover up the splatter. One of the chairs is pretty bad. You might just want to throw that out, but the couch seems fine. The coffee table and end tables you can just bleach, too. Might hurt the wood some."

"Okay. Wow. Thanks. Um . . . You're sure there won't be criminal charges?" I ask, even though I'm kind of afraid of the answer. The thought of Mrs. Jennings in jail or on trial is just too much to imagine.

He eyes me like he's trying to decide how to answer, and finally says, "I'm almost positive. It's pretty cut-and-dried self-defense, special circumstances. It'll have to go to the attorney general's office, but I can't imagine anyone is going to make a big to-do about a woman shooting down men who broke into her house and threatened her kids with guns."

I swallow hard. Hearing it from an officer makes me really believe it. But it doesn't mean everything is one big happy fun land. "What about the third guy?"

The cop's hazel eyes narrow. "We'll be looking for him. Don't you worry. And we're going to post another deputy here in the driveway tonight, too."

"Good, thanks," I say. That's another relief. It feels much safer with a police car here, especially with Mr. Jennings in the hospital. It felt good to have them here all morning, actually. "So, you're leaving now?"

He nods. "We're done here. You've got a ton of neighbors around, lots of good people working outside. You'll be okay."

"Sure," I say a little too brightly, I guess, because he gets a reassuring look and puts his big hand on my shoulder for a second.

"We're just a 9-1-1 call away."

First, I rip up the rest of the carpet that they haven't taken for evidence. Fortunately it's pretty easy to pick up. Then I spend over an hour trying to scrape and bleach the dried-up blood off the walls. When you shoot someone, the blood splatters. I hadn't watched enough crime shows to realize this. I manage to not gag and sort of disassociate from all of it, but it's still . . . It sucks.

When my cell phone finally rings, I grab it without looking at the display because I think it's got to be my dad or Logan and also because I could really use a break from cleaning.

It turns out, this was not the right move.

"Hello?" I say.

"Chrystal Lawson Smith?" The voice is gruff, with a twangy drawl that is more exaggerated than Logan's.

I sit on the couch, a Clorox bleach wipe in my free hand. "Yes?"

"You don't know me, but I have a friend who thinks you're pretty special. I was thinking you could maybe give me a moment of your time?"

"Who is this? How'd you get my number?" I answer.

Thunder whines to come into the room and I nod at him. He rushes in and lies across my feet.

"Those aren't questions you need to bother your pretty little self with, Chrystal."

That's when I know. It's the guy from last night. The guy who got away.

The back door opens and I jump up off the couch. Thunder leaps off my feet and charges toward the kitchen just as David yells hello.

"What's up?" he says, stepping into the room. "You cleaning?"

I hold up my hand for him to be quiet, then realize I have the wipe in it. I throw it on the floor. I must look shocked or something because he mouths the words, *Are you okay?*

I shake my head as the man on the phone says, "We have the antidote."

"Antidote!" I repeat. "What is it?"

He laughs. David strides across the room in two steps. I turn the phone so he can hear it too. Our heads are super-close together. His breath smells like beef jerky.

"You think I'm going to just tell you, little girl?" the man says.

"Well, it would be the nice thing to do."

"I don't believe in nice."

"Obviously," I say. My hand is shaking so much that the phone wobbles back and forth. David takes it from me, but holds it in the same place between our heads.

The man laughs again, a Wicked Witch kind of laugh, sharp and full of venom. Then he says, "Well, aren't you going to ask me what I want?"

"What you want?" I repeat.

"Yep. Quid pro quo. Something for something else. The antidote for . . ."

I make big eyes at David. "For what?"

"For you," he says.

I shudder. David makes like he's going to yell something into the phone, but I take it from him and say, "When and where?"

"Tonight. Half a mile up the road. Away from town. Go out of the house and turn left. No police. Any cops, no antidote. Got it? Or else we'll kill the little one the first time she's alone."

The little one? Katie?

"What time?"

He hangs up. I stare at the phone in disbelief. I open the call log, but the number is listed as unknown. I stare at it for a little too long not to be in shock. David is walking around the living room in circles just saying, "Holy . . . Holy . . . Holy . . ."

Swallowing hard, I grab the bleach wipe off the floor and start in again on a spot on the wall. I rub and rub and rub until David's voice breaks through.

"Chrystal," he asks. "What are you doing?"

"Cleaning."

"We've got to call someone. We've got to tell someone," he says.

I nod. "I know. It's just . . ."

He whips out his own phone. "I'm calling Logan. And I'm calling my dad."

"Tell them no cops," I say. "We'll make this work. We'll make a trap for them, right? They think they're trapping us, but we'll do the opposite, right? And trap them, right?"

"You have to stop saying 'right.' It makes you sound crazy."

I push my lips together and nod. I don't trust myself to speak. I'll just clean. I grab a new bleach wipe and start scrubbing at a new little spot in the splatter. This one is smaller than a dime. It's right below a picture of the entire Jennings family. It's the kind of picture that you get at a photo studio in Sears or Walmart or something. They are all a few years younger. Logan's hair is shaggier. Katie is tiny. Kelsey's got bangs. Mr. Jennings looks strong and happy and slightly embarrassed to be posing while Mrs. Jennings's hand is on his shoulder. She looks proud. They are perfect and beautiful and they can't be hurt anymore.

"We're going to stop this, David," I say when he hangs up the phone.

He nods, but he doesn't look too positive.

"We are," I repeat.

"Do you want to call Logan or do you want me to?" he asks.

"Me," I say because I want to hear his voice, and I want to know that he's okay with this. I say it because Logan feels like a tiny bit of sanity in a world that's just suddenly gone crazy bad. I say it because last night Logan said he likes me, and I've been trying not to think about those words all day, because they are big words, important words. I've seen the way he takes care of his sisters, the way he tries to help his mom before she asks, the way he walks like he's half in the clouds and half on the ground.

So I call him, and I try to be as brave as I can as I tell him what's happened, and what has to happen, and what we have to risk if we want to save his dad.

"We have to take action ourselves," I say. "It's not going to be easy."

"Nothing good is easy," Logan says, his voice breaking just the tiniest of bits, a slightly missed fingering on a fret.

David starts working on the bloodstains as I talk, because now he says he needs something to do. After a minute I hang up and look at the time. Only a few more hours until night and still no word from my father.

21

LOGAN

Everything has just gone to hell in a handbasket. I don't understand it at all. Really, when school ended in May, everything was normal and routine and even a little boring. Now I'm sitting in the intensive care unit of a hospital in Tahlequah, hoping to see Dad again while my mom and sisters sit across from me, hollow-eyed with worry and exhaustion, and a girl I didn't even know in May is in our house, worried about her missing father. And she's promised to meet some werewolf lackey creep and trade herself for the antidote to keep my own father from becoming a monster. My father, who she didn't know a couple months ago. She is willing to risk her life to help him.

It's all just too weird. I want to cry. I want to cry for Dad, but I also want to cry for the very idea that someone like Chrystal exists, someone who would make that sacrifice for another person.

"Is Chrystal okay?" Mom asks a few minutes after I pocket my phone. It's like the fact that my conversation ended has just now penetrated the fog she's been in since we got to the hospital. She's hardly the same woman who pulled the trigger and dropped two men dead on the floor of our house yesterday.

"Yeah. No. I don't know," I say. I explain how the guy who got away last night somehow got Chrystal's cell number and has offered her a trade.

Mom's face had changed a little as I talked, but when I indicate the creep wants Chrystal, some color rushes back in and she sits up straighter, her eyes hardening.

"No." She says it sternly, in that voice you just don't argue with. "She is not going to meet that man. Call her back." I don't get my phone out fast enough for her. "Call her now."

"All right, Mom." I get the phone out and tap on Chrystal's number. She picks up on the second ring. "Hey, it's Logan again. I'm just—"

Mom is beside me suddenly and she snatches the phone out of my hand. "Chrystal," she demands, "you are not, I repeat *not*, going out to meet that man. Do you understand me?"

Chrystal must not understand. Or, more likely, she doesn't understand she's arguing with a brick wall of determined mother. Mom listens to her, but her face never changes. If this was something simple, like arguing the morality of skinny-dipping, it would be funny to watch one side of the standoff. But it isn't. And it isn't at all funny. I know Chrystal can't go out there.

"He said what?" Mom asks. She then looks over at Katie, who is slumped over in a chair with her eyes closed, dozing. This must be where Chrystal said the creep would get Katie if Chrystal didn't meet him. "Did you tell the police?"

Chrystal's answer to that is negative. The cops left. One will come back in the evening. That won't be good enough for Mom. I count off the seconds it takes for Chrystal to argue her point. On ten, Mom has heard enough.

"I'm calling the sheriff," she says. "No, Chrystal. No. You are not going out there. You can't trap him." She pauses. "No, I'm not saying that. I'm saying the risk is too much. The answer is no. You're not doing it. No. I'm calling the police now, Chrystal. If you don't promise me right now that you won't try this crazy plan, I'm going to ask that they put a guard over you day and night."

She waits.

"Do you promise?" Mom demands. "Okay. Here's Logan." She hands the phone back to me, pulls out her own, and moves out of the waiting room.

"Chrystal?" I ask.

"She is a hard-core mom," Chrystal says. Her voice is dead and defeated.

"Tell me something I don't know." I pause. "But my mom is right. Dad told me about that woman they found, the girl from Walmart. It's bad, Chrystal."

"I know it's bad, but your family was so perfect and now I'm here and everything is so bad for you and I just want to help and— Katie and—"

"This isn't your fault," I cut in. "Remember? The monster was here before you. That's why you're here."

"I know, but now it seems to be targeting me and it just isn't fair that your—"

"Chrystal, no," I say, and I know I sound just like my mom. Chrystal knows it too, and she laughs at me a little, which is very good. "I think you're the most—the nicest person ever, and I'm really happy you're willing to run the risk to help us, but I can't let you."

"When those men came in last night," Chrystal says slowly, "they wanted me and/or Kelsey. They didn't seem interested in Katie. I think he wants me. Or Kelsey. Or both. But if I go, then maybe they'll leave her alone."

"Why?" I ask. "Why would a werewolf in Oklahoma want a girl from Maine? I mean, if he wanted you, wouldn't he go to Maine?"

"That isn't important right now. He's here, his pack is here, obviously, and so am I, and he's targeting me. I'm sure of it. I'm going to look through the books and papers my dad left here. Maybe I can—" She stops for a minute.

"Chrystal? What's wrong? Chrystal?"

"Your mom called the cops, didn't she?"

"I don't know. Yeah, probably. Why?"

"They're here." Her voice gets high and sharp and she doesn't sound like the nicest person ever right now. "This is why I didn't want you to tell anyone."

"Oh. I'm sorry." I'm not, really. "It's probably for the best, Chrystal. You didn't like the guns, so it's better if there's at least one cop there."

"Maybe so," she says, but I'm not so sure she agrees. "He's coming to the door."

"I'm going to come home for a while. I'll see you pretty soon."

"All right. Bye." I can hear the doorbell ring in the background, then she's gone.

Mom is back, though. The crisis is averted, at least in her mind. Her face has lost some of the color it had when she was arguing with Chrystal.

"I called the police," she said.

"I know. They got there while I was talking to her."

"Good. She'll be okay now." Mom lowers herself back into her chair and stares ahead.

A nurse pokes her head into the small waiting room and says two of us can go in to see Dad for ten minutes.

"I want to go," I say.

"You went last time," Kelsey argues.

"I have to go home," I tell Mom. "I want to see Dad before I go."

Mom nods and starts to stand up.

"Can I go alone?" I ask.

She looks at me, and there's a whiff of suspicion in her eyes, but she settles back into her chair and nods.

"I want to go if you're not going," Kelsey says to Mom.

Mom shakes her head at Kelsey. I follow the white-uniformed nurse into Dad's room.

It smells. Yes, there is the usual hospital smell of disinfectant, sterile equipment, and medicine, but there's another smell—wild, animal. It's the smell of that monster from the woods. It's here, in my dad's hospital room. It's here because . . . No, that *will not* happen.

I go to the bed and look down at my father. He has heavy stubble on his cheeks. It registers that this is more stubble than he would normally have at this time on a day when he hadn't shaved in the morning. The old, rational part of my brain suggests that maybe he didn't shave yesterday, either, while the new side that realizes fairy tales can be real argues that he's growing wolf hair.

Besides the hair, his face is pale. A bag of clear fluid hangs on a gleaming steel stand at the head of his bed, dripping its solution drop by drop into a tube that feeds into Dad's uninjured arm. I don't know what all is in the bag, but I know they've been giving him morphine because of the pain. And antibiotics because of the infection they can't identify.

They can't identify it because it's the werewolf disease and no one who hasn't seen the monster would ever believe that's what it is.

Dad's right arm is wrapped in fresh, clean white bandages and lies on top of the covers at his side. Under the covers, I know, his chest and stomach are wrapped in bandages too.

I take the hand of his uninjured arm and squeeze it tightly. His eyelids flutter, and for just a second I think he's going to open them. I wonder, if he does, if they'll be his eyes or the eyes of the monster I saw rip the head off a calf. Then he seems to settle back into sleep.

"Dad, I'm so sorry this happened," I say. "I'm sorry, too, that I have to go, but Chrystal needs me. That thing wants her. They're going to try to hurt Katie if they don't get Chrystal. I can't let that happen. I wish you could help me, Dad. I wish—"

I don't even feel the sob coming, but suddenly it explodes out of me. I hang my head and let the tears run. When I use my free hand to finally wipe them away, I see that Dad's eyes are open and he's watching me. His eyes are alert but clouded with pain.

"I heard," he says. "Don't you let the girls anywhere near—" He grimaces in pain and his face becomes even paler as he squeezes my hand in a brutally tight grip, then he relaxes a little. "Don't let them do it," he says.

"I won't," I promise.

He's taking deep, ragged breaths. "Logan, I want you to know you're a good boy. A good son. I love you. I love your sisters, too. I'm proud of all of you."

"Don't say that, Dad. You're not . . . you're not going to die."

"Listen to me," he insists. "I can feel it in me. It's changing me. It hurts. You can't let me become like that thing. Do you understand?"

I nod.

"You talk to Chrystal's dad. You find out what you have to do, then you come back here and do it."

"The guy who called said he has an antidote," I say.

Dad shakes his head, more like he's fighting off pain than disagreeing with me. "Stay away," he says, gasping. "Stay away from them. No deals. You find out—" A strangled little cry of pain comes out of him. He's trying hard to keep it quiet, to hide it, but as strong as he is, he can't completely do it.

The nurse appears suddenly. "You're awake," she confirms. "And in pain. I can't give you anymore morphine for fifteen minutes, Mr. Jennings." She looks at me. "I'm afraid you need to leave. I'm sorry."

I look from her to Dad. No way I want to go.

"No antidote," he says. "The other. You know."

His body convulses in pain again and the nurse physically separates our hands and pushes me out the door. My face gives me away to my family. Mom is on her feet instantly, her hands on my shoulders, demanding to know what's wrong.

"He woke up. I got to talk to him. He's in a lot of pain," I say as Mom looks over my shoulder to the door, like she wants to burst in and see him. "The nurse won't let you. She pushed me out. I . . . I have to go home."

Mom's hands fall off me. I'm not ready, though. I put my arms around her and hug her tight, as tight as I can, and I make her back pop when I do it. She hugs me back and when she's able, she asks me, "What are you doing? What did he say?"

"I have to go," I repeat, but I can't. I go to Kelsey and bend over her and I hug her, too, where she sits in the chair. "Dad loves you," I whisper in her ear. I stand up and look at Katie, who is still sleeping in her chair.

"Logan, what is going on?" Mom demands, her voice quavering.

I reach out and touch Katie's head as gently as I can. She doesn't stir. I pull my hand away and look at Mom.

"It's going to be okay," I promise. "It's going to be okay. I swear it."

I lose about ten minutes sitting in my truck in the parking lot, crying a little bit, trying to get a grip. I can't help it, though. At least nobody sees me. I mean, I think nobody sees me. I don't really care. Finally, I wipe my face, start the truck, and head toward home.

I used to love driving the highway between Tahlequah and home. The woods are dense, and I would imagine all the game hiding just out of sight of the highway. I'd think about hunting some of those ten-point bucks or following Thunder while he chases coons through the trees. Now, though, all I can think about is monsters.

Maybe that's why I think I see it about halfway home: running through the trees to my right, moving as fast as my truck, upright like a man—a dark, dark shape in the shade of the woods. Moving with me. Moving toward my house.

When I slow down and focus hard on the trees, though, I don't see him.

I stop the truck hard, set the brake, and jump out.

"What?" I yell. "What else are you going to do to us? Huh?"

Still, no visual.

But I hear him. Far off, out of sight, I hear his long, unnatural howl, and it sounds like he's laughing at me.

22

CHRYSTAL

The police take my cell phone, call the phone company, try to trace the call back to its origins, but things like that are never quick and rarely work, they tell me.

The big Shrek-like officer with the blond crew cut and hazel eyes is here. He gives me most of the information, and I nod and listen and wish I could fix this somehow.

"They threatened his sister," I say.

We're sitting in the kitchen because I just can't handle the living room right now. The state cop's Smokey Bear hat is on the table. His dark-brown shirt and tan pants are crisp and sharp despite the oppressive summer heat outside.

"And that's your only motivation." He says it like it's a question and a statement, like he knows it isn't.

I bite my lip and watch the clock on the wall above the stove click away some seconds. Even with all the bleach, I can still smell the blood. Galahad whines to go outside. "You know how Mr. Jennings was bitten by him last night?"

The cop nods.

"And . . ." I continue. I don't know how to pick the words. "And he's sick in the ICU right now. He's really not doing well."

The cop nods again. They must teach that at the Criminal Justice Academy or police school or whatever. He probably got an A in nodding. I read his nameplate. It says SGT. MITCHELL.

I try to keep going, even though the totally blank face on Sergeant Mitchell isn't making me feel super-confident about sharing this with him. "And . . . well, he's turning into a were-wolf now. The bite infected him with some sort of virus. This guy said he had the antidote but he'd only give it to me if I went there."

The cop lightly bangs his head on the wall. Just once. "You want my advice?"

Now it's my turn to nod.

"My advice is you get out of here. Make the Jennings family stay at the hospital where it's safe. You and your dad just get out of town. If they've targeted you, there is no way you're going to be safe here until we capture them."

"But won't you capture them if you know where they are going to be tonight?" I ask.

"Possibly. But we aren't about to use you as bait. It's noble of you to think of it, but there's no way we could possibly do that." He lifts a finger. "Hold on."

Pivoting, he walks into the living room and talks into his portable radio. Unfortunately, he speaks too quietly for me to hear. He comes back and says, "We'll have a patrol presence here through to the morning, but our men are strapped. The local sheriff is having to use reserve officers now, and half of those are busy trying to keep looky-loos out of the woods. So if you and your dad could go somewhere safe, preferably out of state, that might keep you off these creeps' radar. I'll alert Mrs. Jennings about what we think her best option is to ensure the safety of her family as well. Okay?"

"Okay."

He studies me for a second and then pats my arm. "Buck up. It'll all be over soon."

"I know," I say.

But "all be over" doesn't mean "awesome outcome." "All be over" doesn't mean "everyone is safe and not a werewolf and not dead." "All be over" just means that: all over.

The police sergeant leaves after giving me my phone back, and the next person to come through the door is Logan. His face has paled. He's got ridiculous dark circles under his eyes. I put the kitchen knife I've been clutching down onto the counter and rush at him, jumping against him. He doesn't even stagger back, just circles his arms around me and sniffs so loudly, I can actually hear it. I think he's smelling my hair.

"You okay?" I ask. My voice is muffled against his T-shirt and collarbone.

"Yeah . . . no . . . I don't know."

We let go of each other, but hold hands and sit at the table. The dogs all scoot around our feet. Logan tells me what his dad said and I listen, because that's all I can do right now: listen. The inability to magically fix everything, or even *logically* fix everything, just kills me.

"That's so hard, Logan," I say, and then I tell him about my conversation with Sergeant Mitchell. "I wish you hadn't told your mom. That wasn't cool."

He stares at me and there is nothing at all in his eyes. It's like when I am learning a new progression on the bass and I've messed it up so badly that my teacher can't think of what to say.

"Maybe you should go," he says after a silence. "It would be safer for you."

How can he just say that? My heart feels like it's turned into a lump, a painful, crappy lump.

"One, I don't know where my dad is. And two, I'm not going and just leaving you all here with this mess." I stand up, walk away from him, angry that he'd think that was a solution at all.

"You haven't heard from your dad?" His eyes grow big. He untucks his shirt, crosses his legs at the ankles, and leans forward in the chair. "Is that normal?"

"It's a little long," I admit, but I can't let myself worry about it too much, not when there are so many other things to worry about. "He'll be back."

I text my dad using other people's phones, just to mix things up.

Nothing.

Kierkegaard said, "The proud person always wants to do the right thing, the great thing. But because he wants to do it in his own strength, he is fighting not with man, but with God."

I call my dad again.

Nothing.

Kierkegaard said, "The task must be made difficult, for only the difficult inspires the noble-hearted."

I walk from room to room in this damn house, trapped and stuck and pointless.

I need a car. I need to look for my dad. I need to find a way to save Logan's dad. I need. I need. I need.

Kierkegaard said, "The tyrant dies and his rule is over; the martyr dies and his rule begins."

I have no choice.

Night comes quickly. The patrol car idles in the driveway and Logan and I stay in the house with Sam and David. We are all restless, roaming around. Logan and David play video games to pass the time, but it's obvious neither of them is into it. I make excuses and go upstairs to bed.

If anyone notices that I'm distracted, they don't say anything. Maybe they figure it's because my dad hasn't called. He has to be missing for twenty-four hours before the police will file a missing persons report on him. I learned that today. I've been learning a lot about police procedures lately.

I grab a pen and a piece of notebook paper out of one of Kelsey's half-used school notebooks. The paper is fluorescent pink, so no way anyone will miss that in the morning. Guilt makes my hand shake as I write. Whatever I do, I'm going to feel guilty, but this one isn't quite so bad. No matter what the outcome, I'll know I did all I could do.

Logan,

Please don't be too mad. Okay. I know you'll be mad, but you have to understand. I couldn't live with myself if I didn't try to save your dad. I know it might be a trap. I know I might die. Or worse. But my dad's missing . . . and . . . there aren't a lot of options here.

But if I don't go and there's no cure for your dad, then I'll never be able to live with myself. Your family is so beautiful and so good. They deserve every chance to stay whole.

Chrystal

I put it on my pillow. That's a pretty obvious place.

Kelsey's room is at the corner of the house. The porch goes around the front and one side—the same side as Kelsey's room. So I pop out the window screen and lean it against the wall. The sky is dark as I crawl onto the porch. I put the screen back in place as best as I can from the outside before I creep to the edge of the porch roof and shimmy down the support pole. I jump off and land on a flower, which makes me feel bad. There's so much death. I try to straighten the stem, but the flower part just pops off completely, landing in my hand. It doesn't seem like a good omen.

I start to step away, then pause, looking at one of the other plants. It looks familiar. I saw a picture of it in my dad's folder of information for this investigation. Monkshood. Also known as . . . I grab a cool green stem and rip it out of the ground, putting it, roots and all, into a hip pocket.

Crouching down, I peek at the patrol car. The officer isn't moving, isn't looking this way at all. His head is kind of tilted back. He must be asleep, which is completely lucky for me. But the window is open, so I'll have to be quiet.

Something is wrong, though. Something is really wrong. I can't tell how I know. I just know. I stand up straight and walk toward the patrol car. Nothing happens. There's no movement of the head. There's no "Miss, what are you doing out here?" There's nothing except a sinking feeling that is spreading through my stomach.

"Sir?" My voice is a whisper. "Officer?"

No answer. I move one more step and peer in. The light from the console illuminates the cab of the patrol car enough for me to see it: his head—a chunk of his head is missing. It's like someone bit a piece of it.

I turn away and throw up without even thinking about it. For a second I try to think of my options.

I can scream.

I can go back inside, but then I can't go meet the evil thing that did this to the officer.

I can go on ahead and probably lose half of my own head. But then the officer will just be sitting out here and a fly is already buzzing. And he could be someone's dad or husband or . . .

Trying not to look at him, I open the door of the car. He's actually buckled in, so he doesn't fall out or anything, which is good. I couldn't handle that. I reach around and grab the radio. It unclicks from its holder pretty easily. It's attached to it by a springy cord that reminds me of a Slinky. It grazes the dark fabric of the officer's uniform, right above his knees. I refuse to look at his head. I refuse to look at his head. . . . Instead I press the button.

"Um . . . officer down . . . you have an officer down at the Jennings residence on the 720 Road," I say. I swallow hard. The fly buzzes so loudly. It's like it's roaring. I unclick the radio.

Static blares back at me. Then a man's voice comes on. "Unit calling. Did you say 'man down'?"

"Yes. There's an officer down at the Jennings property. He's dead."

The moment I unclick the radio I hear, "Attention all units. We have a 10–23, possible signal 7 at—"

I back away and run down the street. The meeting spot is a half mile from here. A half mile should take me four minutes at the most to run. Four and a half, maybe. A half mile and my fate will be sealed, I guess. A half mile . . .

I pause for just a second to look back at Logan's house. The lights are still on. I can hear Galahad barking. It's funny. I can recognize his bark. The cruiser's driver's-side door hangs open, waiting. I could just go back.

No. It's just a half mile.

But I don't make it that far.

23

LOGAN

Y ou're lucky, man," David says as he explodes the head of a
video game zombie.

I club another ghoul in the head while trying to figure out what
the heck he means by that. Lucky that my dad is in the hospital
and might become a werewolf? I pause the game and look at him.
"How?"

David nods toward the stairs. "I've barely seen Yesenia at all
the last few days. Your girlfriend is living with you. And tonight
there are no parents in the house."

I look at the stairs and remember Chrystal's bare legs and little
shorts as she went up to bed. She is so beautiful, and so nice, and
we get along amazingly well. I turn my eyes back to the TV, un-
pause the game, and release a barrage of bullets at a lurking horde
of the undead.

"She's not my girlfriend," I say, my voice dull.

Now David pauses the game. "What? You're crazy. You two sure act like boyfriend and girlfriend."

"When this stuff is over, one way or another, she'll go back to Maine with her dad. We can't very well go to a movie or make out through Snapchat or a webcam or whatever. She'll go home, go back to her school, her friends, forget about me and Oklahoma and all of this craziness, and we'll never see each other again. Plus, she's mad at me for telling about her plan."

I stare at the still screen, at the scowling, hungry, greenish faces of the zombies, at the buildings that make up the setting, at the blood and brains frozen in mid-splatter, like the pattern made by the liquid insides of the guys Mom shot. David is staring at me and I can't face him. I swallow a lump in my throat, and I'm afraid he heard it.

"Man. That does suck," he offers. "I hadn't thought of that."

"Yeah. Well, it seems like a waste to get serious about a girl who'll be almost two thousand miles away before school starts."

"You like her, though."

I shrug again. "I don't know."

"Man, sometimes you gotta take life by the balls. Live for today. She's here now," David says, leaning forward so he's in my peripheral vision. I turn my head to face him. "You know what I mean? She's here now and you obviously have feelings for each other. Maybe you admit how you feel, then find out you can't stand her laugh or that she thinks you should eat more broccoli or something, or maybe she goes home. Anything can happen tomorrow. Take what's there today."

I grin at him. "Getting philosophical, ain't ya?"

"Just being real. I wouldn't have thought I'd have to tell a poet anything about love," he says. "Now, are we gonna kill zombies or talk about our feelings some more?"

We blast away for a while longer, but I'm just not into the game anymore. Something about shooting zombies on a television screen just isn't so much fun when there are real werewolves roaming the woods outside and my dad's in the hospital and my mom has killed men in front of me in my own living room. The undead horde drags me down and my screen goes red as I die again.

"It's all yours, man. I'm out." I drop my controller and leave David blasting away.

Mr. Davis is reclining on our couch, mostly asleep. He snores, and he's not quite out of it enough to not wake himself up with his snores. So he drifts to sleep, starts to snore, and when a really big snort comes along, it wakes him up. Sleep apnea, I think they call it.

I wander to the window and look out. It appears our guardian deputy is also getting some shut-eye, as he's sitting with his head back and not moving.

Sleep. I consider it for myself, but I know I'd just lie in bed and toss and turn. So I go over to the table where Mr. Lawson Smith has been working. Is it Mr. Smith, or Mr. Lawson Smith? I'm still not really sure. Chrystal Smith? Chrystal Lawson Smith? I should ask her. I don't even know her full name, really. Crap. That's ridiculous. I pull out his chair and sit down, looking over the stuff he's got spread out on the table.

The microscope he'd been using so much is pushed away now. A thin, ancient-looking book holds the prime spot. It's opened to a page with a drawing of a man on all fours, a baby hanging from his mouth. Nice. More books and some stapled, photocopied pages are stacked around the corners of the desk. Beside the microscope on one side is the piece of shirt and the hairs Galahad found in the field. On the other side is a newer book, like a college textbook, showing close-ups of hair samples. The microscope is loaded with a slide that has some hair on it, so I put my face to the eyepiece, but it's all dark. I find an electrical cord going to the microscope, so I figure there's a switch, and start looking for it.

Before I find the switch, I find a paper, partially covered, but I see Chrystal's name on it. I pull it from the pile of documents and see that it's an email conversation between Mr. Lawson Smith and someone named Monty Borgess. The Borgess email address has the university in Tahlequah as its domain name. I scan the part where I saw Chrystal's name. Her dad had said he was worried about bringing her on the Oklahoma expedition, not only because of her age but "because of her maternal heritage."

Matt, I understand your concern, but if we are right and this "Bigfoot" our local boy saw really is a werewolf, it's pretty unlikely any werewolf in the woods of Oklahoma will have any knowledge about your ex-wife's ancestry. I'm sure your daughter will be safe. Please don't delay. The next victim might not be a cow.

I start reading it again.

"Did you hear that?" David asks. He pauses the game. The house is way too quiet.

"What?" I ask.

"I heard a scream."

"It was the game."

"No, man, it wasn't the game."

Mr. Davis jerks awake on the couch and sits up. "What?" he asks. "What happened?"

Then we all hear it, high and shrill. My name. Chrystal's voice.

"Logan!"

I don't even pause to curse. I fly out the front door, grabbing my shotgun as I go. Even before the screen door slams against the house, all three dogs go wild, scrambling from under the porch and rushing toward the police car. The door is open now. The deputy is still inside, but now his head—what's left of his head—is turned, looking at us.

David runs into my back, knocking me forward. I catch myself on the rail around the porch.

That's when the werewolf lands on top of the patrol car.

My blood turns to ice and goose bumps run up and down my arms as I face the thing again.

"Holy—" David says.

"Dear God a'mighty," Mr. Davis says from behind us.

The beast is sort of crouching, but not all the way—it's more like he's getting his balance. He's looking right at us, his face not all wolf, nowhere near all human, with a short snout, black nose, and hate-filled black eyes. Slobber drips from his mouth as he snarls at us.

I don't hesitate this time. I bring my shotgun to my shoulder, flicking off the safety as I do. The thing's attention is diverted as Galahad jumps at him. No way Galahad can reach on top of the car. But the thing can reach Galahad. With one swipe of his long, muscular, hairy arm, the monster smacks Galahad across the head and shoulders, sending him flying over the yard.

I take my shot.

The shotgun roars thunder and spits fire.

My 12-gauge slug finds its mark right in the center of the creature's chest. The impact causes the thing to stagger back a step. Blood runs from his chest.

But he doesn't fall over.

He doesn't drop dead.

He roars at me, instead. Challenging me.

I pump my shotgun and fire again.

David opens up with his rifle.

But this is no video game.

It's so much worse.

I hit the thing three more times in the chest. David's .30-caliber bullets rip into it. There are exit wounds. I can see blood spraying from the thing's back. I swear it. But the monster doesn't go down.

I only have one shot left. I jack my pump, sending the spent shell casing flying to my right. Carefully, I plant the single sight on the thing's throat while David pops off two more bullets.

"I'm out," he says.

I pull the trigger.

A big chunk of meat flies away from the monster's throat. Blood sprays over the white top of the cop car. The werewolf's howl drowns in a gurgle of blood. He clamps one hand/paw over his throat, and now he's had enough. He jumps off the far side of the car and runs.

His speed is incredible. He must be moving at thirty-five or forty miles per hour as he cuts across our yard and vanishes into the night.

"Chrystal!" I scream after him. "Shells! I need more shells!"

"I'll reload you." Mr. Davis pushes his own shotgun into my hands while jerking mine away from me.

"I'm good," David says, pushing another bullet into the chamber of his rifle.

We take off after the werewolf. Thunder and Daisy are ahead of us, baying like crazy as they race after the monster.

Police sirens are approaching. That was fast. Too fast.

The werewolf's trail is easy to follow. The grass is tromped down and there's a steady trail of blood. Plus, the dogs are picking it up with no problem at all. But about a mile from the house we hear something moving to our right, toward the road. I stop and grab David's arm to stop him. The dogs are now angling to our left.

Then I hear it again. It's the sound of a struggle.

Without thinking, I start running. The grass is really tall here, up to our chests, because the ground is low on either side of the road and water stands here for a long time.

"Leave me alone!" It's Chrystal's voice. Dead ahead.

I almost trip over her. She's lying on her back, her wrists and ankles bound with silver duct tape, another strip of tape hanging from her cheek. I stop short just as she pulls her knees back and shoots her feet forward. A man grunts.

It's the third guy from our home invasion. Chrystal's feet catch him in the groin and he doubles over.

She yells something again, but I can't hear her over the sound of sirens. The air is flashing red and blue, red and blue, and the sirens are screaming.

The injured man's eyes fix on me and David and our guns. I jerk the shotgun to my shoulder and fire, but miss. The man gives Chrystal one hate-filled final look, then runs to our right.

A second later we hear the squeal of brakes and a solid thud, followed by a moan.

"Take care of her!" David yells in my ear, then he jumps over Chrystal and runs toward the road.

"Drop that gun!" a strange voice screams.

I fall to my knees and pull my little lock-blade knife from my pocket to cut the tape holding Chrystal.

"My God, Logan. I can't believe it's you. I can't believe you found me. He lied to me. He—"

As soon as her wrists are free she throws her arms around me and pulls me down on top of her. She has a grip like a boa constrictor, and she's still talking, almost hysterical, but without tears or sobs, just hot words pushing through the flesh of my neck.

"I knew I was going to die. I was going to die and it was going to be useless because there isn't an antidote, just lies. He lied to me. I heard the shots. I heard the guns. Did you shoot him, Logan? God, tell me you shot him. Did you?"

She pushes herself away and looks at me. Before I can answer, there are two cops towering over us, shining flashlights at us. One reaches down and grabs the shotgun off the ground where I'd dropped it. David appears beside them.

"That guy we just hit, he's the one who tied you up?" I recognize the cop as one who was at the house this morning.

Chrystal nods.

"Damn it, girl, didn't I tell you not to go through with that harebrained plan?" he asks, and his voice is bubbling with fury.

Chrystal hangs her head, and now the tears do flow. "I had to," she whispers.

"That was you who called about an officer down, wasn't it?" the deputy asks.

Chrystal nods again.

"Was that a lie? Something to get us back out here in case you needed us?"

She shakes her head, and then looks up, her eyes wet but defiant. "I would never do that," she says. "The deputy at the house. He's dead."

The man curses a long stretch of the best swears, turning away.

I reach down and cut the tape off Chrystal's ankles, then help her up. We follow the remaining deputy, the one holding Mr. Davis's shotgun, back to the road. Chrystal is limping a little.

"Are you okay?" I ask her.

"Bruises," she says. "I made him work to get that tape on me."

I put my arm around her waist and hug her as we walk on. But she turns towards me and grabs my face. Before I know what's happening, her lips move against mine and I . . . I pause for a second, but then I'm kissing her back. She breaks for air, but then I pull her back. I can't have enough of her, of this. Her hands are clutching my shirt and my arms are all the way around her, moving, and then she's kissing me even harder, deeper. I feel helpless and strong all at once, but I break away and look down at her quiet, brave face and she's staring up at me. And this time I start the kiss, soft and then it becomes so intense that I'm shaking and dizzy.

She pulls away this time, shaking her head. "Wow."

"Wow?"

She bites her lip. "Yeah. Wow."

I don't know if it was the adrenalin or the . . . the panic of everything that's happened, but I can't imagine a kiss could ever be anything like that.

"We should get going," she says, tugging me forward.

About five feet in front of the patrol car with its flashing red and blue lights is the man who had been in our house. The man who had attacked Chrystal, tied her up, and was going to take her to the werewolf. One of his knees is bent the wrong direction. Blood leaks out of his mouth and nose, glistening in the headlights of the cruiser.

"He's dead?" I ask.

"Deader'n the devil," the deputy with Mr. Davis's gun answers.

"Can we check him?" Chrystal asks. "Just in case there was an antidote that he wouldn't give me?"

The first cop, the one who got so mad at Chrystal, is inside the car, talking on the radio. The one with Mr. Davis's shotgun turns and looks at us. He's older, with a gray mustache and brown eyes. He puts the gun on the hood of the car.

"I should check him for ID, I suppose. We took pictures already, right?" he says, then goes to the body, and checks the pockets of the man's sleeveless flannel shirt, then the faded jeans. He pulls a ring of keys from the right hip pocket, then reaches under the body to check the back pockets.

Nothing. No wallet. No driver's license. No bottle of magic medicine that will make my dad all normal again.

"He had a gun," Chrystal says. "A pistol. A big one. It was in the back of his pants, but he pulled it out when we heard the shooting. He was taking me a different way, but when we heard the dogs coming, he changed direction and started for the road. He slipped, though, and that's when he dropped me."

"She kicked him in the nuts," David adds.

"That thing was at our house," I tell the cop who is still squatting by the dead man. He looks up at me. "The . . . monster. Werewolf. Whatever he is. He was on top of the dead cop's car.

We shot him. I mean, we shot the hell out of him, but he just jumped off and ran away."

"You shot him?" The cop stands up. The other cop is out of the car now, standing with his hands on the open door, listening.

"Yeah, we shot him," David says. "I put five rounds in him, myself. Saw two hit the shoulder and two in the chest. I might have missed with the first one."

"I shot him five times with twelve-gauge slugs," I tell the cops. "The slugs were ripping out his back. I saw the blood. I put the last one into the side of his throat. Tore off a big piece of skin . . . ."

More sirens are coming toward us. Far off down the road I can see more red and blue flashing lights.

Mr. Davis appears from the other direction, huffing and puffing up the road, holding my shotgun in one hand while he swings his arms as he sort of runs in an old man way. He stops near the dead man, bends over, and puts his free hand on his knee as he struggles for breath.

"Dear God," he says, panting. "What happened?"

24

CHRYSTAL

The local police call in the state troopers to help them out, and I guess I look sufficiently traumatized, because the tall blond sergeant doesn't even yell at me too much for blowing off his directions. Instead he just interviews me in his squad car, gets the facts, and writes them down in a little notebook with a spiral that's at the top instead of the side. Then he makes me write out my own witness statement.

The sergeant? He swears a lot. I can't blame him. One of his cop friends is dead and that's got to be beyond hard. While we talk, we sit in the car with the air conditioning blowing full blast, but the windows are down. The engines are running on every single car like they are all prepared to run away or chase after anything that moves.

The sergeant clears his throat while I stare at my shaking hands. They clutch each other like that will hide the shaking. There are wounds around my wrists. The ambulance people didn't check them out, though. They are too busy with the dead.

"We normally have one murder a year. One. Thirteen reported rapes. A few dozen assaults, either domestic or bar fights. Most of our calls are dogs at large, noise complaints and thefts from vehicles. This . . . what's going on here . . ." He seems to search for words, stares ahead through the windshield like the sight of the other cops working out there in the dark might somehow magically help the words come out. "It affects all of us . . . all of the community . . . You're not from here, so you may not realize how it is."

He takes his hand and rubs it across his face. It's the only time I've seen him show any weakness. Then it passes.

"I'm from a pretty small town," I say. "It's not the same, but . . . it's a lot of death. I . . . I've never seen so much violence. Not ever. I've never even seen a gun in real life before."

I swallow hard and try not to think about it, but images flash into my head. *The officer's head bitten . . . the dead guy's eyes . . . running down the street . . . hands grabbing me by the waist . . . howls . . . duct tape . . . the ground beneath my body as he drags . . .*

"Your father still hasn't shown up?" the sergeant asks. His voice snaps me out of the memory suck.

I shake my head because I don't trust myself enough to speak. It's like all this fear and sorry and worry are ready to burst out of my lungs, and if I just say that little word, then it will start escaping me and I won't be able to stop it.

He nods slowly. "This all just sucks, doesn't it?"

"Yeah," I make myself say. "Yeah, it does."

I run Kierkegaard quotes through my head. I think of what could be keeping my dad from coming back, from answering his phone. I imagine playing the bass, detailing out every sound, every finger position. Nothing calms my mind. Nothing.

I am tired of being at the whims of the bad guys and the good guys. I am tired of hoping things will resolve. Yes, I failed and fell into a trap, but maybe next time I'll be the one to make the trap.

When the police are done with us, Logan and I huddle together on the porch, just sort of watching the cleanup and the investigation. There is a tarp over the dead officer. They haven't removed his body yet. There is yellow crime scene tape pretty much all over the driveway. They've blocked off the road, too.

"Are you all right?" Logan asks, stretching out his legs across the wood boards.

"Yeah." My knees pull themselves up to my chest.

He shakes his head at me. "You're such a liar."

"How can you tell?"

"One, nobody can be okay after that, and two, whenever you lie, your mouth twitches in the corner, just at the left."

My eyes look at him full-on then. He's got lines by his eyes and they weren't there before. It's like all this is aging him. And he still notices that about me. He knows something about me that I don't even know about myself. I kissed him. I look away again and say, "I'm sorry I didn't tell you what I was doing."

"Yeah."

He didn't see the note, I guess. I should go crumple it up.

Police radios crackle in the background. Someone coughs. They've put up giant lamps on poles like highway workers do when they do nighttime construction. It's like daylight in the front yard. I didn't imagine this.

I say, "I didn't think it through well enough. I thought the werewolf would come get me, not the human."

He actually scoffs. "And that would have been better how?"

"I brought wolfsbane." I show him the plant. "I took it out of your mother's garden."

He holds the plant gently in his hand as if he might kill it accidentally. "Wolfsbane?"

"My dad kept muttering things about flowers, right? And he was really interested in the flowers outside your house, so I started thinking about it. And then I looked it up on Google and it's mentioned in some of my dad's books. It's supposed to kill them."

The ambulance attendants start to take the dead cop out of the car. The body is limp. One of the officers turns away and curses the killer as they move it.

Logan's hand goes to the side of my head. He turns my face so it is against his chest. "Don't look."

"It's all so wrong."

"I know . . . I know . . ."

We sit there rocking for a second, and then I say, "Wolfsbane is poisonous to them. At least that's what everything I read says. Maybe you could put it in a shotgun or something."

"Shoot him with wolfsbane?"

"Yeah."

"You didn't bring a gun, Chrystal. What were you going to do with it?"

"Throw it in his mouth when he tried to bite me."

"That makes no sense."

I shrug. "Like any of this does."

While we are sitting on the porch, I tell him everything I know about wolfsbane, but I know that's not what he really wants to hear about. He wants to know about the attack. I tell him to wait until we go inside, until the cops are mostly gone, and he agrees.

Sam, the feedstore guy whose last name I can never remember, says he's sleeping downstairs tonight with the dogs, who have all come back, even Galahad. He's bruised up, but his little doggy self is okay.

We say good night to Sam, who has taken the back door. A state trooper is stationed at the front. I wonder how Sam stays awake for so long, but I'm not going to ask. There's so many other, more important questions.

Logan and I go upstairs. I'm dead tired. It's like all my body parts weigh eighteen thousand pounds. It kind of feels like when you have the flu. I walk up a couple steps and Logan gasps.

"What?" I say, stopping. All my senses are on super-alert.

"You're all bruised up," he says. "The backs of your legs."

That's all? I thought he saw the werewolf, or someone else dead or . . . I don't know.

"They're just bruises." My feet start up the stairs again.

"They are not *just* bruises."

We go into his room and sit on his bed. He inspects the damage to my wrists, scowls, and leaves the room, telling me he'll be right back. I flop onto his bed, stare up at the off-white ceiling. Some of the paint is peeling a little bit. The shape of it looks like

Oklahoma. No, it looks like a gun. Something shudders inside me, right near my stomach. Even though I'm afraid, I close my eyes.

Logan comes back in the room and starts working on my wrists. He puts Neosporin on them, then wraps them in gauze.

"You look like you tried to slash your wrists," he says.

I give him a half-hearted smile. Then I grab his hand in mine. "Thank you. It was nice of you to fix me up."

"No problem."

He's so close. His lips are just about six inches away. When he speaks, I can feel the vibrations of his words, the sound waves against my skin. His eyes meet mine.

"I'm never going to let anything hurt you again."

"You can't promise that, Logan."

He cocks his head, listening. "Do you hear that?"

I listen too. "The cricket? Or something else? Do you hear the wolf thing?"

"Sh . . . No. The cricket."

It chirps, steady, just one voice.

"I do," I tell him. My hands go to his cheeks, hold his head steady. I swear I could stare into his eyes forever. They're the only things that don't make me think of what just happened. "I hear it."

"It's lonely. There's just one of them." His eyes crinkle a little bit. "That's what I was like—a lonely cricket. Then you came."

I stare at him.

He blushes and pulls away, plopping next to me on the bed, saying, "That was stupid."

"No! No! It's sweet," I insist, snuggling into his side.

His arm goes around my waist, pulls me in closer. I listen to the cricket. One chirrup-cheep. Another. It's hopeful. That and our kiss are the only hopeful things going on here.

"Tell me what happened," he says.

I tell him the basics of it: how I was running and the guy caught me before I got a half mile away. I don't tell him about the fear, or how the guy's hands felt so rough. I don't tell him how scared I was or how much it hurt, how being bound with duct tape was almost more frightening than what had happened in the hotel room because it made me so much more helpless. I don't tell him how I had to chant Kierkegaard quotes and chord progressions to myself just to keep from passing out. Instead I tell him the basics: *He caught me. He hit me across the face so hard, I fell down. He taped my wrists together.*

Logan's body is still and riddled with tension as I talk, but he is obviously pretending he's not upset. His hand keeps moving in little circles around my shoulder, which is something my mom used to do to me when I was little and she tried to comfort me. I keep talking even as I realize how much I miss my mom and my dad, being a family.

"He told me that the wolf is looking for a mate. Then he said he doesn't see what's so special about me."

"Holy crap," Logan sputters.

"Yeah."

For a second his hand is still, but then it starts moving again, pressing me even closer into him, and he says, "Is there more?"

I nod, inhale the smell of his deodorant and farm boy skin and coconut hair. "I asked him why they were helping him and he said that they had pledged allegiance to him, that they were going to start a lupine army. That they were his lieutenants and eventually he would turn all of them, but they had to help him get me first."

"My God." He coughs. "Wait. Why? Why not just bite you or scratch you and turn you like he turned my dad? Why kidnap you?"

"They can only do that with men. There are no female werewolves, I guess. If he wants to make pure babies, he has to find a mate."

I sigh against him. He is so unlike a wolf. So human and warm and fur free. My hands wrap around his arm and the side of his chest. I wish I could crawl inside of him and hide there somehow, and just sleep.

He breathes in so deeply that my head moves about three inches as his chest does. He says, "I found a letter on your dad's desk downstairs. It was an email from a professor at the university. Your dad said he was worried about bringing you here because of . . . how'd he say it? I can't remember, but it was something about your mom's side of the family."

"Really?" I say it, but it somehow doesn't seem important right now.

"The professor said you'd be fine. He said no Oklahoma werewolf would know what your mom's ancestors had done. Do you know what that means?"

"No." I snuggle my face against his neck, feel his pulse against my cheek. "That's really weird."

"Do you want me to go get it? The email?"

"No. Not now."

We are silent for a minute, just breathing in each other, and then I tell him the rest.

"The man, the dead man, talked to me at first, when he was carrying me over his shoulder. He said that we won't ever win. He said the only way to keep your father from changing is to have him drink the wolf's blood, and to do that we'd have to catch the wolf. That's when I started screaming your name and he threw me down again and we struggled some more while he tried to tape my mouth."

He pulls away a little so he can look into my face. "Catch the wolf?"

I sputter out a bitter laugh. "I know. I know. It seems impossible."

"Nothing . . . Nothing is impossible."

25

LOGAN

From the far distance comes a long, angry howl. We both jump off the bed and rush to the window, throwing the curtains aside and pressing our faces against the glass. We can't see much. I dash over and turn off the bedroom light, then go back to the window.

The last few cops are lined up at the edge of the light in the front yard. They have their guns drawn, not that their little handguns will do anything to that monster. The blond highway patrol sergeant has a rifle now.

On my front porch, our dogs are barking. I still can't believe Galahad escaped with only bruises and a couple scratches. I thought for sure he'd be dead. He is limping, and that's keeping him from jumping around the way he usually does.

"I don't see how that thing can be running around that fast after taking all the bullets me and David put in him," I say. "Okay, so they didn't kill him. They weren't silver, didn't have wolfsbane, whatever. Still, my last shot ripped out half his throat. Even if the movies are true and they grow everything back, wouldn't it still take a while?"

"I don't know," Chrystal says.

Heavy, slow steps trundle down the hallway, then Mr. Davis appears in my door. "Everything okay up here?" he asks.

"Yes, sir," I answer.

He rubs a hand over his sleepy face, then seems to realize we're standing in the dark. "You two ain't gonna do anything your parents wouldn't like now, are you?"

"No, sir," I answer, and I can feel my face reddening as memories of our kiss rush back.

"Okay. Good. I'm gonna go back downstairs. I trust you," he says, giving me a pointed look. "Turn this light back on when you're done there at the window."

As soon as he turns away, Chrystal jabs me in the side with her elbow.

Outside, the dogs have stopped barking. The central air unit is still running in the house because Oklahoma in late July is hot all the time, even during the dead of night. Still, I can occasionally hear the static of a police radio and sometimes a snatch of conversation. I'm very, very tired. We sit on the bed, don't talk. Chrystal lies back first, then me. She rolls into me and I put my arms around her. The cricket is quiet, and I imagine for a moment that it's found a lady cricket and isn't alone anymore.

Chrystal suddenly twitches in my arms, and that makes me jerk.

"What?" I ask. "You okay?"

"I think I kind of fell asleep," she says.

I kiss her forehead. "You get ready for bed. I'm going downstairs for my shotgun. It didn't do much good earlier, but I still feel better having it close."

Mr. Davis is sacked out on the couch, snoring at an unbelievable volume. My shotgun is lying across the coffee table with his. I pick it up and start back to the stairs, then detour to the kitchen and look over the stack of books Mr. Lawson Smith left there. Where is he? Has something happened to him? I hate to think about that. I pick up an old, thick volume with pages turning brown around the edges, put the email between the open pages, snap it closed, and take it upstairs with me.

Can Mr. Lawson Smith really read this? The book is written by a priest who died about a hundred years ago. There are pages and pages of notes for each chapter, and every chapter has paragraph after paragraph in foreign languages without any translation. I skim through several pages, and some passages seem to jump out at me.

The eager lover to the boy aspires,
Just as the wolf the tender lamb desires.

What is that all about? I don't know, but I'm suddenly extremely aware of Chrystal's bare leg touching mine under the thin blanket. I flip a few pages.

Lust, then, as well as blood, is associated with the wolf.

Lust?

I flip over a chunk of pages and find a little story about a Norwegian guy named Ulfr Bjalfason, also known as the Evening-Wolf. I read two sentences over and over:

When the werewolf fit came over him and his companions their exploits were bloody with the most ferocious savagery. Whilst the passion endured none could withstand their might, but once it had passed they were weak as water for a while.

Weak as water
After
None could withstand . . .

The sun is up and streaming into my room when my eyes snap open. I'm lying on my side and the first thing I see is the butt of my shotgun.

The cows! I'm sooo late for the morning milking.

"Logan? You awake?"

I roll over, and there's Chrystal, standing on the other side of the bed and holding the little tray with the short folding legs that Mom uses to serve us food when one of us kids is sick. I suddenly smell the scrambled eggs and my mouth waters.

"I have to milk the cows," I say, ready to throw the covers off.

"No, Sam and a couple the deputies already did it," she answers. "We slept through it."

"We did? They did?"

"Will you sit still so I can put this tray on your lap?"

I stop fidgeting. She lowers the tray with two plates of eggs, bacon, toast, and two glasses of orange juice. She's put on the shorts Mom gave her. The bruises on her legs stand out, dark and ugly, as she carefully sits on the bed next to me.

"My dad's still not back. The cops are all gone," she says. "Sam said he saw us sleeping up here when he came to get you for the milking. He moved the book and turned off the light and just let us sleep. When he went outside, the cops were pretty much finished, so a couple them offered to help."

"That was really nice of them," I say around a mouthful of eggs. "Did you make this?"

"No. Sam's wife is here. She made it." She nibbles at her toast. "It's so cool how everybody just jumps in to help."

"Yeah," I agree. "It is. Your neighbors would do that, wouldn't they?"

"I don't know," she says. Her eyes get this faraway look. "I would like to think so, but I don't know. Everyone here just seems so nice."

"They say country people are that way."

"I slept well," she says after we eat for a while. "It seems like forever since I slept well, you know?"

"Me too," I say, but I'm not totally sure it's true. Bits and pieces of Mr. Lawson Smith's book must have influenced my dreams. "I found something in your dad's book that might help us. I don't know. It's a really hard book to understand."

"What was it?"

I look around and find where Mr. Davis put the book on the table beside my bed. I pick it up. It's closed. I let it fall open, hoping it'll go back to the little story about the Norwegian werewolf. I get close, but I have to thumb through a few pages to find it. I read the two sentences to her.

"We have to find someone who is weak and tired today?" she asks.

"Well, that would be nice. But I was thinking of my dad. We

have to get the werewolf's blood, if that guy was telling you the truth last night. I couldn't find anything about that in this book. If we can figure out who it is, maybe we can kill him after his werewolf episode."

"Do you have any idea who it could be?" she asks.

I shake my head, then sip orange juice. "I didn't know any of those three men who are dead now. Whoever the werewolf is, he's probably a stranger too. Otherwise this stuff would have been happening forever. It just started, though."

"Who would know? I mean, who would know if new people moved in around here?"

"I don't know. Mr. Davis usually knows that kind of stuff, but he didn't know those guys Mom shot."

"Anyone else? Were there any farms for sale?"

"No. Nothing right around here. But that thing has killed livestock all over the county. And who says it lives on a farm when it isn't a werewolf? Maybe . . ." I pause, thinking.

"What?"

"Well, there is one place where new people show up all the time."

"Where?"

"The college in Tahlequah."

"You think it's a college student?"

"I don't know," I say. "I just don't know."

"That's where my dad was going. He was going to visit a professor there." Her voice is too quiet, completely unperky and un-Chrystal.

We eat, finishing the last of our breakfast.

"Any news about your dad?" I ask.

Before she can answer, though, my phone rings. I grab it off my table. It's Mom. She's probably calling me back from when I tried to call her last night. She didn't answer.

"Logan? What is going on? Are you all right?"

"Yeah, I'm fine. Why?"

"It's on the news. Our house is on the news right now. They say a man was killed on the road right outside our house and that thing was back in our yard and Chrystal was kidnapped. What's going on?"

As briefly as possible, I tell her what happened the night before.

"Everyone's all right?" she asks.

"We're fine. Chrystal has some bruises. David went home after it was all over. His mom was about to have a fit."

"I'm sure she was," Mom says, and now her voice is calmer. Sadder.

"How's Dad?"

"Not good. They—" She chokes on the words, then tries again. "They've had to put him on a respirator. He's having some minor convulsions, too. They still don't know what it is."

I'm quiet for so long that Mom has to ask if I'm still on the line. "I'm here," I say. "I just don't know what to say."

Downstairs, someone's leaning on the doorbell. Mr. Davis's booming, raspy voice is telling someone very firmly that no one in this house wants to talk to whoever is at the door.

"How are Kelsey and Katie?" I ask.

"Tired. Bored. Worried," Mom answers. "Beth Thompson is going to come up and get them and take Katie back to her house so she can get some sleep today. Kelsey insists she has to come home for a bit. I want them back up here tonight, though. If . . ." She sniffles. "If we're still here. I think you and Chrystal should get out of the house."

I want to tell her I don't think it would do much good. The thing is locked onto Chrystal and, unless we could mask her scent, he would follow us wherever we go. "I'll think about it," I say.

Mr. Davis is still arguing downstairs. Chrystal gets up and goes out of my room. A second later she comes back in. She's limping a little. The bruises must be making her legs stiff.

"Reporters," she whispers.

"I have to go, Mom. I'm going to try to come up there today, but we have to look for a cure, too."

"What do you mean?" Mom asks.

I can't tell her about getting werewolf blood. "In Mr. Lawson Smith's books," I answer. It's not a total lie. I do want to look in more books to see if they say anything about such a cure. "Call me if there's any change, okay?"

"I will," she promises.

Chrystal goes to my window and looks out, then drops the curtain and quickly steps away from the window.

"I have to go, Mom. Bye." I barely wait for her to acknowledge me. I jump up and put an arm around Chrystal. "What?"

"More reporters. One was aiming his video camera right at the window when I opened the curtain."

26

CHRYSTAL

Reporters are not the worst things in the world, obviously, and I know some really, *really* nice ones back at home, but when you're struggling with survival, it's not who you want to see, you know? It's just another hurdle we have to deal with—that we will deal with," I tell Logan. "We can do this."

"Do what?" He's so scruffy-looking from sleep. It's adorable. I rough up his hair—I just can't resist.

"We're going to go to the college, ask around about a guy with burns on his face, maybe a neck wound, or if he heals quickly in human form, just about someone who is acting funny. If we get stuck there, we'll go to rooming houses in that *T* city. Tecalumeh?"

He makes a face.

"Do not make a face at me," I tease. "It is an unpronounceable city!"

He presses his lips together like he's trying not to laugh. I toss him his pants and walk out of the room so he can get dressed.

Downstairs, after I greet Kelsey, I sign in to our phone account and check to see if Dad's made any calls. He hasn't. His data usage is practically nothing since we maxed it all out by using GoogleMaps and the GPS getting here. Dad never turned on his Find My iPhone because he thought it was a government conspiracy to keep tabs on people, or a big business conspiracy meant to tap into consumers' habits for marketing purposes.

But we have family sharing.

I click on "all devices."

The green dot appears next to both of our phones and my computer.

I select dad's phone.

"Holy crap," I whisper.

"What is it?" Kelsey's leaning over my shoulder.

"It says that Dad's phone is still at the college. At that college in that town whose name I can't pronounce."

"What?"

I point at the screen. "That's where he was going, so it makes sense."

"Maybe he forgot it there."

"Maybe," I say, "or maybe he's still there."

Swallowing hard, I turn to her. "Dr. Borgess said he never showed up, but what—"

"What if he did?"

"Exactly."

I'm just putting on my clothes after a shower when I bristle.

Something's happening.

I pull the door open a tiny bit and listen.

There's a shuffling noise downstairs.

"Kelsey? Logan?"

Nobody answers.

But then there's a hard banging like someone being pushed into a wall.

I thunder down the stairs and into the kitchen. The computer's missing. The tables are overturned and the back door is open.

"Kelsey!" I scream, and push through the door and out to the back steps. "Kels!"

In front of me, heading into the woods, is a man. Kelsey's dangling over his shoulder. "No!" I yell, running after them.

Two seconds later footfalls come racing around the house. There's hollering and Logan and a cop have caught up to me and passed me, heading toward Kelsey. I can't see her anymore. I can't see anything.

A motor roars in the woods, almost as terrifying as a beast.

"No!" I say again, picking up the pace, but it's too late.

She's gone.

Apparently, whoever it was waited until one of us was alone in the kitchen and the police presence was all positioned in the front of the house. They knocked Kelsey out after a scuffle, judging by her body position as the man ran to the woods. There was an ATV out there. They've followed the tracks to the road.

"Why would they take her?" I say with a gasp.

But we know the answer isn't anything we want to hear.

After, Logan and I are lectured by the police about being careful, and questioned about why we're such targets. After far too long explaining that we don't freaking know, we slip out the back door and run to the truck. People turn and film us, but we don't stop. It feels like we can't ever stop, like if we stop, we'll be dead.

The cameras roll and the voices start.

"Miss Lawson Smith! Is it true your father's missing? Do you think he's part of this? Did he abduct the Jennings girl?"

"Mr. Jennings! Logan! What does it feel like to have your own dad mauled by the beast?"

Logan tenses. I grab his hand and yank him toward his truck. He hauls open the door and I climb in first, avoiding the stick shift and then settling into the passenger seat. He follows me. Both windows are down and there are cameras filming from both sides. Logan is tugging keys from his jeans pocket. I turn to the camera outside my window.

"We are all hoping," I say in my best news camera voice, which is supposed to sound measured and sincere, I think, "for a speedy recovery for Mr. Jennings. We mourn the loss of the women who died last week and our local law enforcement officer who died so bravely in the line of duty."

They all stare at me. I try to quickly think of something else that will satisfy them so they can have their three-minute clips and thirty-second sound bites.

"And we also pray for the quick location of the beast who did this to all of them." I nod. "Thank you."

Logan makes the truck's engine roar. Some keep filming. It seems like there are actually three film crews here, with three big cameras on various-sized cameramen and three white vans with call letters on the sides and mini satellite dishes on the tops.

"Are you two a couple?" one asks. "You were holding hands. . . ."

Logan swears under his breath and shoves the gearshift down. He guns the engine again, muttering more curses. The truck rumbles like a spaceship getting ready to lift off and take us into the land of zero gravity.

"Try not to run anyone over," I say as I pull the seat belt across my chest.

"Wouldn't be any loss," he grumbles.

"Logan!"

He does a half laugh that's mostly anguish, then slips from between the cameras and up the driveway. Then we're off, away from his house, away from the reporters, away from the deaths, hopefully, away . . . away . . . away . . .

We hold hands as he drives. Logan has to keep letting go of my hand in order to shift. Every time he does, I check the phone the cops gave back, looking for a text from my dad, but there's nothing. It takes everything I have to not keep calling him. Good news? He is now officially a missing person, so they are looking for him and the Subaru. Sort of. I can't imagine it's on the top of their list of things to do when there's a cop-killing werewolf on the loose.

"You okay?" Logan asks.

"Pretty much," I lie.

"You okay?" he asks again.

"Nope."

He shifts at a stop sign. The thing about letting go of a hand is that it's so much better when you grab it again. It's like the letting go makes you appreciate it more.

"We're going to find them," I say.

"Yep."

"We will."

"Yep."

Kierkegaard wrote: "Trouble is the common denominator of living. It is the great equalizer."

My dad likes that quote. It's on our fridge. He made me print it out and put it there when I read it to him the first time. I think I was, like, eight then. I stuck it on with a bass magnet.

"Do you think evil exists, Logan?" I ask as we pass a doughnut shop and a car wash. Worry pushes the insides of me around, making everything feel misplaced. My nerves are jangled and every time I think about Kelsey, panic threatens to overwhelm me.

"Yeah." He glances over at me. So much pain lurks in his eyes. "Well, now I know it does."

I grab the handle above the window as we take a left turn. "I never used to believe in it. I thought it was just something we made up to make ourselves feel like we're good. I figured you couldn't have good without evil and that maybe people weren't either, you know? Like we just were in the middle, but that wasn't cool, or didn't make for good stories, so we invented evil to have something to compare ourselves to."

"And now?" he asks as we pull into a student parking lot at the college. We don't have a sticker. I hope it doesn't matter, since it's the summer.

"Chrystal," he says, like I'm forgetting something.

"What?"

He pulls into a parking space. "And now? What do you believe?"

"I believe that beast is evil to us, but to him? Maybe we're the evil ones, keeping him away from what he needs to survive."

"Seriously?" He looks at me like I'm totally crazy. "It took Kelsey. It killed so many people."

I unbuckle my seat belt. "Maybe. I don't know. It doesn't matter. I think I define evil as this: something that hurts me or my friends. Something that kills or tortures to get its own needs met. Something without a conscience."

"So like a tiger?"

"No. Like a werewolf."

The heat presses against my shirt, against my skin, against everything, really, as we get out of the truck and step into the parking lot. The campus sprawls in front of us. Brick buildings line the quads of grass. Concrete buildings hover behind them. Even though it is summer, some sort of programs or classes must be going on, because student-looking people walk by alone or in groups. Some throw Frisbees. Some lounge on the grass, eyes closed. Some are reading, or pretending to.

"Busy place," I say.

Logan points. "Those big, ugly buildings are campus housing."

"So, what do we do? Just sort of knock on people's doors?"

He makes a face. "I'm not sure."

I rub the sweat off my forehead. "I know you want to be looking for Kelsey. I do, too. I just think . . ."

"My dad's running out of time and this is our best bet. We find the werewolf, we save my dad, Kelsey, maybe find your dad."

"Exactly." I cringe. "I'm so sorry all this is happening."

"Me too. But there's no time to be sorry. We've just . . . We've got to get looking."

The first door we try needs a key card to get inside. We don't have one, so we wait all of 30 seconds for someone who does. It's a girl in short-shorts and a tank. She smiles at us and says, "I hate when I forget mine."

"It sucks," I agree, sliding in behind her as Logan holds the door open for both of us.

We walk up and down the halls. It smells like beer and pot, stale. There are little signs on people's doors announcing who they are in big block letters. There's hardly anyone in the lounges, and nobody matching the werewolf's human description.

"This isn't going too well," I tell Logan once we leave the building, which at least was air-conditioned.

"I know." He pulls his t-shirt away from his chest because the humidity is making it stick. "But I don't know what else to do."

I don't either. So we check out another building and another. It's hard to imagine going to school here. It's so big and empty all at once, but again, I guess that's because it's summer.

"Are you going to college?" I ask Logan.

"I'm applying. I'm a senior this year."

"Me too."

For a second I want to ask him where he's thinking of going. Maybe we're applying to the same places. But the truth is, I don't know if we're going to make it to college, the way things are progressing. We'll probably end up dead. I grab his hand in mine and squeeze.

"I just realized something," I tell him.

"What?"

"My dad is gone. Your dad is out of action. It's like the monster's going for all the alpha men—the leaders. Like he's systematically taking out the strongest men. Or maybe just the men in my life. Dad's not super alpha, but he's my dad."

"And?"

"And that means you're next."

We stand there for a second. He shakes his head. "You're the one he wants, Chrystal. He's trying to kidnap you. I don't know why they took Kelsey instead."

"I don't know either." I know nothing.

There's a man walking across the grass toward Quality Market, this tiny little convenience store. We're heading there to get some water. The guy? He's limping a little bit and he's wearing a leather jacket. He's wearing a leather jacket in this weather.

I grab Logan's arm. "Look."

He looks and stops walking, frozen for a second. Then he says, "You think?"

"I can just feel it," I whisper as all the campus people stroll around us. A Frisbee flies through the air and is caught. "I know it. It's him."

27

LOGAN

My heart is hammering in my chest as we approach the tiny store. Emotions surge through me. If that's him . . . if that's the werewolf . . . he's the one responsible for putting my dad in the hospital, for taking Kelsey. He killed those women. The livestock. He terrorized Chrystal. Anger makes me walk faster. Chrystal holds me back. At first I almost pull my hand away from hers because I don't want anything standing between me and that guy.

That guy whose blood could be Dad's only hope of living.

"Wait, Logan," Chrystal says, pulling harder.

I stop dead and turn to face her. "What?" My voice is harsher than I meant it to be.

She looks startled and steps back a little.

"I'm sorry. It's just . . ." I look back at the store. "What he's done."

"I know," she says. "But we need a plan. What if we barge into that tiny store and surprise him? It's small, and not many other people are going in or hanging around outside. What if he changes inside and attacks us? We don't have any weapons. He could kill us before we get out of there. Nobody would even know."

"Can he do that? Can he just change whenever he wants?" I ask.

"I don't know. He obviously doesn't need the full moon. It was only half full last night. It wasn't even full-on nighttime when he attacked me in the hotel. Maybe something else triggers it. I just don't know."

"So what do we do?"

"Play detective," she says.

"Follow him?"

She seems to think about it for a minute. I keep an eye on the door of the store, wondering if it'll be a man or a monster that comes out.

"I think one of us should follow him while the other goes into the store and talks to the clerk," Chrystal says at last.

"Split up?" I don't like that idea at all. "That never works out well in the movies."

"This isn't a movie," she reminds me.

"But it means leaving you alone," I insist.

There's nowhere to hide. Still holding Chrystal's hand, I drag her toward the largest cluster of people I can find, a group of students walking toward us. They stare at us as we hurry toward them.

Chrystal doesn't see the guy leave the store, but I do. He hesitates for a second when he comes out, carrying a small paper sack. When I peek at him, he's holding his head high, like he's sniffing the air. He's way older than I imagined.

"Crap," I whisper. "We're upwind from him."

Chrystal starts to turn, but the students are blocking our view now, which is good because they're hiding us, and not so good, because they're blocking our view of him.

"Hey," I say to the guy in the middle of the students. He seems to be the leader of the group. There are two other guys and four girls.

"What's up?" he asks me, his eyes going over me and Chrystal. I bet he's a football player. He's got the shoulders for it.

"Do you go here?" I ask. My voice is full of tension.

"Yeah. I'm a junior. They're subfrosh." He indicates those around him. "I'm showing them around campus. Are you freshmen next year?"

"No, not yet. We're seniors in high school, but we're thinking about coming here next year," I say. "We were just wondering if you like it here. You know, the advisers and people in the office make it out to be great, but I wanted to ask a student."

"Oh yeah, I get it," he answers. "Sure, it's a great school."

"Are the dorms nice?" Chrystal asks. "I can't stand mold and bugs and stuff like that."

"Nah, they're good. Oh, I'm Matt, by the way. Matt Craig." He shakes my hand, then Chrystal's.

"All right, well, thanks," I say. "I don't want to keep you, since you're showing them around. Maybe we'll see you next year."

"I hope so, brother. It's a good school," Matt says.

We step aside and let the group pass. Our friend in the leather jacket is still in sight, but just barely. He's limping across a lawn toward a space between two buildings.

"I'll follow him," Chrystal says. "You go see what he bought. Ask if the clerk knows his name."

"No way. No way at all," I argue as we start walking back in the general direction of the store. "I'm following him. You go in the store." She starts to protest, but I cut her off. "No, Chrystal. He can obviously smell you and . . . whatever it is about you that's making him want you. You're not going near him. Who knows where he's going? Plus, you're not super fast still."

"Fine," she gives in. "Hurry. People are depending on us. Keep your phone with you."

Catching up with the guy is no problem. He's walking really slowly, and as I watch him it seems like he's barely using his right arm. I stay at least twenty-five yards behind and do my best not to be obvious. As soon as he gets between two buildings that look like they must house classrooms, he stops and leans against one of the buildings, his head down. I step behind a huge shade tree and pull out my phone like I'm reading a text message.

The guy is hurt pretty badly. It looks like he's panting while standing there. How he can stand to wear that heavy leather biker jacket when the temperature has to be close to one hundred today is beyond me. After a couple minutes he pushes himself away from the wall and kind of staggers for a few steps before going back to his off-balance shuffling pace.

I wait until he's just about at the back edge of the building, then leisurely move after him.

More students mill around behind the buildings. A handful are holding books and seem to be acting out a scene from a Shakespeare play. Matt and his group of freshmen are still on the tour, with Matt pausing to point out a statue of Sequoyah, a Cherokee silversmith who wrote his nation's alphabet. I keep my guy in sight, and I notice a few other people looking at him as he stumbles by in his leather jacket.

The guy rounds another corner and disappears for a second. I walk straight, going past the corner, and feel lucky I did. He's collapsed onto a park bench and I'd swear he's moaning as I go by the space between the two buildings. I find another spreading shade tree and plop down as casually as I can, pulling out my phone for the old reading-text-messages trick again. I can just barely see the probable werewolf because of a thick green shrub at the corner of one of the buildings. If he was to move a little to his right, I couldn't watch him.

He takes a bottle of water from his sack, twists the lid off, and chugs the whole thing. But, while he's chugging, he puts a hand to his throat, like it hurts to drink. He drops the bottle to the ground and slumps forward like the act of drinking exhausted him. Then he reaches into the sack again and pulls out a brown bottle of hydrogen peroxide and a thin white-and-green package. He tears the package open, throwing the wrapper on the ground, and unfolds what looks like some white gauze. He pours peroxide on it, then presses it against his throat. On the right side.

The side where I blew off part of the werewolf's throat.

If I had a needle and syringe, I could just walk up and take his blood right now. He's obviously too weak to do anything about it.

I'd rather cut his throat and bleed him into a bucket the way we do when we buy a hog to slaughter for a big barbecue. Chrystal wouldn't like me thinking that way, even though the guy is a creep and a killer. Probably.

What if he isn't the werewolf?

No, I agree with Chrystal. He's the one.

The guy just sits there for a long time. Finally I can't take it anymore. I get up and walk toward him. He acts like he doesn't know anyone is around him. I don't really have a plan. It's just a sudden urge to see him up close. I'll just walk by and look at him. He sits there with his head down, his hand pressed against his throat. The gauze wrapper flutters and blows away. He doesn't move.

I am right in front of him, but his head is still down.

I walk slower.

He looks up and our eyes lock.

"You don't know what it's like," he says, his voice hoarse and raspy.

My heart and feet all stop. I stare at him for a moment. Our eyes seem to pull at one another. His face is thin and drawn and pale. He has a scraggly black beard and dark, dark eyes. His lips seem very red.

"What did you say?" I ask.

He waves at the end of the bench, like he wants me to sit beside him. Like we're old friends meeting on the quad to talk about our English class or something.

"What did you say?" I demand.

"Sit down. Talk to me," he rasps.

"Why?"

"I have what you want. And you have what I want."

I look around. Sitting down with a werewolf has to be the stupidest thing I could possibly do. This place is in pretty deep shade from the buildings and nearby trees. Some students pass by where I was sitting a few minutes ago, but there isn't much foot traffic here. I shouldn't have approached him.

"You're safe. For now," he says.

I stare at him, angry but confused. He looks so weak. What did the book say? He'd be weak as water after his spell as a werewolf.

I sit down.

"That jacket must be hot," I say sarcastically.

"It is. But I'm still leaking from the wounds you gave me last night." His voice has a slight intonation. It isn't strong, just enough to be a little different and it fades in and out even as he's talking.

"You hurt my dad," I accuse. "He might die because of you. And those others. The women . . . Kelsey. You took my sister."

"I didn't take your sister."

"What?" I'm the human, but I'm practically growling. "You liar. I swear, if you hurt her."

"I did not technically take your sister and I assure you I am no liar. I'm many things, but not that. She is safe. As for her abduction? My pack does that sort of thing for me. I hate to get the paws dirty." He laughs like the ultimate douchebag. And then adds, "I am sorry about your father."

That surprises me. Really, I didn't expect that at all. "Sorry?"

"He was in the way. The strong, fearless father, the alpha male who protects his cubs—real and adopted. He could make a great wolf."

He's still holding his hand to his throat. He pulls it away and looks at the gauze. The bandage is stained pink. As he pours more peroxide on it, I think to look at the wound. It's sort of hard to really make out behind the upturned leather collar, but what I can see is nasty. It looks like somebody's slammed a mess of hamburger between his head and shoulder. But . . . it's nowhere near as bad as it should be.

"You do regenerate, don't you?" I ask.

He nods and presses the white cloth back to the wound. I can see tiny white bubbles dribbling from his throat to soak into his black T-shirt.

"Why are you doing this?"

"You don't understand," he repeats. "You can't." He pauses and looks away from me, up to the green leaves of the tree. "The beast has everything. Power, speed, courage, strength, but . . . but it's a very lonely existence."

"Lonely?"

"Yes." He looks back at me. "I can turn other men. I can turn them easily . . . just look at your father. A mere bite. But the beast needs a mate. Only certain women will do. Most die. It is unfortunate. I don't really care about killing people. The beast is happy enough killing deer and elk, or cattle sometimes." He pauses again, and I remember him tearing the head off our calf. "I want children. Not children that I turn, but that I sire. I want a companion to share my days with, to nurse my wounds."

"You're looking for a mate? Seriously? This isn't, um . . . a little overkill? Most guys go to a bar or online. Tinder. That's a thing, right?" I ask, still incredulous. At that exact moment my cell phone goes off. It's Chrystal. I slide my finger across the screen to answer, and just say, "Stay where you are. Stay there. I'll call you in a minute."

"Logan, what's—"

"Trust me. Just stay put. I'll call." I end the call before she can protest again.

"She's close," the werewolf says. "I can smell her."

"You can't have her. I won't let you."

"You could stop me?"

"You haven't got her yet."

"Is that a challenge?" he asks. He grins, and in that grin I can see the wolf. Then his face relaxes and the pain returns. "You want to cure your father. Have your sweet sister back all safe and sound and untainted."

"Yes," I answer after some hesitation. It's taking all my restraint not to hit him.

He smiles as if he's gloating. "You need my blood to save him."

"That's what your goon told Chrystal before we killed him last night," I say, stretching the truth of the circumstances just a little.

"I'll give it to you," he says, shrugging like it's nothing at all.

"You will?"

"A trade," he says.

"No!" The reality of what he's asking comes quickly and is too horrible to consider.

"Your father for the girl. Chrystal. Such a perfect name. I'm surprised her idiot father agreed to it."

My head snaps back around to look into his face. "What? What do you mean he agreed to it?" I demand.

The monster chuckles. "Mr. Lawson Smith is a gullible man. He changed the spelling of the name, but . . ." He lets the sentence trail away and shrugs his shoulders.

"Do you know where her dad is?" I ask.

"Don't worry about him," the werewolf says. "I am positive that he's getting all the research he needs. Your sister is still alive and you . . . you could save them both by helping me get the girl."

"You're disgusting."

"She may like the life I could offer her."

"No. She wouldn't. You don't even know her," I argue.

"I can sweeten the deal. Your father has no choice. He'll become like me unless you help him. You can make your own choice, though. If you want the power I have, I'll give it to you."

"What?"

"Think about it before you refuse it," he says. "Think of what you did to me last night. Look at me now. I'm hurt, yes, but I should have been dead many times over last night. Soon I'll be back to full strength."

"I should kill you right now," I growl. "Kill you and bleed you."

"Right here? You'd spend the rest of your life in prison. You have a lot of life ahead of you, Logan Jennings. Maybe."

"You can't have Chrystal."

"You don't get to decide her life choices for her. Her father has refused to tell her, even when he decided to bring her into an obviously dangerous situation. Amateur researcher, going off half-cocked, too caught up in what he believes he'll never really find. You should have seen his face. . . ." He pauses, smiles, then returns to his original line of thought. "Explain my offer to her. Let Chrystal make up her own mind," he says.

"You're probably lying, anyway," I accuse.

"I already told you. I'm not a liar." He smiles at me, then puts his gauze pad on his thigh and carefully bends over to retrieve his water bottle. I watch, stunned, as he raises his stiff right arm to his face. His teeth have changed. They're not human teeth. They're wolf teeth. The canines are long and curved. He bites into his own wrist with one of those wicked teeth. Blood rises to the surface of the wound and spills out. He holds it over the water bottle, letting the slow, thick blood run into the bottle for a few minutes. Then he turns his wrist and presses the bandage over this new wound.

Leaving the bitten wrist turned up, he lifts the bottle and hands it to me. The blood is sluggish and very bright in the bottom of the plastic container.

"Boil water," he says. "When the water is at a rolling boil, add one fresh leaf of that wolfsbane that grows in your mother's flower garden. Leave it in the water for sixty seconds. No longer. Take out the leaf and add the blood. Make your father swallow a teaspoon of it. It won't be strong enough to cure him, but you will see that I am sincere in my offer."

"Wolfsbane is poisonous. I'm not doing that."

"Give me what I want and I will tell you the formula to reverse the curse completely," he says, ignoring my concerns.

"How do I know this won't kill my dad, then you'll come after Chrystal again anyway?"

Suddenly, with more strength than I would have guessed he has, he pushes himself off the bench, reels for a moment like he's dizzy, then gives me one final look.

"You are an incredibly stupid boy. There are forces at work, lives entwined, that reach back for centuries. You and your family are just tiny pawns to be used along the way."

He limps away, leaving me sitting on the bench, alone, holding a water bottle with a little bit of blood in the bottom.

My phone rings again. I answer and put it to my ear without looking at it. My eyes are still on the werewolf as he walks away.

28

CHRYSTAL

What the heck is wrong with you?" I don't shout it, but I want to because I'm so mad at him, at the risk he just took. "You were just talking to him. You were sitting. Right. Next. To. Him! He could have killed you!"

"I know . . . I know. . . ." Logan holds a water bottle in front of him like it's a magic elixir. "It's just . . . He wasn't that bad. Tormented. Not downright evil."

I think my mouth must drop open. I shut it. Someone's listening to hip-hop in a nearby apartment. The bass booms of it only make me angrier. "He has killed people. Your dad is in massive pain. Your sister is kidnapped so do not tell me that he's not quote-unquote downright evil."

"He's . . . He is evil, but I sort of get it."

I stare at him. "And now you just let him walk away. We don't even know where he lives."

"Yeah, but—but . . ." Logan lifts the water bottle. Bright-red stuff fills up about a quarter inch if it. "He gave me this. He said it's a partial cure."

"It's his blood?" It makes me feel sick to my stomach to even think it.

"Yeah. He said it's a partial cure!" Logan repeats this like he's trying to convince both of us, but it's obvious that he believes it. He's so psyched, he's practically bouncing all over the place. He almost reminds me of my dad in hyper mode.

I talk slowly to make sure I get through. "Good. That's beyond good, if he's telling the truth, but, Logan . . . don't you understand?"

He looks clueless. "Understand what?"

A plastic bag, the kind you get at the grocery store if you don't bring your own canvas bag, rolls across the sidewalk. The hot wind catches it and blows it up into a tree. It snags on a limb and stays there—a dirty yellow thing mixing with the green leaves. It doesn't belong, just like the werewolf doesn't belong.

I turn away from it, scan the area once again, looking for the guy, for a clue. Giving up, I turn back to Logan and say, "He obviously has Kelsey. He might have my dad. This is the school my dad was coming to when he was meeting his friend. I have to follow him and see who he is. With my own eyes."

Before he can say anything, I take off in the direction the creature went, but when I round the corner, there's nothing except buildings and trees. It's a dead end. Still, I make note of the location. We're off campus now. There are a lot of two-story houses, all with a twenty-year look of rundown. It's the kind of landscape that people write blues songs about with all its peeling wood siding, chipped paint trim, roofs that look like they can barely withstand a gust of wind.

Logan catches up to me in a second. Sweat marks his T-shirt. "You see him?"

"No," I say. Dread fills me. It's more housing, more streets. He could be anywhere. He could be watching me right now. Something creeps along my skin and I know it's just my own sweat, but it still freaks me out.

He could be anywhere.

He could be laughing at us right now.

I'd really like to give him the finger. But that's only half of me. The other half is truly freaked out and expects him to come bashing through a window or rushing down the road at any second, teeth bared, howling, ready to kill us both.

"Tell me about what happened. I want to check to see if Dr. Borgess is in his office, and then we can go see your dad." I pause. "And Kelsey. We have to find Kelsey. How are we going to find her?"

"I don't think he's going to hurt her, not yet," he says.

"Why?"

"Because of you. He wants you."

Hurrying, I take Logan to an academic building and directly to Dr. Borgess's office, but he's not there. I call his cell. He doesn't answer. I knock on the door. It swings open. "Let's go in. I'll leave a note on his desk."

"That sort of seems like trespassing."

"Seriously, Logan? We have bigger things to worry about here than breaking baby laws."

"That's not it. I just . . . I want to get out of here—soon. That guy was . . . He was creepy. And Kelsey . . . Let's just hurry."

"I want to get out of here too, but this is where my dad was going."

"Dr. Borgess already told you that he hasn't seen him. He told you that when you called."

I sort of crumple against the desk, leaning over it. "I know. I just . . . I still have hope, okay?"

The word leaves his mouth slowly: "Okay."

I straighten up and finish scrawling out a note. My finger taps the computer screen. It's one of those giant monitors that's connected to a laptop. "Look at this."

"A giant picture of a wolf is the screensaver?"

I move the mouse, but the screen is locked. "Damn it."

"You were just going to go through his files?"

"Yeah. Wouldn't you?"

"In a movie one of us would be a hacker or a computer genius."

"We need new identities." I leave the desk, motioning for him to follow me to the office door. "I thought being a bass player was the ultimate end goal, you know. But now?"

"You want to be something else?"

"I want to be the person who ends this," I say. "What do you want to be?"

"I want to be the guy whose family is safe."

"Good goal."

"Yours too."

I give him a weak fist bump. I don't know what else to say.

We hustle out of there, quick and fast like a good riff in a very bad song—we stick out, and it's time for us to leave.

But even as we drive, it's all bothering me.

"Why does he need a mate if he can just make little werewolves?" I ask.

"He wants his own family, I guess." Logan shrugs. He puts his free hand on the seat next to his butt, but I don't grab it. We feel distant all of a sudden. I don't know why. Maybe because we're both stubborn. Maybe because I'm mad that he went and discussed my fate with the werewolf guy and then just let him go. If anyone is going to make a bargain about my fate, it should be me. If anyone is going to decide if a trade is okay, it should be me. It's my life. Not his. He's not even my official boyfriend. Just a guy. Just a guy I kissed. Just a guy we live with now.

And I know that's not quite right. Even as I swallow my anger, I know that it's not quite right. Family is important. My family is so broken and I've liked Logan's so much. I mean, I just trusted his mom right off, telling her and Kelsey pretty much anything they wanted to know. I even like his dad. They've all been so kind. It can't be easy for them to have strangers in their home.

My mom would never do anything like that.

My mom . . .

I whisk out my cell with one hand, and tap on her name in my contact list. Yes, she is in Europe. No, I have no idea what time it is there. It doesn't matter.

She answers. There's a lot of background noise.

"Mom?"

"Chrystal!" she yells into the phone.

"Dad's missing." I guess maybe I should have started it off easier.

"Oh, honey . . . You know how he is. He's probably just lost track of time."

Logan looks at me. I sigh, and push the back of my head into the headrest. "No, Mom. He's been missing awhile. Things are crazy here."

"Where are you, honey, Indiana?"

"Oklahoma."

She starts laughing at something someone said.

"Well, we are having the best time," she says after a good twenty seconds. "It is just beautiful here. And everyone is so lovely and foreign."

"They think your mom is beautiful," Husband #3 yells into the phone.

She starts giggling again.

"Mom . . . Mom . . ." I work to get her attention. "Mom, can you listen?"

"I am! I am listening." She laughs again, which makes me doubt it.

I forge ahead anyway. "Look, what do you know about your family being werewolf lovers or something?"

She is silent for a second and then says, "Please don't tell me your father has started to believe that crap."

"It's not crap, Mom. Things are happening."

"It's a wives' tale. An old wives' tale. Look up my maiden name. It's a fairy tale, baby. Made up by silly people who wanted to believe their lives were worth more than they were."

"So we mated with werewolves?"

"Oh my gosh, the words you choose, young lady. 'Mated'!" She snorts through the phone line. "No! It's all rubbish. Look it up on the Internet, baby. Our food is here. Kiss! Got to go. Love you! Your father will be back soon," she says, rushing this last sentence out as an afterthought. "Do not worry."

The line goes dead even as she starts laughing about something again.

"She tell you anything?" Logan asks.

"Nope." She never does.

I hold the container like a holy grail all the way back to the house, which is where we are going first, not the hospital. It turns out we have to make a little spell first, which is not good, especially since it takes time where we could be actively searching for poor Kelsey. Not so good? The fact that this is only supposedly some kind of half cure. Also not so good? The fact that the wolf guy offered Logan a chance to turn. What? Is he really trying to make some sort of werewolf army? It makes me shudder imagining more than one werewolf.

"Would you do it?" I ask him.

"Do what?"

"Turn."

He stares at me for a second and his hands clutch the wheel. "No. Not unless . . ."

"Not unless what?" It feels like he's holding something back. It's felt like that this entire trip.

He swallows hard. "Not unless I had to."

I stare at my own hands around the water bottle, the thick blood that swooshes in the bottom of it as we hit a bump. "Why would you have to?"

"To save you or to save my dad or my sisters or Mom or even

David or anyone really, I guess." His face whitens. "I'd hate to, though—hate to be like that."

"Even with the power? The regeneration stuff? All that strength?"

"Honestly, Chrystal. I'm the kind of guy who writes crappy poetry on the front porch, who plays Sorry! with his sisters every damn week. I'm not into power."

"It's not crappy poetry," I say. "It's better than a lot of song lyrics that are popular right now."

"Yeah, it is," he says, laughing. He doesn't ask me if I'd change. I guess we both know I might not even have the choice, not if the beast has its way. But that's not going to happen. We're too smart for that to happen.

The reporters are gone by the time we get back. Logan jumps out of the truck and talks to Sam, who has just returned to the house. He spent the morning at the feedstore. I carry the water bottle inside as they talk.

I insert a long pipette and syringe that I found in my dad's stuff into a bottle. I click and extract one molecule of the thick, bright blood. I remove the syringe and put it on a slide, then place a protective slide cover over it. Doing the same procedure, I get two more drops before Logan even comes back inside. I put two in the fridge to preserve them. The other one I keep out. Maybe heat will affect it. Maybe not. But I want to see.

"What are you doing?" Logan's at the door.

"Preserving some samples," I say, putting the equipment that's been contaminated in the sink. "I want to see if it's chemically different from our blood, maybe bring a sample to Dr. Borgess. I only took three drops. I'm sure it won't affect anything, Logan. I swear."

He nods. He bounces on the balls of his feet. "I got the wolfsbane."

We boil the water and stare into the pot even though it's so hot out already and the steam is impossibly warm against our red faces.

"It takes forever," Logan groans.

Tiny little dots appear at the bottom. They look like molecules almost, but I know they'll expand into bubbles, rise to the surface.

"It's almost there," I say. "You have the wolfsbane?"

I don't know why I ask it. I know he does. The water boils. "Finally!" Logan breathes, and he drops the soft purple flower in. It curls. I start the timer and we watch as the seconds pass. I have a long spoon to take out the flower. The buzzer dings, loud and angry, and I scoop the purple blossom out before Logan can say anything. It's limp and darker now. He pours in the blood, which gloops out of the plastic bottle. I expect it to separate the way human blood would, or to glob all on the bottom like honey does at first, but instead it turns a bright pink and then crackles before combining with the water. After about thirty seconds it turns into the color of a deep-red wine.

"Weird," Logan whispers.

"Think it's done?" I ask. "You sure he didn't say how long to cook it?"

"He didn't. He just said to add the blood."

I move the pot onto a burner that isn't turned on and shut off the stovetop. "We only need a teaspoon?"

Logan nods.

"Do you think we used too much water?" I ask. "You're sure he didn't say how much water."

Nerves seem to beat through Logan. "Chrystal! I would have told you."

The silence between us is huge. "I know . . . I know . . . It just doesn't seem scientific," I explain. Then I try to make him feel better because I know how stressed he is. "If he didn't say, it doesn't matter. Don't worry."

I pet his arm. He pulls me into a hug. It is a nice hug and it makes me feel a tiny bit better, but not completely.

"I know," he says apologetically. His voice is rough with emotion. "I'm sorry. I just want so badly for this to work."

"It has to work," I say. "He needs us to trust him enough for a trade, so this has to work."

His hands drift up to my face and we pull away so that we can look at each other.

"You're so logical," he says.

"It's self-preservation," I explain with a shrug. "From living with my dad. Someone has to be logical, you know?"

He laughs, but it's short and bitter. I bet he's like me. I bet there are so many emotions stringing along inside him that he can't decide which one to pluck and let loose into the air. Finally he whispers, "We can do this. We'll find Kelsey and your dad. We can save my dad, too, right?"

"Yes," I say, pulling away enough to grab his hand and lead him to the door. "Yes, we can."

29

LOGAN

They won't let Chrystal into Dad's ICU room. I try to argue with the nurse, but Mom simply says my name in a voice that is hollow with defeat and I give up. Chrystal puts a hand on my arm.

"It's okay," she says. "Go ahead."

I give her a quick hug and take one more look at Mom. She's sitting in a very square padded chair, but she's just slumped there, worn-out, dark circles under eyes, her hair unwashed, no makeup. I notice again how she looks twenty years older than she did a few days ago.

She whispers, "Kelsey."

"I know, Mom. We'll find her."

She doesn't meet my eyes.

A surge of hate for the werewolf passes through me. I think of how Chrystal defined evil: something that hurts me or my friends. Something that kills or tortures to get its own needs met. So what if that guy/werewolf didn't mean to do this? He did it. He's torturing my family.

Dad looks awful. They haven't shaved him, so he has a full beard, which isn't so unusual for him after a few days without shaving, but the hair is too long. And worse, it's too high on his face and low on his neck. Tubes still run from bags to his arms. Another runs from beneath the bedsheet to a bag at the end of the bed. Fluid in, fluid out.

At least he's off the ventilator. Before the nurse leaves me alone in the room with him, I ask her about it.

"We took him off it early this morning," she answers. "He was breathing on his own again after a really rough patch in the evening. We're watching him closely," she promises. "If he needs it again, he'll have it. It's right there, ready for him."

She points to a white machine with all kinds of tubes going every which way. I thank her and she leaves with a smile on her face, telling me I have ten minutes.

"Dad?" I say, going to the bed and taking his hand. He doesn't respond. Nothing. Just ragged breath and the soft *beep-beep* of a heart monitor machine.

"I talked to him today," I explain. "That son of a bitch. He gave me this." I pull the little bottle out of my pocket and kind of shake it. It had cough syrup in it before, but it was almost empty. I dumped the little bit left down the sink and Chrystal rinsed it out several times with hot water. "I don't know if it'll work, Dad. He says it will help you, but only for a while. He says . . . he says he'll give me more if we give him what he wants."

I have to quickly swipe a hand across my face. It comes away wet.

"Chrystal would probably do it. I need you, Dad. I can't let her do it, of course. I can't. But I don't know what else to do."

I pause and look at the red elixir. "This might not work. It might . . . it might even kill you. I don't know. Is it worth it? If it doesn't work, is it better that you're dead?"

I can feel my resolve starting to slip. If I keep talking, I'll talk myself out of this. I know Dad would rather be dead. He told me as much.

I rip the lid off the bottle, then take Dad's jaw in my hand and pull it down. I pour at least a teaspoonful into his mouth, close his jaw and cover his mouth and nose. He struggles, but just barely. I see his throat move as he swallows.

"God help me if that bastard lied to me," I whisper as I put the bottle back in my pocket.

Dad doesn't move. There's no immediate change. I wait. Nothing. The door opens behind me and the nurse says, "Son?" I don't turn to look at her. "Son? I'm afraid your time is up. Son?"

Reluctantly, I turn away. The nurse smiles at me and pats my arm as I walk past her. She promises me they're doing their best. I nod and keep walking.

Chrystal is sitting beside Mom, holding her hand. She looks up at me as I approach, and her eyes are big and afraid. Mom is as listless as she was when I went in.

"How was he?" Chrystal asks.

I shrug. "Nothing changed."

"Your mom hasn't been eating or drinking. I told her I'd get her a Coke and she said she'd try to drink some of it." Chrystal looks from me to Mom and says, "We'll be right back, Mrs. Jennings. I'm going to get you that candy bar, too."

Mom's eyes shift toward the sound of Chrystal's voice and she smiles just a little. "You really are a good girl," she says, her voice a cracked whisper. "You feel like family, you know that, don't you? Ever since I first saw you, it felt like you were one of my own."

Chrystal nods. "You too. I think . . . I think you must be the best mother that there ever was."

And I know what she's thinking. She's thinking that she wishes my mom were her mom. I can't blame her, not judging from that phone call I overheard.

"Come on, Logan." Chrystal gets up and grabs my hand, pulling me out of the waiting room and down the hallway toward a bank of vending machines we saw when we came in. As soon as we're out of earshot she asks, "There was no change?"

"No. Maybe it takes a while. I don't know," I say. "He didn't move when I gave it to him. On the good side, he didn't go into convulsions and die. Let's stay here a little bit and see if there's any change."

"We will," she promises. At the bank of machines, she feeds two one-dollar bills into one machine for a bottle of Coke while I pay another dollar for a Hershey bar with almonds, Mom's favorite.

"Now that I think of it, I'm kind of hungry," I say.

"Me too. We can go get something to eat in a while. Maybe we can get your mom to go with us," Chrystal says as we walk back. "But, I also really want to go looking for Kelsey. I've called Dr. Borgess and left another message. He's probably missing too."

She stops abruptly.

Mom is gone.

Chrystal and I both stand there, dumbfounded for a moment, looking at the empty seat Mom had been sitting in just a few minutes ago. Her purse is still tucked under the chair, but she's gone.

"She wouldn't leave her purse," Chrystal says. "Not unless . . ."

"Nurse!" I yell at the first white-clothed woman I see. The thin black lady stops suddenly, like my voice scared her. I try to calm down. "My mom is gone. She was right here." I point at the chair.

My God. What if the werewolf was here? What if he got her?

The nurse steps closer, looking at the chair. "Mrs. Jennings?" she asks.

"Yes," Chrystal answers.

"She's in the room with Mr. Jennings. He asked for her," the nurse says.

"He asked for her? He talked?" I ask. Hope fills my heart.

"Yes."

"Can we go in?" I ask.

"Only two visitors at a time. One of you will have to wait," she says, and smiles again, then goes back to whatever errand she'd been on before I yelled at her.

"Go on." Chrystal pushes at me. "Ask him how he feels. Ask if he feels anything inside. You know, like . . . I don't know. Like the burn of alcohol or something."

Mom is crying in the room. She's holding Dad's hand, her back to me, but her shoulders are shaking with the sobs. I step up next to her and put my arm around her waist as I look down at Dad.

It's amazing. Someone has raised the bed so that he's sitting up. His eyes are almost clear and he's alert, though it's easy to see he's still feeling some pain. The hair, though. I can't believe it. He still has the beard, but it's his normal beard. The hair that was high on his cheeks and low on his throat is gone. Well, not gone, but all loose. Like he's shedding.

"Logan," he says when he sees me.

"Dad." I don't know what to say, and that's just as well because I don't trust my throat to make anything like a manly noise right now.

"RJ, I've been so scared," Mom says. "I don't know what I would have done without you if . . . if . . ." She can't finish.

"I feel a lot better now," Dad says.

"It's a miracle. It's a miracle from God," Mom says through her tears.

I bite my tongue. Dad is looking at me. He knows something. He looks up at Mom. We've promised not to tell him about Kels.

"Will you give me just a minute with Logan?" he asks.

"She hasn't been eating," I tattle. "Chrystal has a Coke and a candy bar for her, and we want to take her to lunch."

"That would be very good," Dad says. He gently pulls his hand away from Mom and looks at her in a way I'm not sure I've ever seen. There's so much love there. "Give us just a minute, okay? Go eat your candy, then come right back."

Mom looks suspiciously from Dad to me, then nods. She leaves us, but I know we've only got a couple minutes.

"What's going on?" Dad asks as soon as the door is closed. "You did something."

"It's temporary," I explain. "The werewolf gave it to me as proof that he can make a cure for you. But he wants a lot for the rest. I don't know how long this will last."

I pull the bottle out of my pocket, look at it for a minute, then press it into his hand. "It's water, wolfsbane, and his blood."

"His blood? Wolfsbane? That's poison," Dad says.

I nod. "I know. We just dropped the flower into boiling water for a minute, then took it out. I don't know how it works. But it does." I remember what Chrystal told me. "How do you feel? Do you feel different inside?"

Dad seems to think about it for a minute. "A little," he admits. "Before, I felt . . . I don't know. Mad. Like there was something in my gut making me real mad. Now I can feel that it's still there, but smothered."

"I don't know if you can just take another little drink of that if you get to feeling bad," I say, and am about to say more when Mom comes back in.

"What's that?" she asks, looking at the bottle in Dad's hand.

"Nothing," I answer too quickly.

"This is medicine Logan made," Dad answers, giving me a semi-harsh look for lying to Mom. "This is why I'm able to talk to you right now."

Mom looks from the bottle to me. "What is it?"

"It's anti-werewolf medicine," Dad says before I can speak. "Logan, I want you to take your mom to eat, and I want you to tell her everything you know. She's been safe here. I want her to stay. Where are the girls?"

"With the Thompsons," Mom lies. "For the day. They'll come back and sleep in the waiting room with me. It just seemed safer to keep them away from the house at night."

Dad nods. "That's fine. Logan, what about you and the Lawson Smiths?"

"Chrystal's dad is missing. Me and Chrystal have been staying at home. Mr. Davis has been staying with us. There have been deputies, too."

"I don't like that," Dad says. "Not at all."

30

CHRYSTAL

I part my hair down the middle and braid it as tightly as I possibly can, trying to create a new look, a new me, somehow—a me that a werewolf doesn't want. The mirror in the hospital bathroom is warped and smudgy and the flickering fluorescent light doesn't help me examine my image. I look older, I think . . . maybe . . . tired but determined. Or maybe I just want to think I look like how I feel. When it comes right down to it, nobody knows what they actually look like—mirror images are not true images. They flip us. Nobody really knows how the world sees them.

I am what a werewolf wants. Who would believe that? Who would think that these are the secrets I am hiding? Certainly not the elderly lady who just shuffled into the accessible stall; her rubber-soled shoes made little *plip-plop* noises as she walked across the linoleum floor.

These two braided pigtails are all I have right now, all I control. My hand shakes when I think about it, think about Kelsey, how scared she must be. I finish up and leave the bathroom, head down the lime-green halls to the doors of the ICU ward, and push the button to open the door. It swings open and I walk past the desk that is the nurses' station, past the carts of medicine, the movable IV lines, and to Mr. Jennings's room. I step inside before anyone says anything.

He lifts his head. "Chrystal?"

"Mr. Jennings." My courage wavers a little bit, but I move toward the bed. His skin is pale but human-looking. "How are you feeling?"

"A bit better, thanks to the concoction." He eyes me. "Thank you for that."

"I heard what you told them. How you don't want me to be bait. How you would rather die than feel guilty."

"I meant that, Chrystal," he says, his voice gruff.

"I know you did, but it's awful selfish of you."

His eyes widen. "What?"

"The way I see it, we know that if nothing is done for you, you will become a werewolf and you will ask Logan to kill you before that happens. If Logan can't do it, you'll ask one of your friends. We know that we have no way of stopping the transformation. Your outcome is inevitable." I take a deep breath. "But with me—we don't know what will happen. My plan could work. I could be bait and we could get the antidote and save you, or the other option is I could be bait and we could fail."

"And you'd die."

"It's a possibility with me, but not the *only* possibility, not like you."

He closes his eyes. Machines blip. A door buzzes open. A phone rings. People keep living their lives.

"You can't live with the guilt of my death, Mr. Jennings, but neither can I live with the guilt of yours." I lean forward and kiss his forehead. "You have a family. You have a wife and three kids. They can't make it without you. They're in jeopardy because of me."

"How do you figure that?"

"The werewolf has it in for me, for my family. So what does he do? He creates a little craziness here in Oklahoma, knowing that my dad is into cryptozoology. Everyone knows that. So my dad comes out here. My dad brings me. It's all just this elaborate trap for me. All of it. Your family's terror. The dead cops. The missing women. Even the dead cows. It's all to get me and my dad out here. And then . . . then he takes out the men who protect me. You. My dad. Who is next? Logan? I can't let that happen."

Moments pass. In those moments the truth that I've finally articulated weighs in the air, heavy and horrible. He grabs my wrist. Even though he's weak, I can feel the strength in his fingers. "Chrystal, you're so young."

"I know," I say, "but that doesn't make my life worth more than yours."

He lets go of my wrist. I tuck the thin blanket around him.

"You rest," I say. "It'll be okay."

But we both know that's probably not true.

I told Mr. Jennings that I had a plan, but that's complete bull, because I don't have anything of the sort. At least, I don't until Logan and I are back in the truck and headed home.

"I don't think he'll come tonight," he says.

And that's when I get the plan. "So we strike tonight."

His eyes open wide. "What?"

"If we strike tonight while he's weak, we have a chance. We find his human self and restrain him and—"

"How are we going to restrain him?" he interrupts.

"Good question." And I have no answer. "Isn't there some sort of livestock thing that would work for werewolves? A cage or something?"

"The cops might have something."

"The cops think I should go back to New England without my dad, Logan. I don't think they'll want to help us with this." I rub my hand across my eyes. My whole face feels dirty. I'll have to shower again when we get back to the house. I let my head drop back against my seat. "Maybe David?"

"He'd help us, but I don't know if I want to put him at risk," Logan says after a second.

"Yeah. That makes sense."

Logan reaches over and grabs me by the arm. He tugs like he wants me to lean into him, and I do, but the stupid stick shift makes it awkward.

"I don't want to put anyone at risk, especially you." His voice is hoarse with emotion.

"I know." I trace a circle on his jeans, right where the center of his thigh is.

"But you're pretty determined, aren't you?"

"Yeah," I say. "I am."

When I take my shower, I try not to think, *This is possibly the last shower of my life.* When I shampoo my hair with the Jenningses' shampoo, I try not to think, *I will die smelling like coconut.* When I grab the soap, I try not to think, *I miss my loofah and I miss my dad and my mom and my friends.* I try not to think, *I want Kelsey to be okay. Please let Kelsey be okay. And my dad.*

I try not to think of anything, just let the water wash the grime and the sweat away and come out clean.

I have texted all my friends a silly I LOVE U GUYS. ROCK HARD. xoxox <3 text, which is normal for me. So nobody will wonder about it. I have riffed on my bass just the tiniest bit and left a note that Katie should have it. I suspect she'll have some musical ability. I know she eyed it before, and if there's anything I know, it's that a bass needs to be loved.

I have done all these things and even written notes for my dad and my mom and Mrs. Jennings, sealed them all up in envelopes I found downstairs. I studied the chemical composition of the blood as much as I could before I packed up one of the samples and mailed it to Sergeant Mitchell.

I was going to mail a sample to my dad's professor friend, Dr. Borgess, but when I went to the university website to get his mailing address, I found something that showed me just how futile this whole thing is.

I left the rest of the samples for my dad, in case he ever comes back.

Logan has found a trailer that David's dad uses to move bulls. It's sturdy, but they're retrofitting it with extra plates and steel. David, Mr. Davis, and David's dad are both in on it now. Logan felt like we had no choice, and the more help the better. I hope that's the right decision. I hope no more people get hurt.

Kierkegaard wrote, "What is a poet? An unhappy person who conceals profound anguish in his heart but whose lips are so formed that as sighs and cries pass over them they sound like beautiful music." That is Logan. Even his breaths are music to me, a low melody that soothes.

When I get out of the shower, I wrap a towel around myself, walk down the hall to Kelsey's room and put on the cleanest clothes I can find, which seems ironic. I try not to think, *This is what I might die in—a pair of baby-blue shorts and a T-shirt from the Oklahoma state fair.* I can't stop the thinking though, can't stop the wondering. In twenty-four hours it should be all over—one way or another—and I'm going to hold on to that thought.

There is wolfsbane in my pocket, just in case. We've made a squirt bottle full of boiled wolfsbane mixed with water, but we want the werewolf alive at least long enough to get a cure.

A cure.

I brush out my hair but don't bother to dry it. It's too hot. Instead I tug it back into a high ponytail. I put earrings in every single hole in my ears. And I start to head downstairs. The dogs bark. First it's just one bark that belongs to Galahad, but the others join in and it becomes an insane cacophony of sound.

Someone is banging on the door.

"Hold on!" I hear Logan yell, and I rush down the stairs. A dust bunny made of dog fur tumbles after me.

Logan peeks out of the curtain and whispers a swear, but runs to the door, quickly works the locks, and throws it open.

A girl tumbles in. She's dirty and bloody. Her clothes are ripped. Dust and dirt cake her crazy dark-brown hair.

"Holy . . ." Mr. Thompson swears.

"It's Kelsey," David whispers.

Kelsey looks around all crazy-eyed. One shaking arm reaches up and her finger points. It points at me.

31

LOGAN

Chrystal and Kelsey are staring at each other. Kels is crying and she sways and it's none of us men who catch her. Nope, it's Chrystal who wraps her arms around her and settles her on the couch. Kelsey is all dirty and Chrystal's fresh out of the shower. The dirt from the torn clothes and exposed skin is getting ground into Chrystal's clothes and all over her bare arms. And her tear-streaked face.

I suddenly feel self-conscious for gawking at them during this emotional interchange, so I turn away, pretending to straighten the make-shift drapes Chrystal's hung over the window. Yeah. Like anyone would believe I care about drapes right now.

"Someone needs to call the police," Mr. Thompson says, leaving the room and pulling out his cell phone.

Chrystal asks, "What happened?"

They are holding each other at arm's length, both with wet, dirty faces.

"He has your father—the wolf—he . . . he's coming for you. I . . ." Then Kelsey promptly passes out.

Sitting at the dining room table with a jug of cold water, a pitcher of sweet tea, and our glasses, Chrystal and I tell Sergeant Mitchell our story first. As we talk, his animated face transitions between looks of intense interest to shock, fear, pride, and determination.

"You would use yourself as bait to help a fellow human?" he asks Chrystal when we're done. She nods. He lowers his head for a moment, and when he raises it again, there is steel in his eyes. "Did we not talk about this?"

She waves his anger away. "Anyone would do it."

"No, they wouldn't," I argue.

But it's pointless. The sergeant wants to hear what happened to her. Kelsey is sitting up again and an ambulance is on its way. She tells us that she was held in a cage with Chrystal's dad. He'd been abducted at the university, he said, while trying to find a professor friend of his. He didn't see who did it.

But she saw. Kelsey's voice becomes a whisper as she talks about the wolf. And then the men who helped him.

"When I woke up, I was in this closet. It was super small. There was duct tape over my mouth and around my wrists and ankles.."

"They like their duct tape," Chrystal says.

Sergeant Mitchell gives her a look.

"So they open the door and drag us out. Then, they're just

throwing us into the back of a pickup truck and we all drove out to the woods somewhere. They yank me out and sit me next to this tree and just wrap even more duct tape around me. So now I'm totally stuck to this tree and they drive off with Mr. Lawson Smith."

Chrystal makes a horrified noise and she keeps patting Kelsey's leg. Galahad comes over and flops across Kelsey's feet. She doesn't even react. I think she's in shock.

"Go on," says Sergeant Mitchell.

"When we were in the truck, he told me the wolf was looking for you. He wanted me to warn you that you were the prize. That's what he called it—the prize." Kelsey's voice shivers, but Chrystal doesn't flinch.

"How long were you tied to the tree?" Sergeant Mitchell asks.

Sirens sound in the distance.

Kelsey shakes. She seems so tired. "Until, like, an hour ago."

"And this was the closest house?" he asks.

She nods. "It felt like I walked forever."

"Interesting coincidence," Sergeant Mitchell says.

"I saw him change. He showed me. While we were at the tree. He stripped off his clothes and took several deep breaths, like he was getting ready to lift a heavy load, and then hair started to sprout all over his body. His arms and legs thickened, like someone was blowing him up. Like an air mattress or something like that. His face was contorted with pain. He fell to his knees first. His jaw got longer and I could see his teeth growing in his mouth. His mouth was like growing and moving to make room for the new shape. Then he fell flat on the ground, rolled to his side, and curled up in a fetal position for the rest of the change.

"Afterward, he stood up and howled. He ran off into the woods. I haven't seen him since."

"How did you get away?" Chrystal asks.

"A rock. I got a rock from the ground. It was under my butt and it was super uncomfortable. It had a jagged edge on it and I used it to saw through the duct tape. It took a so long because they used so much freaking tape to hold me against the tree." She gulps her tea, refills her glass, then looks at Chrystal. Her hand is shaking. "I—I—I'd like to call my mom."

The ambulance comes. Kelsey heads to the hospital. Mom will meet her there. Sergeant Mitchell takes a stern tone with Chrystal.

"Do not do anything stupid," he orders.

"Of course not," Chrystal lies.

The sergeant leaves. The sheriff's two deputies who had remained in the yard most of the time get in their car and follow Sergeant Mitchell up our driveway.

"We have work to do," Chrystal says. She goes to her dad's work area and starts riffling through his papers. She pulls one out and shows it to me. "Start reading from the bottom. That's my name and my mom's. And my grandma's. Every seventh generation they are in all caps. Mine is in all caps."

She rubs her palms over her hair and pushes hard at her head like she's trying to force something to go past her. "If you count the names between Adelind Gersten and Krimhilde Rothstein. There are six."

"Krimhilde is the seventh," I say, and I remember the email I read, what the werewolf said. "Seven generations?" I ask.

"Yes, Logan," Chrystal says. "Now count the names between Krimhilde and mine. Six—I really am the seventh. Krimhilde Rothstein is my ancestor, and she was allegedly the mate of a werewolf. But she wasn't. . . ."

"I don't understand," David says.

"I was on the phone with my mom and she laughed at the mate thing when I told her," Chrystal says. "My mom laughs at most things like this, so I wasn't—you know—surprised that she didn't believe it, but she insisted this was wrong."

"What was wrong? Your dad's chart?" David asks.

"No. Who Krimhilde was. What she did," Chrystal says. Her eyes have an almost fanatical gleam. I've never seen her like this before, honestly. "She wasn't a werewolf's mate. She was a hunter."

"Ha! And you don't even like guns!" David slaps his leg. It's the most happy any of us has been in a long time.

Chrystal doesn't crack a smile. "Not that kind of hunter. A werewolf hunter. She killed a werewolf."

She pulls up a webpage that she's bookmarked on her computer and there are words in another language and a sketch of a woman holding the severed head of a wolf. "I translated it."

"So the werewolf isn't trying to mate with you?" I ask. "He's just trying to kill you? He's going to an awful lot of trouble."

"He's playing me. He's playing us. This is about revenge. He wants us as scared as possible, as betrayed as possible," she says. "But there's more. I know. I'm pretty sure I know who it is."

Another click. The screen shifts to the same guy I sat with on the bench, the same one who gave me the blood.

"Holy—" David *and* Mr. Thompson *and* Mr. Davis swear simultaneously, which normally would be humorous, but not now.

"That's who you talked to, right?" Chrystal asks me. "On the bench."

"The professor? It's been the damn professor. I told you that you can't trust those professors," Mr. Davis says. To be fair, Mr. Davis says you can't trust anyone who doesn't work with their hands. David starts to argue the point with him.

Chrystal holds up her hand to stop them. "According to my dad's research, and this book I found"—she waves at a pile of papers on the corner of the desk—"a werewolf lives for about ten generations of men. That is to say, about two hundred and fifty years." She pauses. "According to the translation of that story I just showed you, that werewolf had a child."

"Whoa. Badass," David says.

I glare at him, but Chrystal just nods.

She sifts through papers and moves a couple other books until she finds another battered book with an old library call number handwritten on the spine. She opens the book to a page marked with a purple sticky note and begins to read.

"'It's explained that these women,' like my ancestor, 'in order to preserve their health, suck the blood of men they have seduced. The men fall into a kind of lycanthropy. They are characterized by excessive body hair, index fingers that match the middle finger in length, and typically have hollow, mournful eyes and fingernails much thicker than the average man. At the waxing of the moon they are doomed to become beasts when God's light vanishes from the land. Such a curse will last nightly until the waning of the moon leaves the sky dark. Being larger and stronger than the natural wolf, these creatures become "wolf-kings," and their subjects must supply them with the finest meats.' And that's how it allegedly started."

Chrystal turns the page. We all sit transfixed, waiting for her to continue.

"'A story from the Balkans tells of one such witch, Lanya, who seduced and attacked a priest of the church named Heinrich Lanzkranna. This priest was a convert to Christendom and had risen to his current position through much pious devotion. Upon awaking from his cursed slumber and finding himself defiled, he cast off his priestly office and summoned the wrath of his old stone gods, cursing Lanya and her descendants so that in every seventh generation they can find no love save after they kill the beast he himself became. He then took Lanya as his wife and returned to the mountain village of his pagan youth.'"

She pauses and I have to speak up. "Wait! What does that mean?"

"It means Chrystal can't love anyone until after she's killed one," David says. "Even I got that. But that's totally stupid. Sorry. A lot of this is totally stupid."

"I'm not arguing with you, but in this hyperbolic stupidity, there's some truth. That's the point. You have to look past the stuff that makes no sense, the hyperbole, and go find the nuggets of truth. Right? There's more," Chrystal says, interrupting David when he tries to speak again. "Let me finish. It says this German historian and preacher, Johannes Geiler, reports finding a written confession sent to a church in Hungary in which a woman admitted to being the bride of a known werewolf. In the confession, she said it was a curse of her ancestors that every seventh generation would kill the *ruvanush*—that means 'wolfman'—or be killed." Chrystal pauses and looks at each of us. "That confession came from Adelind Gersten, who said her mother and grandmother told her she was descended from a witch mother and sacred man of the mountains remembered only by the name Wolf-King.

"Then it says that, according to the tenets of the pagan belief system, the curse would continue until the last male progeny of the original *ruvanush* was destroyed. Then it says he will probably kill her. But that might not happen," she adds quickly. "I mean, obviously, one of my ancestors succeeded. It's just that the wolf she killed wasn't the only one left."

We all sit quietly for a moment, sipping our tea. Mr. Thompson has rejoined us. He breaks the silence to say, "I can't believe this. I mean—I do. I'm not saying you're a liar, girl, but—"

"Something about that doesn't add up," I say. "If these women had babies that were werewolves . . ."

"It sounds like a fairy tale for kids to me," David's dad says.

"Or an episode of *Supernatural*," Chrystal adds, but her voice is strained. "Believe me, I know how it sounds."

"But it's our lives," David says.

"Yeah. Or our deaths," I groan. "Both of our dads' lives are on the line, Chrystal. You know that, right?"

She nods. Her face is fierce like a warrior's. "Oh yeah. I know."

32

CHRYSTAL

My plan? Well, that's changed a bit now," I tell them. There are all these men with guns in this tiny kitchen space. Add in the dogs, and I feel sort of claustrophobic. I get up and pace over to the sink before I turn around again and face them. They stand there, all different heights and shades of skin, and every single one looks tired and worried. They have identical expressions on their faces—like they are waiting for orders. I don't have orders. I have thoughts. "I thought we could hunt him out and capture him before night, before he turns."

"Why has the plan changed, then?" David asks. He's impatient like me, much more alpha than Logan.

"Because of what Kelsey said . . . ," I start to explain.

Logan says it for me. "She saw him change during the day, which necessitates a much higher level of caution."

"It means we can't count on him staying human," I finish. "But he's still weak, right, Logan?"

He rubs at his ears, takes a big breath, and blurts out, "Most likely."

"And on the bonus side, we know his name now, we know where he works, we know how to trace him—" I add.

"But . . ." Logan interrupts. He looks into my eyes. His are so beautiful. I want to stand next to him, touch his arm, anything to make sure he's real. "If he knows that Kelsey escaped, then he also knows that we can find him at his normal haunts."

"Exactly." Mr. Davis leans back against the counter. Galahad whines for treats at my feet and Mr. Thompson tries to shoo him away. He doesn't budge.

I turn to Mr. Davis and say, "So I'm bait again. Instead of surprising him, we have to lure him."

For a minute we are all silent and thoughtful.

I start thinking aloud. "How do we make a cure? Do we know that? That's the most important thing. That's our primary objective; then our secondary objective is stopping him."

"Primary objective? Only Logan would fall in love with a rocker chick who talks like a commando." David looks at me like I'm speaking a foreign language. Logan elbows him in the gut.

"Th-th-the cops have rubbed off on me," I stammer, motioning toward the cruiser parked outside. Logan shakes his head like he wants to kill David, but it's really okay. I try so hard to be normal and logical and talk like a regular person, but sometimes I just fail. It doesn't matter. I turn back to check on Mr. Davis, who looks like a wild man with his too-big, worried eyes.

David starts in on the Internet while Logan rushes through

books. Mr. Thompson and Mr. Davis and I start looking too. Then Logan yells, "Got it!"

We huddle around him as he reads through a page of an ancient, smelly book. His finger points at lines as he talks. "For one dose? One person? A quarter of a cup." He turns away, paces two steps, pivots, does it again, rubbing his forehead the way he does when he's upset about something or deep in thought. "Yes, yes. Right. A quarter cup should do."

David and his dad exchange a look. Galahad flops onto his side, wagging his tail.

"Here's how it goes." I rub Galahad's side gently with my foot and say, "We are going to shoot him with animal tranquilizers. Mr. Davis said he can get us some of those, and a couple guns to shoot them. Then we're going to shove him into the trailer. When he's subdued, we'll take some blood. When we're finished . . . We'll kill him with wolfsbane or silver bullets."

"How?" Logan asks.

"We'll use one of my dad's needles," I say. He has needles. He's weird like that. He also has ancient texts and silver bullets and crosses and holy water. I pull one of Dad's bags from under the table. It's open from when I got into it earlier. I pull out a wooden box and open the lid to show the silver bullets. "Will these work in any of your guns?"

Logan pulls a bullet from the box and holds it up. "It's a .30-.30," he says, looking to David, who nods. Logan hands the bullet to him.

"So I should load up with these?" David asks.

"Yes," I tell him.

"What if . . . ," Logan begins, then stops, thinking. I wait him out. "I have my bow upstairs. What if we squeezed some juice out of the wolfsbane onto one of my arrows and I shot him with it? Would that kill him?"

I shrug. "Probably. I don't know."

"What if we really kill him?" Mr. Thompson asks. "If what you say is true, and he's really a man. Well, I mean, that could be seen as murder."

I look him straight in the eyes. "Then he dies."

"But there will be consequences," Mr. Thompson says.

I swallow before I say, "There always are."

I wash up before we go. Logan meets me at the top of the stairs, takes me by the arm, and says, "Chrystal?"

I stare up at him, at his big eyes and all-over-the-place hair. He's washed off a bit too, but not a real shower. He's just stuck his head under the faucet and put on new clothes. He looks a bit silly in a skater T-shirt, holding his bow, but adorable, too.

"What, Logan?"

He cocks his head. "Did you mean that? About killing Dr. Borgess?"

"He isn't Dr. Borgess. He's a monster. He has killed people. He has no qualms about killing people, about letting your dad die, about taking Kelsey, about killing women and cops. I knew he was creepy when I met him . . . I just . . . I trusted him to help us anyway. He played us so hard. I mean, seriously, when I met him he flat out told me the monster's motive was vengeance. I was too busy being a skeptic to even realize he was actually giving us a hint." I meet Logan's eyes. "I hate that. And I hate that I resisted believing my dad for so long. If I hadn't, maybe everyone would be safe. Maybe this would have ended a lot earlier. I was just so stubborn and selfish. All I wanted to do was get to New York and to not believe, you know? It hurts to think I caused this."

"You didn't cause this. Dr. Borgess caused this. I caused this. I didn't want to believe it either and I actually saw it and I still didn't want to believe it."

Someone coughs downstairs. There's a low murmur of men's voices. Mr. Davis has arranged for some other guys to watch the farm, but I figure if I'm not here, it's pretty safe.

I focus on Logan. He wants so badly for everything to be good, for life to fit into poetry lines, for the landscape to be beautiful, and for the people to match that beauty. He reaches out and touches my hair. "What happened to the girl who didn't believe in me, who didn't believe in werewolves, who shrank away from the thought of violence?"

"She saw a monster, Logan. She saw a monster and she knows she has to stop it to protect the people she loves." I kiss his cheek and hurry down the stairs before I have to look into his eyes again. "And once I do that, I will have a lollipop and play a little bass, and maybe we could actually kiss again, okay?"

He smiles and snorts out a laugh. "Okay."

There's a place in the woods, not too far from the Jenningses' property. There are tree stands in multiple positions there. Tree stands are these wooden platforms where Logan and his dad and sometimes their friends will hunt deer. Because they are hunters, they have things that mask their human scent. They rub this stuff all over their clothes and bodies and hair. They did this back at the house, but they do it again now that we're in the woods. The sun will set pretty soon, and if the monster is stronger in the dark, we have to hurry.

"Deer pee," David explains, grinning. "Elixir of the hunting gods."

"It's gross, but it works," Logan adds, smiling.

"Like him enough to hug him when he smells like deer piss?" David asks.

"If he smelled like deer *poo*, I would still want to hug him," I say, and to prove it I wrap my arms right around Logan's trunk, pressing myself against him. I whisper, "I wish I could stay here forever."

He kisses the top of my head even though everyone is watching. "Me too."

I let go and we exchange a look. I don't need to tell him how scared I am; he can tell by the way my hands shake, I know, and how my voice is this forced, dead calm that's totally unlike my normal up-and-down, excitable voice. I don't need to tell him how much I like him either, but I do.

"I really like you, Logan. In a love kind of way."

He smiles. It's heartbreaking and slow. Maybe the last smile I'll ever see. His eyes are as intense as his voice. "I like you that way, too."

I punch him in the arm for effect. It seems appropriately rah-rah tough for the drama of the moment, but everything inside me is imagining losing him and all the things we won't ever be able to do. We won't be able to go to a movie or really make out for hours or watch fireworks or get harassed by Katie or any of it. . . . He could die. I could die. It could all end now.

For a second I allow myself to give in to all the pain and worries and doubt. I bow my head to lean the top of it against his chest. His hands instantly go to my shoulders. He really does smell horrible.

"Chrystal . . ."

I swallow hard, press my lips together, fight the urge to cry.

"You don't have to do this," he says. "We can find another way. You don't have to—"

I lift my finger and press it against his lips to stop him. His lips still against my finger. We both know that I have to. He sighs and sags his body against me. I'm holding him up.

"This all sucks so much. . . ."

I stagger under his weight, but I don't fall. I'll keep us both up.

"It'll be okay. We'll be okay." I rub my hands along the sides of his face. "Let's just do this."

33

LOGAN

The hours tick by. Varmints and night birds go about their business all around us. The sound of an owl snatching a mouse from the ground creeps me out the way it always does. Death from above. On the other side of the ridge, our cattle low and chew up their winter alfalfa in a lighted pasture.

Mr. Thompson dozes and David has to nudge him to wake him up so he'll stop snoring. Mr. Thompson has a tranquilizer rifle in his lap, as does Mr. Davis. David has his Winchester .30-.30 loaded with silver bullets. I have my bow with the arrow tips moistened with sap squeezed from the stems of the wolfsbane growing in Mom's flower garden. Four guys. Three different kinds of weapons. I hope at least one of them works.

The police have promised to visit the university and talk to Professor Borgess, but they never called back to tell us what happened. All we told them was that he might know something about where Chrystal's dad is.

Chrystal said she loves me.

And I said I love her.

We may die tonight. She may live, but leave tomorrow. Either way, I am in love with a beautiful girl who loves me back. No one should die without feeling what I feel right now. Without the fear, of course.

Coyotes yap and howl off to the east.

A huge mama possum with five babies clinging to her back trundles through the clearing, not fifteen feet from where Chrystal sits cross-legged. In the light of the moon and stars I can see her eyes get huge as she watches the possum family. She doesn't move, and that's good, because a frightened mama possum can be a mean thing to deal with.

No werewolf howls. No werewolf crashes into the clearing to claim my beautiful, brave girlfriend sitting there like a worm on a hook.

In short, nothing happens.

At about two a.m. Mr. Davis calls it off for the night. We're all stiff and tired and disappointed, but at the same time I think we're all more than a little relieved.

"He must still be recovering from last night," I say as I throw my arms around Chrystal.

"I guess so," she says. "But that just means we have to do this again."

"Yeah."

Back at the house, we send Chrystal upstairs to sleep. Mr. Davis and Mr. Thompson try to get me to go to bed, too, but I insist on staying up and drinking coffee with them until it's time for the morning milking. After the cows are milked, then I go upstairs to my room. Chrystal is sleeping in my bed. I'm dirty and I stink from the milk barn, so I gently kiss her cheek, then settle onto the floor with my pillow and a spare blanket.

I wake up to the feeling of being kicked. Not hard, just a gentle, persistent kick to the legs. I peel my eyes open to the bright light of late morning and find Chrystal standing over me. She's wearing shorts and a T-shirt, nudging me with her bare foot.

"Wake up, sleepyhead," she says. "Go take a shower, then come back and talk to me."

Sitting, I rub at my face. "What's up?"

She drops to the floor in front of me. "I was thinking. It took me forever to get to sleep because I was thinking about the same thing I thought about the whole time I was waiting out there being bait for that werewolf thing."

Her face is so serious and so pretty. I want to lean in and kiss her, but I know my breath must be atrocious.

"Thinking about what?" I ask.

"That you should take a shower," she says.

My shower is quick, although I'm so nervous, I drop the soap twice and the huge bar of green Zest sounds like a boulder when it hits the porcelain of the tub each time. I finally rinse, turn off the water, and towel dry. The whole process takes about ten minutes, or half of my normal time. I like a good, hot shower, where I can think under the water.

Wearing just a pair of boxers and a T-shirt, I slip back to my room. To my surprise, Chrystal is in bed. I listen closely as I close my door. There's not a sound coming from anywhere in the house, other than the steady hum of the air conditioning. I push the door closed and lock it.

"Everyone's still asleep?" Chrystal asks.

I turn around and nod. "I think so. Didn't hear anybody."

"Good."

Our bodies sort of pivot toward each other and then it just happens—our lips meet. Her hand grabs my bicep. Her hand is small but strong and cool. My hand goes to the small of her back. My palm presses against her skin. Her shirt's ridden up a bit, but I'm glad, really glad, because I like the feel of pressing against her. But that's not what I'm focused on, not really.

The lips.

It's not like our lips are just kissing. They hint at things, at good, good things: gesturing out our souls and wants and aches and fears. She is nice and strong and kind. Her lips move a little more solidly against mine. My hand slides up her arm, to her shoulder and then to her hair. I want to press her lips into mine as hard as I can, so I can only think about them and nothing else, just her, her lips.

"It's like coming home," I say against her mouth, then I pull away and collapse against the bed. "Oh, that was so corny."

"It was nice," she says.

"No, it was corny."

"And nice? It's totally corny, too, though." She just waits. "Want to try again?"

I hold up my hand because I do, but there's something . . . something not right. A noise.

Barking.

The dogs are barking.

Chrystal's gaze moves from me to the window, so I look there too. I don't want to, but I go to the window and move the curtain aside. A silver Toyota Camry is pulling up to the house. Thunder and Daisy are baying like crazy, their teeth showing, while Galahad rushes at the driver's door, snapping and growling before backing away to do it again.

"What is it?" Chrystal asks.

I can't actually see the driver, but with the way the dogs are acting, there's really only one person it can be.

"I think it's him. Professor Borgess."

"What?" Chrystal sits up on the bed.

"I'm going downstairs. Wake David up. I'll get Mr. Davis up. He's human if he's driving a car, and I don't think he'll get out with the dogs there. Hurry." I start to rush out, but stop. There's a werewolf in my driveway and a girl in my bed. This is just too bizarre to ever happen to anyone else, ever.

I lean over Chrystal and kiss her hard on the lips. "We'll get back to this," I promise.

Then I slip out of the room, closing the door behind me.

"Galahad! Come here!" I yell at the dog. Thunder and Daisy are already beside me, still growling, but waiting. They're hunting dogs. They know to wait for a command to attack. Galahad is just a sweet, dumb mutt. Still, he's a good dog, and eventually he comes to me. I turn to Mr. Davis, who is standing in the doorway with his shotgun in his hand. I'm holding my own shotgun. "Will you call Galahad and keep him inside?"

He does. Galahad doesn't want to go, but when I gently pop his rump with the butt of my gun, he goes up the porch, looking over his shoulder at the car, promising pain if he's allowed to give it. Mr. Davis lets the dog pass him, then he steps onto the porch and closes the door.

Professor Borgess opens his car door and steps out. He's wearing hiking boots, jeans, and a short-sleeved denim shirt. There are no signs at all of his face being burned. As he steps toward me, his limp is gone. Only his throat shows signs that anything has ever been wrong with him. The skin there is pink and new-looking.

"You've mostly recovered," I say, crossing my chest with the shotgun.

He looks at the gun and smiles at me. "Yes, I have," he says. "Rest is the key. Rest and water. We must stay hydrated. How is your father?"

"Better," I admit.

"I told you he would be," Borgess answers. "But, as I also said, what I gave you was only a temporary cure."

Behind me, the screen door bangs closed again. I want to turn around to see who it is, but I don't dare take my eyes off the were-wolf professor. He, however, looks past me and there's a tiny bit of shock in his eyes.

"Chrystal Lawson Smith," he says. "Daughter of the pacifist hunter of Bigfoot, werewolves, and alien life-forms, musician, lollipop eater, and nemesis. I never expected to see you holding a gun."

A gun?

I can't help myself. I turn my head just a little. Just in time to hear the gun go off. It isn't loud, though. Not nearly as loud as it should have been. Something whizzes past me, then Borgess grunts. I look back to him.

A tranquilizer dart with a fuzzy end sticks out of the right side of his chest.

Above me there is the sound of wood slamming wood. Glass breaks. Then another muffled pop. And another dart appears in the new pink flesh of the werewolf's throat.

Professor Borgess looks at me, then drops to his knees. "We had a deal," he says, then his eyes roll up into his head and he slumps to the ground.

I look behind and up to see David leaning out my broken bedroom window, holding the second tranquilizer gun.

"He's down!" Mr. Davis calls out, then he whoops. "Whoo-ee! We got him. Let's get him in that cage."

34

CHRYSTAL

The moment that Dr. Borgess falls down, I remember to breathe. David's arm muscles are tight and the gun quivers a little. He's just standing there at the window above me, rifle at his shoulder, yelling like a crazy man.

"Holy . . . holy . . . oh man . . . oh man . . . oh man . . ."

Two darts stick out of Dr. Borgess's body. I hope it's enough.

"David, keep your gun on him!" I yell. I race down the porch stairs before I can even think about shoes.

Logan and Mr. Davis approach Dr. Borgess. The professor isn't moving.

"I shot a man." David's like a zombie, repeating it from the window.

"Dude, it was a tranquilizer. It was okay. I did it too." I step farther onto the driveway. It's too hot for my feet to bear for more than a second. I hop onto the grass and step forward. The bottoms of my feet touch the wide, thick blades. The air smells of hot tar, hot metal, the sweat of people's fear. It's like it's gone into slow motion as I move forward.

One step.

Logan and Mr. Davis are lifting Dr. Borgess. Neither of them are holding guns.

Another step.

A bird caws from a tree. Another answers. They must be crows.

Another step.

I'm by the garden. I reach down with my free hand and grab some wolfsbane, tuck it into my shirt pocket right next to the collapsible mug I found with other camping gear in Logan's bedroom.

Another step.

Mr. Davis jerks back, dropping Dr. Borgess's arms. Dr. Borgess doesn't fall, though, not like he would if he were really asleep.

Another step.

"I don't have a shot!" David yells.

Mr. Davis scurries backward. Logan's still holding on to Dr. Borgess's legs. You'd think the man would fall backward, hit his head on the driveway, but instead he bends upward, reaching for Logan. As he reaches, his body starts to change.

"Drop him, Logan!" I'm screaming the words without thinking, charging forward.

Logan drops him and runs backward. The moment Logan lets him go, Dr. Borgess twists, lunging toward Mr. Davis.

I struggle with the gun. It jams. "David!"

A shot goes off. It hits. Nothing. It doesn't even slow Dr. Borgess down. Hair sprouts everywhere and he's bigger. His body twists as it moves, reshaping itself into something insane and disgusting and wrong . . . just wrong. He grabs Mr. Davis and throws him. The nice feedstore man's body flies soundlessly through the air. He doesn't scream, just lands in the grass with an oomph.

Another step forward. I try the gun again. Logan yanks it from my hands.

David shoots. The tranquilizer lodges itself in the fur.

It's not enough.

The wolfman turns and meets my eyes. He brushes away the few remaining scraps of clothing. I'm what he wants. Logan and I? We're too late; our timing was bad.

Still, I step forward again.

Someone yells my name.

I never believed in bad, but now I do.

I never believed in my father, but now I do.

I never believed in monsters, but now I do.

I can control this. I can choose my own destiny.

"I'm right here," I say.

"Chrystal!" It's Logan. He yanks at my arm, but it's too late. The wolf grabs me around the middle, tugging me with him. He smells—it is horrifying—and he's all hard muscle and fur. His teeth elongate and grow even as I watch, but something in his eyes is still a tiny bit human. Not for long, though. I know it's not for long.

"You don't want to do this," I whisper.

He tucks me into his side and runs. My arms are clamped down. He's so strong. Still, I don't struggle. My feet don't touch the ground, just dangle there as he takes off down the road. He detours across the lighted field, jumps a fence, and runs into the woods, but he doesn't go too far in, just twenty feet or so, zigzagging around trees, blasting through shrubs. Twigs snap beneath his paws. My chest feels like it's about to explode. And then he stops.

He stops.

I'm not scared for some reason. My brain is calm. I think of what to do, what I can do against something so huge and so wrong. The wind beats down on us, hitting the world. The sky is cloudy, so cloudy, and smells of dirt.

He grunts and loosens his hold a bit. I land on the ground. Twigs rub hard against the soles of my feet.

"You made a promise," I tell him. My voice is barely a whisper, but I know he can hear. "You promised a cure. Give me your blood first."

I pull out the collapsible mug I stashed in my pocket.

He snarls. The tiny hairs on my arms stand up, but I keep holding the mug, searching those monstrous eyes for any tiny bit of human.

"You promised," I say again. "You promised."

He howls and lets me go completely. Then, before I really comprehend what he's doing, he slashes his forearm with his own claw. It rips through fur and skin. Blood streams out. Some dribbles on the ground before I come out of shock enough to capture it in the mug. It fills quickly.

"There," I say as calmly as I can. "Good. Just let me put it down."

I place it in the roots of the tree and think as quickly as I can what to do. I turn to face him, stepping away from the tree, protecting the precious blood that will put the Jennings family back together.

"I don't want this," I tell him. "I'm not like my ancestors. I don't want to hunt you. I don't want to mate with you. Don't you care?"

He snarls again—this primal, evil noise that pretty obviously indicates he doesn't care.

"I know you really don't want me for a mate. That was just lies and mythology and trickery. I know you want to be in control, the way you weren't then, when you were young, when my ancestor killed one of you 250 or so years ago. Who was it? Your father?"

He doesn't move.

"Your mother?"

He unleashes another snarl. The wound on his arm is already starting to heal, which is not good. I need that wound.

"Fine," I say, opening my own arms wide. "Come and get me."

He flings himself toward me. I try to jump away, but he knocks me hard against a tree trunk. Pain ricochets through the base of my neck, the back of my skull. I fight to stay conscious. I have to stay conscious. Consciousness is part of the plan. He growls above me, all wild, all teeth and fur and claw, brute strength. I kick at him, try to distract him, fight him off, but I'm no match to really fight him. Of course, that's not what I'm trying to do.

As he works to get a better hold on me, I take the wolfsbane that has been in my hand since I took out the mug. The purple blossom is warm and damp with my own sweat. Limp and dying. I shove half of it into his wound, push it inside the red muscle and blood, the ripped skin. He howls and I throw the rest in his mouth. His teeth snap and graze my hand, tearing the skin of my wrist and all along my pinkie. It doesn't matter. It can't matter, because he swallows. He is not smart enough to spit the flower out. He lets go of me and claws at his face and throat.

Two seconds later he falls backward. Black foam comes out of his mouth. He heaves it up again and again. His eyes roll back into his head and he shudders all over. I scoot backward, against the tree, sliding down to a sitting position. I take the mug in my hands, clutch it to my chest.

There is too much noise. It's like a pack of werewolves are all around us. But I have to stay focused on the one that is right in front of me.

Foaming and snarling, he gets to his knees. He sways, but forces himself to his feet, where he stands towering over me, unsteady but huge and sick and very, very angry.

Then a whisper hisses through the air and makes a loud, wet *thunp* as it slams into his shoulder. The werewolf screams in agony and claws at the arrow—Logan's arrow—protruding from his shoulder. He falls to his knees again.

I watch him turn back into a man, a naked, ugly man.

His hand reaches toward me.

"You're a killer, just like the rest of them," he whispers. "I knew it the first time I saw you in the office with your father. Before then. I knew. I knew when he sent me that email, a picture of him and you in the icon. You had death in your eyes."

He collapses at my feet.

"You're the killer," I say.

"We both are. What did your dead philosopher say, Chrystal? 'Purity of heart is to will one thing'? My heart is pure. Yours is divided. It makes you weak. You want too many things, do too many things."

"Kierkegaard was not perfect. He was just a man, Professor Borgess. I know that," I gasp out. "But he makes me think. I wish he had made you think too. You've wasted your life, hurting people for what? Hurting me for something my ancestor did? I thought you were smart, at least."

"I am smarter than you."

I shrug. "You have lost yourself."

"So have you." His words are quiet now, still full of anger, but not . . . He's dying. I know he is.

His eyes close.

I step away.

Have I lost myself?

Who is he to say? Who am I to listen?

Kierkegaard said, "The greatest hazard of all, losing the self, can occur very quietly in the world, as if it were nothing at all. No other loss can occur so quietly; any other loss—an arm, a leg, five dollars, a wife, etc.—is sure to be noticed."

There is barking and howling all around me. Deep inside my mind it registers that this canine noise is not a threat. Tree branches fight to stay attached to their trees as the wind picks up more and more. Rain will fall soon. And I can't let it get in the blood. I put my hand over the top of the mug, protecting it from pending rain, and sit there, watching, waiting, but still he doesn't move.

"Chrystal!" Something is crashing through the brush nearby.

"Logan," I whimper. He can't see me. He might think I'm already dead.

I manage to pull myself back into a standing position and stagger a step away from the body.

"Logan," I call again, without volume. "Logan."

Something is howling.

Something is calling my name.

Stopping to check behind me, I see Borgess is still not moving. The wind is swirling pine needles and old, dry leaves all around him, a sea of decay. I totter a bit. I don't trust myself to carry the mug, so I bend to put it down again, thinking I'll put some leaves over the top to protect the blood inside.

"Chrystal!"

It's Logan. He is so sweet, so kind. Nothing like the wolf. Nothing. I should have just liked him for real right away. I wasted so much time.

35

LOGAN

'm close to the place where Chrystal and I first saw the three trespassers and the other man who turned out to be the were-wolf. I'm halfway up the slope that leads to one of our ponds and there, fifty yards away from me, is the monster. Something's wrong with him. It looks like the thing is vomiting.

He's on his knees, trying to stand up. I stop and put an arrow to the string, pull the string back until the tension is released. I hold it, watching. The thing rises and stands there, wobbling, growling. I tell myself to concentrate. To breathe. To aim for the head.

I hit him in the shoulder.

But he goes down again, and out of sight behind some shrubs.

Then I see Chrystal. She stands up, leaning against a sycamore for support, one hand against the white trunk while another holds something . . . a cup? Then she begins walking. Not toward me, but down the slope to my left, carefully holding something in both hands.

"Chrystal!" I yell to her, but she doesn't acknowledge me. I go crashing through the brush after her. Behind me, I hear David veering off in her direction too.

My side is sending sharp stabs of pain all through my torso from running so long and hard. I watch as Chrystal bends over, then stands up again with empty hands. Then I'm there with her, taking her hands in mine and calling her name.

Her eyes find me, but they're empty at first. Then, slowly, recognition fills them. She smiles. "Logan?"

"It's me, Chrystal. It's me. Are you okay?"

"I killed him," she says. "And I got the blood. Your family can be whole again. I got it." She bends over and picks up a cup. It's my camping mug, the one that collapses down to fit in a pocket. It's full of dark-red blood with bubbles around the edges.

"What's that?" David asks.

"Werewolf blood," Chrystal answers.

"Is he really dead?" David asks.

"Yes, I said I killed him. You never listen," Chrystal says, but she didn't see him staggering up behind her when we shot him again.

"Monsters tend to come back to life," David says, "Plus . . . um . . ."

I give him a signal to shut up. He actually shuts up.

The dogs are still barking.

"Let's go have a look." I watch Chrystal. She nods once. The three of us start walking. From the bottom of the hill, Mr. Davis calls to us. I wave him forward and he starts laboring up the slope.

Professor Borgess, stark naked, is lying on his stomach in the dirt. The wind is blowing leaves around his body and whipping his hair. The loose wolf hair blows away from his skin. Black foam is drying around his mouth, and a thick black fluid oozes from a gaping wound in his arm. A trickle of black leaks around the shaft of my arrow.

"So is he dead?" David asks again. "Really dead?"

"You really have trust issues," Chrystal says. "Or is it belief issues?"

"It's a monster. I want to be sure," David wipes at the end of his nose with his shaking fingers.

"One way to be sure." I take another arrow and nock it, then aim at his back, where his heart should be.

"No!" Chrystal grabs my arm. "No, Logan."

She kneels beside the body and puts a hand to his throat, holds it there, then looks up at me and David. "No pulse."

I clip the arrow back into the quiver and help her up. That's when I see the wound on her hand.

Her face is pale and she's sweating. It's hot outside, but we're in pretty deep shade. Something is definitely not right.

"You're hurt," I say.

"It's nothing," she lies.

Mr. Davis joins us, huffing and puffing. "What's wrong?"

"Chrystal's hand is hurt."

"Look, nothing's wrong, okay?" Her voice is short, cranky. "He's dead. I got the blood we need to treat your dad. Let's get back to the house and make the cure. We have to—"

Mr. Thompson calls in the distance. He comes running, pulling along another man who has duct tape hanging from his wrists and clothes. It's Mr. Lawson Smith.

"Dad?" Chrystal yelps. Her hand comes out to me and she passes off the cup of blood.

"Chrystal!" Mr. Lawson Smith yells, then charges at her and throws his arms around her. Chrystal puts her arms around her dad's neck and that's when I get a good look at her wound.

It's a long gash on her hand.

"You're hurt *and* bleeding," I say, almost accusingly.

"What? Where?" Mr. Lawson Smith asks, pushing Chrystal away to look at her.

Chrystal puts her hand behind her back. "It's nothing. I cut it on a branch. We have to go. We have to hurry. For Logan's dad."

"You're pale, Chrystal," Mr. Lawson Smith says. He puts a hand on her sweaty forehead. "You have a fever, too. That was no tree branch."

"Dad, come on. We have to go. We have to hurry . . . For Logan's—He's such a nice man. . . . Their family . . . So perfect. . . . We have to go save them." She turns around and stumbles, catches herself, and looks back at us as if to say something.

Then she collapses at our feet.

Chrystal is lying on our couch. She's pale. She's sweating. She is unconscious and moaning in her sleep. Sometimes she has minor convulsions. I want to be with her, holding her hand. Any minute, I know, Mr. Lawson Smith is going to send me out of the kitchen.

"Is it boiling yet?" I ask.

"No," he answers.

I go to the doorway and look at Chrystal, then hurry back to her dad, looking over his shoulder at the pot on the stove. "How about now?"

"Logan, please go check on Chrystal," he tells me. "Put a cool, wet cloth on her forehead. Tell her I'm hurrying, but that it has to be exact. Can you do that for me?" His eyes meet mine, and we both know he's really just getting rid of me because I'm bothering him.

"Yeah." I go and do just what he says.

It seems like an eternity before I smell the sharp, acidic scent of the wolfsbane flower being dropped into the boiling water. I have to really struggle to stay in my place sitting on the coffee table, holding Chrystal's hand. I want to go back to the kitchen and check on things.

Mom would get on me for sitting on the table like this.

"That's the wolfsbane," I say to Chrystal. "Can you smell it?"

I don't know if she can.

Out in the barn, David and Mr. Davis are doing the afternoon milking. Rain, shine, blizzard, or werewolf attack, the cows have to be milked. Farming isn't a Monday-to-Friday job. I wonder what they're saying out there, if anything at all. The wind has continued to pick up. It'll rain before dark.

"Fascinating!" Mr. Lawson Smith says from the kitchen. I assume he must have poured the blood into the water and seen that same weird reaction Chrystal and I saw last time. "That is just incredible. I have never in my life seen anything like this."

I can't help myself. I give Chrystal a quick kiss and return to the kitchen. "Is there enough?"

Mr. Lawson Smith gives me an annoyed look. I've never seen him look annoyed before. "I can't say yet. What you gave your father earlier, it was just like this?" He waves at the pot.

"Yeah. Just the blood and water we'd boiled the flower in."

"And he recovered?"

"Yeah, partially. It was really quick. He was sitting up and talking last I saw him."

"How about since then?"

"I don't know."

"Call your mother. Ask how your dad is."

Is this another ploy to keep me busy? I don't know. His face is pretty serious. I whip out my phone and call Mom. I can tell from her voice that things aren't good.

"He relapsed," she says. Her voice is so tired. So defeated. "Logan, what was that stuff you gave him? The doctor took it away. He thinks it has some kind of poison in it. What was it? Did your father ask you to poison him to end this?"

"No, Mom. It was a temporary cure. He was better. It made him better. Did he drink more of it?"

"No. He was sitting up, having his lunch, when his whole body stiffened up. His heart stopped for almost a minute. They found the bottle while they were resuscitating him."

"How's Kelsey?"

"Fine. In shock about everything, like the rest of us. No. Worse. But physically fine. She was dehydrated. They gave her an IV."

While she talks, Mr. Lawson Smith turns down the heat on the stove. Using a spoon, he gently stirs the liquid in the pot. He was lashed to a tree so close to our house. I don't know why the werewolf would keep him so close. To taunt us? As bait for us? Who knows? Who knows why the twisted do the things they do?

"I'm going to be there pretty soon, Mom," I say. "We killed him. We killed the werewolf. But Chrystal got his blood first, so we can make the real cure. The permanent cure. But she was bitten too."

"Chrystal was bitten? She killed that monster? Little Chrystal did it?"

"Yeah. I don't know how. She got sick and passed out before she could tell us about it. Her dad is making the cure right now. He was tied to a tree. He looks okay. Dehydrated, maybe. As soon as it's done I'll come to the hospital."

"Logan, they're not going to let you give Dad anything else. They might not even let you back in."

"I have to go, Mom. We will make this work. We will get Dad the cure. Bye." I hang up before she can respond.

"The drink you gave your father was too diluted," Mr. Lawson Smith says. "I am sorry to say it, but after that temporary respite, it has made his condition worse because it simply put more werewolf blood into his system. Come, take a gander at this."

What he is stirring is much thicker than what we had. It looks almost like tomato sauce.

"We have to keep stirring this over low heat until it has the consistency of pudding," he says.

"But . . ." I don't want to say it. "But the water is boiling away and there isn't as much of the stuff."

Mr. Lawson Smith nods. "I realize that."

"Will there be enough?"

He looks at me and I can't read his expression. "How much does your dad weigh?" he asks.

"I don't know. Maybe . . ." I think about my own weight and how much bigger Dad is than me. He's gotten a little soft around the middle, but not too much. "Maybe about a hundred and ninety, two hundred."

"We'll see," Mr. Lawson Smith says. He waves at an open book on the counter beside the stove. It's one of the books we'd looked at earlier, open to a page with text and a drawing of a cauldron over a fire. "We need about one ounce for every fifty pounds of body weight. Your dad is, we'll say, two hundred. Chrystal is about one fifteen. That's about seven ounces."

We both look back into the pan. The dark-red brew is thicker than before, more like tomato paste, and now there's even less of it.

There is actually almost a quarter of an ounce extra. Mr. Lawson Smith uses a measuring set he has, along with little plastic tubes he says are for specimen samples, to hold the extra and the dose for my dad. He holds the white tube with the extra up to the light and smiles.

"I have a friend in New Hampshire who will be very happy to have a look at this," he says.

New Hampshire.

East Coast.

Maine.

Chrystal's home.

Better home in Maine than dead.

"Are we ready?" I ask.

Mr. Lawson Smith slowly puts his prize away in a black nylon bag. He doesn't look at me, though. He just stands there, holding the bag.

"What if she doesn't want it?" he asks.

"What?"

"What if Chrystal doesn't want the cure?"

I gape at him. I can feel my eyes blinking as I try to comprehend this. "What?" I ask again. "Are you crazy?" That's horribly disrespectful, I know, but come on!

"Would it be so bad?" he asks.

"Chrystal doesn't want to be a werewolf," I almost yell at him. How can he even think it? He finally turns to look at me, and I can see the fear on his face.

"What if this is wrong?" he asks me. "What if the book is not factual? What if I did something incorrectly?"

I see where he's going. I nod at him. "I understand. But, Mr. Lawson Smith, I know Chrystal. Yeah, I mean, I've only known her this one summer, but I think I know what she would say. We talked about evil. Chrystal could never live like that. She would hate herself."

"She's my little girl." His voice cracks as he says it.

For a second, seeing him break down is just really uncomfortable. Nobody wants to see a grown man cry. But we both love the same girl, in different ways. I know what he's feeling. I feel it, too. I put my arms around him and we hug each other tightly.

"You have romantic feelings toward her, don't you?" he says into my shoulder.

"Yes."

"Does she, toward you?"

"I think so. She said she does."

He pulls away from me and now he's smiling, but it's a little sad. "I always hoped she'd find a nice boy like you. And yes, you're right. She could never live like Dr. Borgess did." He takes a deep breath. "Let's cure my little girl."

36

CHRYSTAL

Pain. It's like my body is a black hole, but in a black hole nothing exists, right? I'm not sure. But the pain exists like some sort of never-ending explosion in every single one of my cells. The pain makes me into nothing. I become it.

Logan's hand holds mine.

My father's voice murmurs.

Open.

But I don't want to open. I want them to kill me. I want . . . I can't turn into that thing. I know that's what's happening. I can't . . .

Open.

Then Logan's voice: "Please, Chrystal."

Something presses against my lips. Pudding? They want me to eat pudding? I can't even move my lips and they want me to eat pudding? The men in my life make no sense.

Chrystal, for me.

For Logan.

My head swims backward into some sort of dream, but it's real: Dad swinging me around and around at the Blue Hill playground. The grass swirls beneath me, the blades of it blurring into one mass of green. My mother laughs, sitting on a swing, watching. We were perfect.

Open.

Another memory: Logan smiling in his boxers, looking beautiful.

For me, Chrystal. Please . . .

My lips open. I swallow. It takes everything I have, all my willpower, but I swallow.

The wolf howls somewhere. He's alive? No. I killed him. The wolf is trying to be me. I am the one howling. I can't tell what's real. I see his mouth. Pain ripples through my pores. Someone screams and screams and screams, and it takes a second before I realize that the someone screaming is me.

Someone sobs in the corner of the room. I can't see them because my eyes don't want to open. It's a man, though, I can tell by the pitch.

My body is a heavy, heavy thing. So I let it pull me back in.

"She died?"

I am not dead.

Are they talking about me?

I try to open my eyes.

I am not dead.

"Her heart stopped."

I smell rain.

Someone pounds on my chest, sobbing.

I am not dead.

The world lurches in. My lungs fill with air and it screams fire through my chest. My eyes open. Logan's face is above me. His hands push against my ribs, pounding pain and life back into me. His face is squeezed tight. Tears stream down his cheeks.

"Chrystal?"

"Hallelujah!!" Dad's standing in the corner. He claps his hands. "I didn't kill her!"

He starts doing a little jig, an Irish jig sort of step dance. I close my eyes. He is so embarrassing.

"Chrystal?" Logan's voice again. His lips against my forehead. "Baby?"

"I'm not a baby," I murmur. "That's sexist."

He starts cracking up, just laughing and laughing, and David stands there behind him and then my dad comes over and says, "You live! You live!"

And I do.

Not much time passes and I grab Logan's hands. He won't let go of me, rocks me back and forth, telling me I'm crazy and good and too damn brave and he likes me in a love way. David cracks up and leaves the room because he says Logan's giving men a bad name.

"You have to go save your dad," I tell him.

"Yeah," he says. "I do."

David and Dad stay with me while Logan goes. I sleep, and when I wake up, people are in the kitchen, talking. The only one with me is Dad. He puts his hands on my cheeks and brings his face right above mine.

"You are conscious!"

"Mmm. Hmmm," I murmur. My lips stretch into a smile. "I'm okay?"

"So okay . . . so beautifully, amazingly okay," he says.

"And Logan's dad?"

"He is well. He almost died, but he came back."

"Oh," I say, "that's good."

He laughs. His entire body seems like it's full of joy. I love it when he's like that. "That's all? 'That's good'? You risked your life to save him, Chrystal."

"It's beyond good," I say, grabbing his hand. I try to squeeze, but I fail. "But I'm a little tired right now."

He starts. "Oh, my poor baby, of course you are! Of course! Sleep."

I nod.

He begins to walk away and then turns back around, returning to the couch. "I didn't tell you how proud I am. When we first came here, I knew you didn't want to come, knew you were anti-Oklahoma and a little anti-me, which is normal, Chrystal. It's normal to feel that way, so don't protest. I'm not offended. When we first came here, you were a follower, but now . . . you're a hero. I could never imagine that my own daughter would be such shining proof of what humanity is capable of. I am only sorry that I've been such a selfish father, that I haven't been able to give you that family, that home you want, that you crave. And I put you in such danger."

I blink back tears. "Dad?"

"What?"

"I love you. I think you are an awesome father." I swallow. It's so hard. "But I don't want to go home. I want a family, Dad. I want people who are solid and real and who are here when I need them."

He cocks his head. "I know."

"Also, I would really like my guitar."

The next time I wake up, I'm feeling much better and I'm in Logan's bed. There are flowers on his bookcase—the orange ones I now love so much, and it must be nighttime because the outside world is dark. There's a night-light on and a little corner lamp, which gives the room a nice orange glow.

Logan's sitting on the floor, touching my bass. He's holding it in his lap. His fingers lightly pluck the strings. It sounds like a mess, but it's also beautiful.

"Logan."

He jumps up, putting the bass against the wall before rushing to the bed. He slows himself and then sits gingerly on the side of the bed. He makes my name a question. "Chrystal?"

I smile. The muscles in my face protest it, feel like they're stretching, but there's no stopping the smile.

Tears stream out of Logan's eyes, but his face doesn't twist up into something sad. He keeps smiling as he says, "I can't believe you. I can't . . . You're okay."

"Yeah. I am."

My hand lifts up to wipe at his tears. Even that is hard, but it's worth it to touch his skin. He reaches up, grabs my hand, and kisses my fingers.

"I thought we were going to lose you. I thought—It was horrible."

"Sorry," I croak out.

"Do you want water?" He gives me some. It helps. He tells me his dad is doing about the same as I am, which for his dad is a great improvement. He had to get Kelsey to bring in the cure, but she did. He's proud of her. He's proud of me.

"I'm proud of *you*," I tell him.

"Me?" he scoffs. "Why? You'd killed that thing long before I shot it."

I shake my head. "No, because you used to try to write poems, and now you live them."

He takes that in for a second and smiles, a slow, creeping smile. "Do you know what your dad said?"

"Oh no . . ." I dread what crazy thing it might have been.

"He said we've all been bound by tragic and adrenaline-filled events, and bonds have been forged that shouldn't be broken and some more things . . . I tuned him out," he apologizes, but he still won't stop smiling. "But he said he won't make you go home. He said it would be detrimental to take you away from the people who experienced these traumatic events with you. At least, he said not right away."

"He really said that?" I ask. My heart beats faster, lighter.

"Yeah."

"Are you good with that?" I ask.

He laughs. "So good. Are you good with that? I know you really wanted to go to New York."

"I still want to go to New York, but it feels . . . it feels a little much right now. I can practice without a mentor for a bit. How about you? You sure you're okay with all of this? Remember how embarrassed you were when we first met?"

"I thought everyone would think I was touched." He coughs and then adds, "In the head. Touched that way. Plus, my poems . . . They're awful."

"They aren't *awful* awful," I say. "And even if they were, that doesn't mean you should stop writing them. Anyway, there are worse things for people to think about you. You know what Kierkegaard said?"

"A lot."

I laugh. "True. But one of the biggest things he ever said is also the simplest. He said, 'Do not forget your duty to love yourself.'"

"That doesn't really seem wordy enough for him."

"I know. Sometimes you don't need words and quotes. Sometimes you just have to be."

We both stare, smiling at each other. Someone honks a horn in the driveway.

"Police?" I ask.

Logan shakes his head. "No. Neighbors have been bringing food all day because Dad's in the hospital and Mom's there with him. Usually they do that for funerals, but Dad came back. Just like you."

I smile up at him. "And I get to stay."

"You think you could handle a kiss? Would it hurt?" he asks, his eyes twinkling.

"Aw, if it did, it would be so worth it," I say.

It is.

ACKNOWLEDGMENTS

Acknowledgments are supposed to be the place where you thank people for helping you to create a book. So, obviously, I have to thank Steve Wedel, who looks like he belongs in Metallica, writes scary things, but has the biggest heart ever.

Thank you to Mel Frain, Zohra Ashpari, and Kaitlin Severeni for making this book so much better. And to Christa Heschke for waiting for me and making me believe in myself and story again.

But acknowledgments are also the place where you thank people for helping you survive and enjoy your life, so thank you to Shaun Farrar who looks like he might kill you with a glare, but is strong and funny, can lift you up in the air with one arm, and who has a knight's goodness, but a raunchy sense of humor. I appreciate you so much.

Thank you to the amazing Emily Ciciotte, who looks like a su-permodel, but could actually kill you with a glare, or with just the sheer force of her brilliant mind, but who really is the most wonderful human I know, saver of birds, lost dogs, fighting sol-diers, and mothers. Thank you always for making me a better human.

Finally, thank you to all the infinitely kind and patient friends and kids and dogs I have in real-life world and social-media world who listen to *Dogs Are Smarter Than People*, who read my posts and tweets, who send me dog, cat, and manatee photos, and who just try so hard to fight the suck that can be overwhelming for all of us sometimes. You are what's good in this world. You give me so much hope. I want you to have hope, too. We've got this. I think.

—CARRIE

Well, I obviously have to thank my gracious, quirky, funny co-writer, Carrie Jones, the best speed-date-the-author partner anyone could ever ask for. Writing books with you is as fun as it can get.

I wish I could thank Wilda Walker, the Enid High School creative writing teacher who put me on this journey as an author and made me want to become a teacher. I know she's still writing poetry in the Great Beyond.

Many thanks to Melissa Frain and the staff at Tor for taking this little story Carrie and I put together and making it better than it was, and for being so amazingly easy and fun to work with. And patient, too.

I appreciate the students I've had over the years more than they'll ever know. You guys are more than just character traits and story fodder. I swear it!

Thank you to Kim, Alex, Sara, Amanda, and Jacob, for putting up with my writing habit and for still being there for me.

My parents bought me my first typewriter a long, long time ago. They've always supported me, but more than ever this past year. Mom and Dad, thank you! This goes to my sister, Rachel, and her family, too.

Lastly, thank you to the readers who have kept me going when I felt like giving up so many times. Your emails, reviews, and comments on social media mean so much.

—STEVE